The most scandalous marriage in London…

If Kit and Eleanor's elopement wasn't enough to fire a frenzy of gossip, it was then heard that Eleanor's new husband had disappeared only a day after their hasty wedding! Five long months later, Lord Mostyn returned. Though not at liberty to explain his departure, he was still determined to win back the affection of his fuming bride. Would he succeed? Perhaps if he continued the marriage exactly where it began—in the bedroom…

"Was there anything else, my lord?"

"Just one more thing," Kit murmured. His gaze drifted from her face, which was becoming pinker under his prolonged scrutiny, down her slender figure and back again. His eyes lingered, disturbingly, on her mouth. Eleanor stiffened.

"I wished to disabuse you of any notion you might have of a marriage of convenience," Kit said slowly. "All this talk of you going your way and I going mine might lead you to imagine…erroneously…that ours would be a marriage in name only."

* * *

The Notorious Marriage
Harlequin Historical #659—June 2003

Praise for Nicola Cornick's latest books

The Virtuous Cyprian
"…this delightful tale of a masquerade gone awry
will delight ardent Regency readers."
—*Romantic Times*

"A witty, hilarious romp through the Regency period."
—*Rendezvous*

The Larkswood Legacy
"…a suspenseful yet tenderhearted tale of love…"
—*Romantic Times*

DON'T MISS THESE OTHER
TITLES AVAILABLE NOW:

#660 SAVING SARAH
Gail Ranstrom

#661 BLISSFUL, TEXAS
Liz Ireland

#662 WINNING JENNA'S HEART
Charlene Sands

THE
NOTORIOUS
MARRIAGE

Nicola Cornick

HARLEQUIN®

TORONTO • NEW YORK • LONDON
AMSTERDAM • PARIS • SYDNEY • HAMBURG
STOCKHOLM • ATHENS • TOKYO • MILAN • MADRID
PRAGUE • WARSAW • BUDAPEST • AUCKLAND

ISBN 0-373-29259-7

THE NOTORIOUS MARRIAGE

Copyright © 2002 by Nicola Cornick

First North American Publication 2003

This edition published by arrangement with Harlequin Books S.A.

Visit us at www.eHarlequin.com

Printed in U.S.A.

Please address questions and book requests to:
Harlequin Reader Service
U.S.: 3010 Walden Ave., P.O. Box 1325, Buffalo, NY 14269
Canadian: P.O. Box 609, Fort Erie, Ont. L2A 5X3

For my grandmother, who introduced me
to historical romances all those years ago.

Prologue

December 1813

When Kit Mostyn stepped through the doors of Almacks Assembly Rooms that night, it was difficult to tell who was the more surprised, the chaperones of the hopeful débutantes assembled there, or Kit himself. Certainly Almacks was not a place where Kit normally sought entertainment, and this evening he had struggled rather incredulously with the compulsion that drove him there. It, or rather *she*, had so strong a hold on him that he could not resist, and being a man who chose not to struggle against fate, he resolved to meet his with a certain equanimity.

He saw her as soon as he entered the room. Miss Eleanor Trevithick, daughter of the late Viscount Trevithick and younger sister to the current Earl. She was dancing with an elderly roué, Lord Kemble, if Kit did not miss his guess, and just the sight of the two of them together made his temper soar dangerously. As he sought to keep a grip on it he was forced to acknowledge that it mattered little who was partnering Eleanor—the fact that it was someone other than himself was all that counted.

Slender, sweet and impossibly innocent, Eleanor Trevithick was the most demure of débutantes, yet there had been something between them from the beginning, a startling attraction that both she and Kit recognised—and knew they had to ignore. It had caught Kit by surprise, and although they had never spoken of it, he instinctively knew that the strength of the attraction both frightened and fascinated Eleanor. As for himself, he had cynically dismissed his feelings at first—a man of his age and considerable experience with the opposite sex was hardly likely to fall in love with an innocent in her first Season. The feelings she stirred in him could be no more than desire—admittedly strong, undeniably surprising, but no doubt of short duration.

He had been wrong. Kit had wanted Eleanor Trevithick for the whole of the past year, ever since they had shared an illicit dance at her eighteenth birthday ball, and his desire showed no sign of waning. Indeed the reverse was true. He was very close to admitting now that he loved her, but he did not wish to be that honest with himself at the moment. It would only undermine him still further. One could not always have what one wanted, and he could not have Eleanor.

Kit, whose title and position would have made him a more than acceptable suitor for any number of young ladies, was the one man whose addresses could never be welcomed by Eleanor's family. There was a feud between the Trevithick and Mostyn families that went back hundreds of years, and the Dowager Viscountess, Eleanor's mother, would cut him dead whenever she saw him. The fact that his cousin Beth was currently engaged in a dispute with the current Earl of Trevithick over the ownership of part of his estate only made matters worse. Kit had had no intention of being drawn any further into the Mostyn and Trevithick feud. Nor was he hanging out for a wife anyway. At the moment he had other responsibilities.

Even so…

He approached Eleanor as soon as he was able, cutting out the young Viscount who had thought this set of country dances belonged to him. Kit knew that all eyes were upon them, knew that Lady Trevithick was swelling like a turkey-cock in a temper and that her rout chair looked set fair to break under the weight. He ignored her, ignored the speculative looks of the other chaperones and the envious, spiteful glances of some of the débutantes, and smiled down into Eleanor's eyes.

'Miss Trevithick… It is a great pleasure to see you tonight.'

Eleanor met his gaze listlessly for a brief second. She did not smile. There was none of her usual vivacity in those dark Trevithick eyes. She avoided his gaze, looking over his shoulder to where her mother and Lord Kemble sat huddled at the side of the floor.

'Thank you, my lord.'

Kit frowned slightly. It was not that he expected her to show her partiality for him, for Eleanor was far too well-bred to make a display of her feelings in public. He was perceptive enough, however, to see that there was something wrong—something dreadfully wrong. Eleanor's face was pale and pinched, all light quenched. She steadfastly refused to look at him.

Kit tightened his grip on her hands. 'Eleanor...' he said urgently.

She looked up. For a fleeting second, Kit saw all the misery and hopeless longing reflected in her eyes and his heart skipped a beat. Then her lashes came down, veiling her expression.

'I believe you must wish me happy, my lord,' she said, softly but clearly. 'I am betrothed to Lord Kemble.'

'No!' The word was out of his mouth before Kit could help himself. His grip tightened murderously on her hands. He saw her wince, and had to force himself to let her go. 'No,' he said again, very politely. 'That cannot be so.'

'I assure you that it is.' Eleanor's dark lashes flickered again. 'The notice will be in the *Morning Post* tomorrow. It is all arranged.'

'It cannot be.'

For a moment her eyes searched his face and this time there was entreaty there. 'Why not? It is not as though you can offer me an alternative, my lord!'

They had been speaking in edged whispers until that point, but now Eleanor's voice rose as though she could not control her anguish. She bit her lip, a wave of colour coming into her pale face then receding to leave her even paler.

'I beg your pardon,' she said, regaining a faltering control. 'I should not have said that.'

Kit's heart turned over. He could see the hopelessness beneath her fragile dignity and it touched him deeply. He felt a rush of protective desire, stronger than anything he had ever experienced before.

'If I could help you—'

'Eleanor!' Lord Kemble's unctuous voice cut across his words. 'I believe that this next is my waltz.'

He bowed to Kit, his hooded gaze watchful. 'Your servant, Mostyn. Ain't you going to congratulate me? This little honey-pot is all mine!'

Kit's own bow was so slight as to be barely there. 'I pray that you will not take your good fortune for granted, Kemble. Miss Trevithick…' He smiled at Eleanor. 'I must bid you good night.'

He watched as Kemble took Eleanor away. The man oozed a self-satisfied lasciviousness that was deeply offensive. The thought of Eleanor's slight figure crushed beneath him, subject to his lusts, was almost too much for Kit to stand. He wanted to call the man out and put a bullet through him. In fact he was not sure if he would bother with the formality of calling him out, just shoot him where he stood. Or he could take Kemble's neck-cloth and use it to strangle him…

He saw Eleanor smile stiffly at her betrothed as Kemble took her in his arms for the waltz. Kit turned away and threaded his way to the door, trying to keep his expression impassive as he passed through the knots of chattering débutantes. The cold night air helped to clear his anger a little. He had to think, had to decide what to do. If only it were not so damnably complicated… By the time he had reached the house in Upper Grosvenor Street his anger had once again been subdued to cool reason but he was no clearer on his course of action. All he knew was that Eleanor Trevithick was his and as such could never be permitted to marry Lord Kemble.

It was later—much later—when the butler came to him to tell him that there was a young lady on the doorstep who was begging to speak with him. By that time Kit had consumed half a bottle of brandy and he simply laughed.

'I don't think that would be a particularly good idea, would it, Carrick?' He murmured. 'In the first instance I am three parts cut and in the second, young ladies…' he stressed the words '…are presumably tucked up in bed…alone…at this time of night, not walking the streets of London!'

Carrick, who was enough of a butler of the world to know that this was true, nevertheless stood his ground.

'Begging your pardon, my lord, but this is very definitely a lady. A young lady, my lord, and in considerable distress…'

Kit sighed with irritation. His first thought—that Eleanor Trevithick had come to seek him out—had been quickly dismissed as wishful thinking. Eleanor was so very proper, so entirely well brought up, that she never put a foot wrong. Certainly she would not even think of entering a gentleman's house alone, especially not in the middle of the night. Respectable young ladies simply did not behave in such a way.

Therefore it must be another sort of lady. An enterprising Cyprian, perhaps, or even a débutante with fewer scruples than Eleanor, intent on catching him. Kit had learned to be cynical. Several young ladies had twisted their ankles outside the house in Upper Grosvenor Street in the last week or two. He had even found a girl in the drawing-room one evening and she had sworn that she had simply mistaken the house for that of a friend. When Kit's housekeeper had ushered her off the premises she had been distinctly annoyed.

Kit's gaze swept around the firelit study, taking in the tumbled pile of papers on the desk, the empty bottle of brandy and the glass of the same amber liquid that stood by his armchair. To entertain a lady here would be the greatest folly. Besides, he had other preoccupations that night, plans that needed serious consideration. Plans that had suffered because of his preoccupation with Eleanor. He shook his head.

'I am sorry, Carrick, but you must turn this so-called young lady away. I am certain that it can only be a trap and I am scarce going to walk straight into it...'

The words had barely left his lips when he heard the sound of running feet on the hall tiles and the scandalised voice of one of the footmen:

'Pardon, madam, but you cannot go in there...'

Both Kit and the butler swung round towards the doorway.

'Kit!'

Kit smothered a curse. He turned to the butler. 'Very well, Carrick, you may leave us.'

Carrick inclined his head. 'Yes, my lord,' he said expressionlessly. He went out and closed the door, softly but firmly, behind him.

'I know I shouldn't be here!' Eleanor said defiantly, immediately the door had closed and they were alone. She was wearing a black velvet cloak over the same dress of pale white gold she had worn earlier in the evening. It was the demure, expensive raiment of the débutante. Her dark brown eyes, huge in her elfin face, were fixed on him. Her hair had come out of it's chignon and rich, chestnut brown curls tumbled about her shoulders, spilling over the cloak and down her back. She looked delectable—and terrified. Kit saw her lock her fingers together tightly to still their trembling. He deliberately looked away from her.

'You are correct. You should not be here. It is madness.' Kit spoke curtly to mask a variety of emotions. He came towards her, keeping his hands very firmly in his pockets. 'Miss Trevithick, I suggest that for the sake of your reputation you should turn around and go directly home—'

Eleanor shook her head.

'Kit, I cannot! You must help me! I cannot bear to be married off to Kemble! That disgusting old man— why, he speaks of nothing but his horses and his gaming, and wheezes and snores his way through every play and concert we have ever attended! And then he paws at me in the most revolting manner imaginable!'

Kit took a deep breath, maintaining a scrupulous distance away from her. Miss Eleanor Trevithick, temptation personified. His mind was telling him to show her the door and his body was telling him to take her in his arms.

'The correct thing to do in this situation is to apply to your brother,' he heard himself say sternly. 'He is the head of the family and could easily prevent such a match…'

'You know that Marcus is away in Devon, and Justin too!' Kit saw tears squeeze from the corner of Eleanor's eyes and she rubbed them impatiently away with her fingers. 'Mama means to marry me off before they return—she is hot for the match! And I have no one to apply to for help! Please, Kit—' she broke off. 'I thought when we spoke earlier that you might save me…' Her gaze touched his face and moved away at what it saw there. 'Perhaps I was wrong…'

'You were.' Again, Kit ruthlessly repressed the urge to take her in his arms. He took a sharp turn away from her and moved over to the fireplace, leaning against the marble chimney-breast. 'Your mama cannot force the match, Eleanor, and certainly not before Trevithick returns—'

'Kemble has a special licence!' Eleanor burst out. 'Oh Kit…' she spread her hands in a pleading gesture and Kit felt himself flinch inside '…you do not understand! I was so sure that you would help me…'

Kit took a deep breath. Every instinct that he possessed was urging him to crush her to him, promise her that he would look after her, swear that all would be well. Yet in the morning she might well regret the whole escapade. In the cold light of day she might realise that she had ruined herself—and the only way to save her from that was to make her turn round now and go home, before anyone was the wiser. Besides, even had there not been such a violent feud between their families, Kit knew he was in no position to marry. He had other commitments, matters that might take him away at any moment. He was not free…

'There is no need for such drama,' Kit said, powerless to prevent the harsh tone of his voice, cursing himself that he could not help her. 'In the morning everything will seem better and you will realise that the situation is far from desperate…'

He saw Eleanor's chin come up as she heard the repudiation in his words. She squared her shoulders. Her dark eyes flashed.

'Very well, Lord Mostyn. I see that I misunderstood you! I will leave now! There is no need to say any more!'

Oddly, Kit found that her pride angered him, got under his defences. He had been able to guard himself against her distress—only just, but he had managed it by telling himself that he simply had to withstand her for her good as well as his own. He would have to deal with his own feelings of helplessness and self-disgust—he did not intend to explain to Eleanor. In the cool light of day he might think of a solution, find a way to help her. But now her danger was intense and she did not even appear to understand that...

She was drawing on her cloak, preparing to leave and looking at him with a mixture of desperation and contempt in her eyes that provoked him beyond reason.

'I thought you a gentleman,' she said, softly but with biting sarcasm, 'but it seems I was mistaken...'

Kit tried to clamp down on his frustration. 'It is precisely because I am a gentleman that I am concerned for your reputation, Eleanor—'

She made a little noise indicative of her disgust. Kit straightened up and came across to her. He told himself that it would do no harm to make her think about what she was doing, frighten her a little so that she would never do it again. The thought of Eleanor throwing herself on someone else's mercy in this trusting and foolish fashion made his anger burn almost out of control.

She was looking down her nose at him as though she expected him to hold the door open for her, as though he were some kind of damned butler. Instead, Kit leant one hand against the door panels and leaned over her. Now there was a flash of puzzlement in her eyes, puzzlement mixed with something more potent. Her lashes flickered down, veiling her expression.

'Excuse me, Lord Mostyn,' her voice trembled very slightly. 'As you have pointed out to me, I should be leaving now...'

'What exactly did you expect of me tonight, Eleanor?' Kit's tone was rough.

She looked up again. Her eyes were very dark brown sprinkled with gold and framed by thick black lashes that the blonde débutantes would give half their fortunes to possess. Her gaze was candid. She had more courage than he had thought and he admired her for it.

'I thought that you would agree to marry me,' she said.

Kit started to smile, despite himself. 'Is that a proposal, Miss Trevithick?'

Eleanor glared. She might be young but she had all the Trevithick pride. Her chin came up and she gave him a haughty glance.

'I think you flatter yourself, Lord Mostyn! The offer is withdrawn!'

Kit laughed. 'A little late for that, Miss Trevithick! You are alone with me in my house—'

'Your cousin's house—'

'A fine distinction! The material point is that neither my cousin nor my sister is here to give you countenance! You are alone with me—'

'That situation can be addressed immediately!' Eleanor said, in arctic tone, 'if you will stand aside, my lord!'

Kit shrugged. 'But I may have changed my mind!'

Eleanor's shrug was a perfect echo of his own. 'Too late, alas, my lord!' She wrinkled up her nose. 'I should have known better than to approach a gentleman in his cups! I see that everything they say about you is true!'

Kit turned so that his shoulders were against the

door panels. He folded his arms and looked at her. Her face was flushed, her delectable mouth set in a tight line. He had noticed her mouth before; it was pink and soft and made for smiling, not for disapproval. Or made for kissing… Kit shifted a little.

'And what do they say, Miss Trevithick?'

'Why, that you are a rogue and a scoundrel!' Eleanor's gaze swept from his face to the brandy bottle and back again with contempt. 'There are those who say that your business dealings are none too scrupulous and your morals even less so!'

Kit's eyes narrowed. 'Yet you are still here?' he said softly.

He saw Eleanor's fingers clench tightly on her reticule. 'I thought…' Her voice faltered. 'I did not truly believe it of you…' Their eyes met. Kit could see the entreaty in hers; she was begging him to live up to her good opinion, prove himself a gentleman. It made him feel sick with self-loathing that he could not help her.

'I thought that you liked me,' she finished softly.

Kit caught his breath. Liking was far too pale a word to describe the feelings he had for her. He felt his self-control slip perilously.

'Eleanor, I more than like you, but there are reasons—' he began, only to break off as she made a slight gesture and moved away.

'I am sure that there always are, my lord. Forgive my importunity and pray let me go now.'

Kit opened the study door for her with immaculate politeness. The hall was dark and empty—one stand of candles cast shadows across the tiled floor. The long case clock struck one.

Eleanor was halfway through the door when Kit put his hand on her arm.

'Eleanor, I cannot let you go like this. I truly wish I could help you, but—'

'Don't!' She shook him off with sudden, shocking violence. He saw the candlelight shimmer on the tears in her eyes, before she dashed them away. 'Do not try to excuse your behaviour, Lord Mostyn! You are not what I thought you and I made a mistake in coming here. That is all!'

Kit could smell her scent, the softest of rose fragrance mingled with nursery soap. Her innocence hit him like a blow in the stomach; her desirability dried his mouth.

'It is not all,' Kit said roughly, knowing he should agree, let it go, let her go. 'Eleanor, you know I care for you…'

She looked him straight in the eye. 'I thought you wanted me,' she said.

Kit was never be sure which of them had moved first but the next minute she was in his arms, her slender body pressed close to his, her mouth beneath his own. Her lips parted slightly and he took ruthless advantage, touching his tongue to hers, deepening the kiss when her instinctive gasp offered him the opportunity. There was a moment when he felt her resist and he was about to pull back, but before his mind had caught up with his body she had softened, melted against him, pliant in his arms. He covered her mouth with his again, drinking deep, until she was as breathless as he. Desire washed through him, hot and sweet. He thrust one hand into her tousled hair, scattering the pins, feeling the silky softness against his fingers. He had so wanted to do that... His other arm was about her waist, the velvet of her cloak slippery beneath his hand. He pushed it aside so that he could hold her closer still, feel the warmth of her body. The cloak fell to the ground with a soft swish of velvet.

'Eleanor,' he said again, though this time it came out as a whisper. He watched as she opened her eyes. They were so dark they were almost black, cloudy, bemused with passion. Her mouth, bee-stung with kisses, curved into a smile.

Kit held on to the last rags of his self-control. 'Eleanor, if you are not certain...'

The smile lit her eyes. She raised one hand to Kit's cheek and he almost flinched beneath the touch, so sharp was his desire for her.

'I am certain,' she said.

And after that there were no more words between them for a long time.

Kit Mostyn woke up with a headache. It was certainly not brandy-induced but it was, without a doubt, the worst headache that he had experienced in a very long time. The room was moving around him, rising and falling with a sickening regularity that wrenched a groan from him before he could help himself.

'How are you, old chap?' a voice asked, solicitously. 'Been out cold for almost two days, y'know—unnecessary force, if you ask me...'

Kit rested his arm across his eyes and tried not to be sick. Then he tried to think, but the effort was monstrously difficult. His head felt as though it were two sizes too large and stuffed with paper into the bargain. And there was something troubling him, a memory at the edge of his mind...

'Eleanor!' He sat up bolt upright, and then sank back with a groan.

'Steady, old fellow,' the same voice said. 'No cause for alarm.'

Kit opened his eyes and surveyed his companion with a distinct lack of enthusiasm.

'Hello, Harry. What the devil are you doing here?'

Captain Henry Luttrell grinned. 'That's the spirit! Knew you'd feel more the thing shortly!'

Kit sat up again, gingerly this time. The room was still swaying, but he realised that that was because he was on a ship. It was a pleasant cabin, well appointed, comfortable. The *HMS Gresham*, out of Southampton, just as arranged. Something had gone spectacularly wrong. He rubbed his hand across his forehead.

'Harry. Where are we?'

Henry Luttrell's handsome face creased into a slight frown. 'Two days out, on the way to Ireland. I thought you knew...'

Kit shook his head slowly. 'I went to the meet at the Feathers, but it was to pass a message to Castlereagh that I could not go...'

Now it was Luttrell's turn to shake his head. 'Don't you remember, Kit? It was agreed to stage it all—the fight, the press gang…'

Kit looked at him. 'I don't remember a thing. What happened?'

Luttrell shifted against the bulkhead. 'You walked in, Benson hit you, we carted you off here… It was all arranged…'

Kit groaned again. 'Harry, I went there to tell Benson it was all off…'

'You never got the chance, old chap,' Luttrell pointed out. 'Benson hit you first, no questions asked.'

Kit rubbed his head ruefully. 'Yes, I can tell! And yes, I do remember we had agreed to stage it that way, but… devil take it, what about Nell! I only got married the day before…'

Luttrell's eyebrows shot up into his hair. 'Married! Thought you were keeping away from the petticoats, Kit!'

'Well of course I was, but it just…happened!' Kit said furiously. His head was aching more than ever now. 'I married Eleanor the day before I went to the meet—that was why I was going to tell Benson I couldn't make this trip!' He put his head in his hands. 'For God's sake, Harry, do you hear me? I've just got married! I've left my bride all alone with no idea where I am…'

Luttrell put a calming hand on his shoulder. 'Deuced bad luck, old fellow, but how was Benson to know? Besides, that was three days ago now…'

Kit raised his head and stared at him, his eyes wild. 'Eleanor's been alone with no word for three days now? Hell and the devil…'

'You can send word when we get to Dublin,' Luttrell suggested. 'Besides, we'll only be gone a few weeks, Kit. All over before you know it and no harm done. Surely your bride will understand when you explain…'

Kit shook his head, but he did not reply. There were two distinct sorts of sickness, he discovered. He had never been a good sailor but could deal with sea-sickness. It was purely physical. But the second… His heart ached. He remembered Eleanor, smiling at him and begging him prettily not to be gone too long… He groaned aloud. Three days ago!

Luttrell was getting to his feet. 'I'll bring you some hot water and something to drink,' he said. 'There's food, too, if you feel up to it, though you still look a bit green, old fellow…'

Kit gave him a half-smile. 'My thanks, Harry. Much appreciated. Is there pen and paper here?'

Luttrell gestured towards the desk. 'Over there.' He went out.

Kit stood up and stretched. He felt bruised all over. It must have been a hell of a blow to the head, but then he had always suspected that Benson did not like him. For all that they had worked together on various operations, he had never quite trusted the other man. Harry was a different matter, of course, dashing, devil may care, but utterly trustworthy. A true friend. If anyone could help him out of this mess…

Kit sat down at the writing desk and drew the paper slowly towards him. This was probably not the best time to write to Eleanor, when his head felt the size of a stuffed marrow, but he had to try. He would never forgive himself otherwise. Probably he would never forgive himself anyway and as for asking her pardon… Kit grimaced, momentarily wishing for a return to oblivion. It was a true nightmare and it had only just begun.

Chapter One

May 1814

Eleanor Mostyn knew that she was in trouble even before the landlord told her, with a sideways wink and a leer, that there was only one bedchamber and there would be no coaches calling until the next morning. Eleanor, following him into the tiny inn parlour, thoughtfully concluded that the signs were all there: they were miles from the nearest village, it was pouring with rain and the carriage had mysteriously lost a spar when only yards from this isolated inn. What had started out as a simple journey from Richmond to London looked set fair to turn into a tiresome attempted seduction.

It had happened to her before, of course—it was one of the penalties of having a shady reputation and no husband to protect her. However, she had never misjudged the situation as badly as this. This time, the relative youth and apparent innocence of her suitor had taken her in. Sir Charles Paulet was only two-and-twenty, and a poet. Though why poets should be considered more honourable than other men was open to question. Eleanor realised that her first mistake had been in assuming it must be so.

She knew that Sir Charles had been trying to charm his way into her bed with his bad poetry for at least a month. The baronet was a long, lanky and intense young man who laboured under the misapprehension that he was as talented as Lord Byron. Still, she had thought his attentions were a great deal more acceptable than those paid to her by some other men during the Season. He might be trying to seduce her but she had believed that the only real danger she was in was of being bored to death by his verse. That had to be mistake number two.

Eleanor removed her sodden bonnet and decided against unpinning her hair, even though it would dry more quickly that way. She had no wish to inflame Sir Charles's desires by any actions of her own, and she knew that her long, dark brown hair was one of her best features. No doubt her hopeful seducer had written a sonnet to it already. At the moment he was out in the yard, giving instructions to his groom and coachman, but she knew that she had very little time before he joined her in the parlour, and then she would need to be quick-witted indeed. The lonely inn, the unfortunate accident, the single bedroom... And he had been dancing attendance on her for the past four weeks and she had been vain enough to be flattered...

Here Eleanor sighed as she looked at her damp reflection in the mirror. Eleanor, Lady Mostyn, passably good-looking, only nineteen years old and already infamous, having been both married and deserted within the space of a week. She could remember her come-out vividly, for it had only been the Season before. Then, she had been accorded the scrupulous courtesy due to all innocent débutantes; now she was a prey to every dubious roué and rake in town.

Her re-emergence into the *Ton* this Season had set all the tongues wagging once again about her notorious marriage, just as Eleanor had known it would. Not enough time had passed for the scandal to die down, but she had been foolishly determined to confront the gossips, to prove that though her husband were gone, squiring opera dancers around the Continent if the stories were true, she was not repining. She had the Trevithick pride—plenty of it—and at first it had prompted her to defiance. Let them talk—she would not regard it.

Eleanor stripped off her cloak and hung it over the back of a chair. Needless to say, she had underestimated the power of rumour. One salacious story had led to another, each more deliciously dreadful than the last. The gossips said that she had eloped with Kit Mostyn to avoid a forced match; that he had deserted her on her wedding day because he had discovered her to be no virgin; that she had told him to leave because she had discovered he was a brute and a satyr who indulged in perverted practices... Eleanor sighed. The gossip had caused a scent of disrepute that hung about her and had the rakes sniffing around and the respectable ladies withdrawing their skirts for fear of contamination. Worse, she was not blameless.

Despite her mama's strictures that a lady always behaved with decorum, Eleanor had decided to scorn the gossips and fulfil their expectations. Just a little. At the start of the Season her off-white reputation had actually seemed rather amusing, much more entertaining than being a deadly dull débutante or a devoted wife. And in a complicated way it was a means of revenge on Kit, and she did so desperately want revenge. So she had flirted a little, encouraged some disreputable roués, even allowed a few rakes to steal a kiss or two. She had planned on taking a lover, or even two, perhaps both at the same time. The possibilities seemed endless for an abandoned bride whose husband clearly preferred to take his pleasures elsewhere.

The idea had soon palled. Eleanor had known all along that she was not cut out to be a fast matron. The liberties were disgusting, the kisses even more so. All the gentlemen who buzzed around her had the self-importance to assume that she would find them attractive and did not bother to check first. Their attentions had become immensely tedious, their invitations increasingly salacious and their attempted seductions, such as the present one, most trying. In the space of only six weeks Eleanor had had to slap several faces, place a few well-aimed kicks in the ankle or higher and even hit one persistent gentleman with the family Bible when he had tried to seduce her in the library. And she was miserably aware that it was her own fault.

Eleanor sat down by the meagre fire and tried to get warm. Now she had to deal with Sir Charles's importunities. If she had found it difficult to decide whether to live up or down to her reputation previously, she knew now beyond a shadow of doubt that she was not cut out for some sordid intrigue. There was enough scandal already attached to her name without some indiscreet dalliance in a low tavern with a man she found boring. Besides, she inevitably compared every man she met to Kit and found them wanting. It was curious but true—he had left her alone to face the scandal of their marriage and she had not heard a word from him since, yet still she found other men lacking.

In the five months since Kit's defection, Eleanor's childish infatuation had turned to anger and misery. When her mother delighted in passing on another snippet of gossip about Kit that had been garnered from her acquaintance, Eleanor hardened her heart a little more each time. However, it did not prevent the memory of her husband from overshadowing every other man she knew.

But that was nothing to the purpose. Eleanor smoothed her dress thoughtfully as she tried to decide what to do. She could appeal to Sir Charles's better nature but that was probably a waste of time as she suspected that he did not possess one. She would not be here if he did. She could play the innocent and scream the house down if matters turned nasty, or she could act the sophisticate, then run away when she had lulled Sir Charles into a false sense of security. Eleanor frowned. She was not entirely happy with either option. There was plenty of room for error.

She could hear voices getting closer—Sir Charles was quoting Shakespeare in the corridor. Oh dear, this was going to be very tiresome. The door opened. Sir Charles came in, followed by the innkeeper bearing a tray with two enormous glasses of wine. Eleanor raised her brows. That was not in the least subtle and somehow she had expected better of a poet. She really must rid herself of these false expectations.

'There you are, my love!' Sir Charles's voice had already slipped from the respectful courtesy of their previous exchanges to an odious intimacy that made Eleanor's hackles rise. 'I hope that you are warm enough—although I shall soon have you wrapped up as cosy as can be, upstairs with me!'

The innkeeper smirked meaningfully and Eleanor looked down her nose haughtily at him. No doubt *he* was warmed by the size of the bribe Sir Charles must have slipped him to connive in so dubious an enterprise. She wondered whether Sir Charles had always spoken in rhyme and why on earth she had not noticed it before. It was intensely irritating.

'The inn is adequate, I suppose,' she said coldly, 'but I do not anticipate staying here long, sir. Surely there is someone who could carry a message to Trevithick House? The others will be almost back by now and will be concerned to find me missing...'

'Oh, I do not believe that you need trouble your pretty little head about that, my love,' Sir Charles said airily. He struck a pose. 'Why, I sense a verse coming over me!' He smiled at her. 'My heart leads me to wed when I spy your pretty head, as you lie in my bed...'

'Pray, sir, restrain your imagination!' Eleanor snapped. 'I do not believe that an inclination to *wed* forms any part of your plans! As for the rest of your verse, I like it not! A work of folly and vivid imagination!'

Sir Charles did not appear one whit put out. Evidently it would take more than plain speaking to deter him. He came close to the fire, rubbing his hands together. Eleanor found herself hoping uncharitably that his ruffled sleeves would catch alight. His dress was very close to that of a macaroni, with yards of ribbons, ruffles and lace, and she was sure he would go up like a house on fire.

'Alas, my dear Lady Mostyn, that you are married already, otherwise I would show you my affections were steady!'

Sir Charles fixed her with his plaintive dark eyes, behind which Eleanor could see more than a glimpse of calculation. 'You must know that my love and esteem for you know no bounds—'

'As does your effrontery, sir!' Eleanor interrupted, before he could finish the rhyme.

Sir Charles pressed a glass of wine into her hand and downed half of his own in one gulp.

'You know that your relatives will not reach home

for a half hour at least, sweet Eleanor, and will not start to worry about you for another hour after that, by which time it will be dark...' His eyes met Eleanor's again, carrying the implicit message that no one would be coming to help her. Eleanor noted wryly that he could speak plainly enough when he chose. 'But have no fear! You are safe with me here!'

Eleanor bit her lip and turned her head away, hearing the innkeeper's laugh as he went out and closed the door behind him. There would be no help from that quarter.

Sir Charles nodded towards her wine. 'Drink up, my love. It will fortify you.' He suited actions to words, gulping the second half of his wine in one go, wiping the excess from his chin. 'This is a charming opportunity for us to get to know each other a little better. Most opportune, my rose in bloom!'

'Or most contrived!' Eleanor said coldly. She looked straight at him, noting that he was nowhere near as good-looking as she had once imagined him to be. His pale brown eyes were too close set to look trustworthy, and taken with his long and pointed nose they gave him the appearance of a wolfhound. Who was it had told her never to trust a man who looked like a hunting dog? It could only have been her aunt, Lady Salome Trevithick, and Eleanor wished she had paid more attention.

She took a sip of her wine, if only to give herself breathing space. Damnation! How could she have been so unconscionably foolish? She had been set up like a green girl and now had very limited options.

The poet was nowhere near as harmless as he pretended and her dénouement looked to be only a matter of time. She shuddered at the thought.

Sir Charles smiled at her. It was not reassuring. His lips were thin and wet-looking. Eleanor, realising suddenly that staring at his face might give quite the wrong impression of her feelings, looked hastily away.

'How far are we from London, sir?' she asked casually.

Sir Charles's smile became positively vulpine. 'At least ten miles, my lovely Lady Mostyn. We are benighted, I fear. You must simply…accept…your fate, my love, my dove.'

Eleanor's eyes narrowed. 'The carriage—'

'Will not be ready until tomorrow, alas.' Sir Charles spoke contentedly. 'Tomorrow will be soon enough. Here we shall stay in our pastoral heaven with only our love, the darkness to leaven…'

Eleanor, privately reflecting that Sir Charles's poetry was the hardest thing to tolerate so far, nevertheless thought that it could be useful. If she could but flatter him…

'Pray treat me to some more of your verse, sir,' she gushed, with what she knew to be ghastly archness. She hoped that his vanity was greater than his intellect, or he would know at once precisely what she was doing.

Sir Charles wagged a roguish finger at her. 'Ah, not yet, my pet! I believe our landlord is waiting to serve us a feast fit for a king…'

'Well, let us see what he can bring,' Eleanor finished a little grimly.

Sir Charles looked affronted. 'No, no, my love, it does not scan!'

The door opened to admit the landlord with the dinner tray. Eleanor, who considered him a most unpleasant character, was nevertheless pleased to see him, for his arrival afforded her time to think—and time when the odious Sir Charles could not press his attentions for a space, unless he was inclined to do so over the dinner plates and with an audience. Eleanor thought this entirely possible. It seemed that Sir Charles was so in love with himself and his pretty poetry that he could not envisage rejection, and probably an audience would add to his enjoyment.

While the landlord laid out the dishes, she measured the distance to the door with her eyes, then reluctantly abandoned the idea of trying to run away. They would catch her, she was in the middle of nowhere and it was getting dark. How had she ever got herself into this situation? Her foolish idea of taking a lover, or even two, mocked her. Here was Sir Charles, proving another of Lady Salome's adages, which was that reality was seldom as exciting as imagination. What folly had possessed her to accept his escort on the journey from Richmond back to London, when only five minutes before, her sister-in-law, Beth Trevithick, had looked her in the eye and told her that Sir Charles was an ill-bred philanderer who would try his luck if only given the chance? Eleanor had tossed her head in the air and allowed the baronet to hand her up into his curricle, and had not even noticed as they had fallen behind the other carriages and finally become separated altogether.

But this was not helping her to effect an escape. She allowed Sir Charles to hold a chair for her, watching under her lashes as he took the seat opposite and pressed her to accept a slice of beef, for all the world as though this were some *Ton* dinner rather than a squalid seduction. Eleanor accepted the beef, and some potato, wondering if either would be useful as a weapon. Probably not. The beef was too floppy and the potato too wet, though she supposed she could thrust it in his face and try to blind him with it. Her first plan, to hit Sir Charles over the head with the fire irons, had been crushed when she realised that there were none. The dinner plate would be a better option but it would probably crack, leaving him undamaged.

Eleanor sighed and tried to force down a little food. Even if she were able to escape Sir Charles for a time, she still had the landlord to contend with and she was alone and benighted in the middle of the country. All the same, there was little time for finesse in her planning. She had to come up with an idea, and quickly, and in the meantime she had to lull her seducer's suspicions by flattering his diabolical poetry.

'I remember a poem you wrote for me but a few days ago,' she began, fluttering her eyelashes. 'Something to do with beauty and the night...'

'Ah yes!' Sir Charles beamed, waving a piece of speared beef around on the end of his fork.

'Oh she doth teach the torches to burn bright, She walks in beauty, like the night, And brightens up my lonely sight…'

'Yes…' Eleanor said slowly, bending her head to hide her smile as she calculated how much the poem owed to Lord Byron and William Shakespeare. 'How many other words rhyme with bright, Sir Charles? There must be so many to inspire you!'

'You are so right, my brightest light!' Sir Charles proclaimed fervently. He seized her hand. 'Lovely Lady Mostyn, your instinctive understanding of my work persuades me that we should be as one! I know that you have your scruples, virtuous lady that you are, but if you could be persuaded to smile upon me…'

Eleanor, tolerably certain that she was being spared the second verse so that Sir Charles could get down to the real business in hand, modestly cast her eyes down.

'Alas, Sir Charles, your sentiments flatter me, but I cannot comply. You must know that I am devoted to my absent spouse…'

Sir Charles let loose a cackle of laughter. 'So devoted that you let Probyn and Darke and Ferris dance attendance upon you! I know your devotion, Lady Mostyn! Aye, and your reputation!'

Eleanor resisted the impulse to stick her fork into the back of his hand. Despite his ridiculous habit of talking in verse and his overweening vanity, Sir Charles would not prove easy to overcome. And all this talk of love was a hollow fiction, to dress up his lust. He was filling his wineglass for a third time now and his face had flushed an unbecoming puce.

'Eat up, my little filly! The night is becoming chilly and I need you to warm my—'

'Sir Charles!' Eleanor said sharply.

The inebriated baronet had come round the table to her now. His hand was resting on her shoulder in a gesture that could have been comforting and paternalistic—for all that he was only two years her senior—but it was neither of those things. His fingers edged towards the lace that lined the neck of Eleanor's modest dress. Her temper, subdued for so long and with difficulty, triumphed over her caution. She pushed his hand away, repulsed.

'Kindly stand further off, sir, and avoid any inclination towards intimacy! I may be marooned here with you but I have no intention of using the occasion to further our acquaintance! Now, is that clear enough for you or must I express myself in rhyming couplets?'

The angry, dark red colour came into Sir Charles's face. He leant over Eleanor's chair, putting a hand on either armrest to hold her in place. His breath stank of wine and meat and his person smelled of mothballs. Eleanor flinched and tried not to sneeze.

'Very proper, Lady Mostyn!' Sir Charles was still smiling, his teeth bared yellow in his flushed face. 'I suppose I should expect a show of decorum at least from one who was raised a lady but has never managed to behave as such!'

He moved suddenly, grabbing Eleanor's upper

arms, and she was sure he was about to try to kiss her. It was disgusting. She pulled herself away, pressing the back of her hand to her mouth. She was shaking now. It was no more or less than she had expected but the reality made her realise how hopelessly out of her depth she had become.

Into this charade walked the landlord, the pudding held high on a covered dish. There were footsteps in the corridor behind him but Eleanor did not notice, for she was too intent on a plan of escape. As the landlord came in, Sir Charles straightened up with an oath and in the same moment Eleanor stood up, swept the silver cover from the dish and swung it in an arc towards his head. It clanged and bounced off, throwing the startled baronet to the floor where he lay stunned amongst the remains of the blancmange. Eleanor staggered back, almost fell over her chair, and was steadied, astoundingly, by arms that closed around her and held her tight.

There was a moment of frozen silence. Sir Charles had sat up, the blancmange dripping down his forehead, a hunted look suddenly in his eye. Eleanor freed herself and spun around. Then the world started to spin around her. She grasped a chair back to steady herself.

'Kit?'

It was undoubtedly her husband who was standing before her, but a strangely different Kit from the one that she remembered. His height dominated the small room and his expression made her insides quail. His fair hair had darkened to tawny bronze and his face was tanned darker still, which made the sapphire blue of his eyes gleam as hard and bright as the stones themselves. There were lines about his eyes and mouth that Eleanor did not remember and he looked older, more worn somehow, as though he had been ill. Eleanor stared, bemused, disbelieving, and unable to accept that he had appeared literally out of nowhere. She swayed again. The chair back was slippery beneath her fingers and she shivered with shock and cold.

'Kit…' she said, trying to quell her shaking. 'Whatever are you doing here? I had no notion… I had quite given you up for lost…'

'So it would seem,' Kit Mostyn said to his wife, very coolly. His hard blue gaze went from her to the lovelorn baronet, who was showing all the spine of an earthworm and was still cowering on the floor, on the assumption that a gentleman would not hit him when he was already down. A smile curled Kit's mouth, and it was not pleasant. Sir Charles whimpered.

'So it would seem,' Kit repeated softly. 'I see that you have indeed all but forgotten me, Eleanor.'

Eleanor barely heard him. Darkness was curling in from the edges of the room now, claiming her, and she gave herself up to it gladly. She heard Kit mutter an oath, then his arm was hard about her and she closed her eyes and knew no more.

'This is all most unfortunate.' Eleanor had not realised that she had spoken aloud until a dry voice in her ear said: 'Indeed it is.'

Eleanor turned her head. It was resting against a broad masculine chest, which she devoutly hoped was Kit's since for it to belong to anyone else would no doubt cause even more trouble. His arm was around her, holding her with a gentleness that belied the coldness of his tone.

'Drink this, Eleanor—it will revive you.'

Eleanor sniffed the proffered glass and recoiled. 'Is it brandy? I detest the stuff—'

'Drink it!' Kit said, this time in a tone that brooked no refusal, and Eleanor sipped a little and sat up. Kit disentangled himself from her and moved over to where Sir Charles Paulet was standing near the door, brushing the remaining blancmange from his person.

Eleanor watched, hands pressed to her mouth, as Kit grasped the baronet by the collar and positively threw him out of the door, dessert and all.

'Get back to London, or to hell, or wherever you choose,' Kit said coldly, 'and do not trouble my wife again!'

The door shuddered as he slammed it closed. Then he turned to Eleanor. She shrank back before the sardonic light in his eyes.

'My apologies for removing your…ah…admirer in so precipitate a manner, my love,' he drawled, 'but I fear I have the greatest dislike of another man paying such attentions to my wife! Perhaps I never told you?'

'Perhaps you did not have the time, my lord!' Eleanor said thinly. She put the brandy glass down with a shaking hand and swung her feet off the sofa and on to the floor. She glared at him. 'We scarce had the chance to come to such an understanding in the few days that we spent together! You were gone before we had exchanged more than a few words and I do not believe that any of them were goodbye!'

Kit drove his hands into his pockets. 'I realise that it must have surprised you for me to appear in this manner...'

'No,' Eleanor said politely, 'it is not a surprise, my lord, rather an enormous shock! To disappear and reappear at will! Such lack of consideration in your behaviour is monstrous rude—'

'And I can scarcely be taken aback to find my wife in flagrante as a result?' Kit questioned, with dangerous calm. His glittering blue gaze raked her from head to toe. 'As you say, we meet again in unfortunate circumstances, my dear.'

Eleanor's temper soared dangerously. Matters, she thought savagely, were definitely not falling out as they should. Her errant husband, instead of demonstrating the remorse and regret suitable for their reunion, was exhibiting a misplaced arrogance that she had always suspected was part of the Mostyn character. It made her want to scream with frustration. Except that ladies did not scream like Billingsgate fishwives. They endured.

'Surely the point at issue is your want of conduct rather than mine, my lord,' she said sharply. 'I am not the one who has been absent for five months without so much courtesy as a letter to explain!'

Kit sighed heavily. 'Eleanor, I sent you a letter—several letters, in fact—'

'Well, I did not receive them!' Eleanor knew she was starting to sound pettish but her nerves were on edge. 'As for finding me in flagrante, surely you cannot believe that I am in this poky little inn by choice!'

'Then you should arrange for your lovers to find somewhere more acceptable, my dear,' Kit observed, his tone mocking. 'I have searched for you in hostelries from Richmond to London, and there are plenty more that could offer you greater comfort!'

Eleanor felt the tears prick the back of her eyes. This was all going horribly wrong, yet she did not understand how to stop it. The anguished questions that she had wanted to ask ever since he had left her—*why did you go, where have you been*—remained locked inside her head, torturing her. She had been told that ladies did not question their husbands' actions in such an unbridled manner and since Kit had not volunteered the information of his own free will she could scarcely shake it out of him. Eleanor struggled to master her anger and misery.

'You misunderstand the situation, my lord,' she said coldly. 'If there have been others who have paid me attention during your absence, that was because you were not here to discourage them—'

'And because *you* did not choose to!' Kit said, between his teeth. His face darkened and Eleanor realised with a pang just how angry he was. 'Do you know that all I have heard since I set foot back in

England is that Eleanor, Lady Mostyn, is the Talk of the Town? The lovely Lady Mostyn, so free with her favours!' His voice was savage. 'They are taking bets in the Clubs, my lady—should Probyn be next, or Paulet? The wager is a monkey against Darke being your current lover!'

His fist smashed down on the table, making the brandy bottle jump. 'Mayhap I am at fault for leaving you for all this time, but you have scarcely been pining in my absence!'

Eleanor turned her back on him. She could feel the fury bubbling up in her like a witches' cauldron after a particularly uncontrollable spell. Here was Kit, firmly, demonstrably and absolutely in the wrong after deserting her with no word for five months, and here was she, being hauled over the coals for something that was not even her fault! She had already found herself trying to justify her presence in the inn with Sir Charles whereas Kit had barely mentioned his disappearance. Apologies, explanations... Clearly they were foreign to his nature.

She sighed sharply and moved away from the window. 'How did you find me here, my lord? If you are but recently returned to England...'

Kit looked up. He raised an eyebrow. 'I am sorry—did you not wish to be found? I must have misunderstood! I thought that you had just been strenuously explaining that you were not here by choice!'

Eleanor gritted her teeth with exasperation, wavering on the edge of abandoning the polite manners bred in her bones and upbraiding him as he deserved.

She wanted to shriek at him, to beat at him with her fists and pour out all the hurt and misery of the past five months. Except that ladies did not—could not—behave like that, no matter the provocation. Self-possession was all. She screwed her eyes up tight and took a deep breath.

'I dislike your double standards, my lord, but I suppose that a husband may do as he pleases, appearing and disappearing if he so chooses!' The words came out with a kind of haughty desperation. She stole a look at Kit. He was pouring himself a glass of brandy and his face was quite expressionless. The misery that was squeezing Eleanor's heart tightened its grip. She stared blindly out into the dusk, where Sir Charles's carriage, its broken wheel spar miraculously restored, was just setting off down the road to London.

'You may have been debauching yourself in all the bordellos from here to Constantinople for all that I care, sir,' she added untruthfully, 'but you could at least have warned me of your return!'

Kit stretched his legs out before the fire and took a long draught of brandy. 'I am sorry if I have spoiled your fun, my dear!' he drawled. 'I had no notion that you had set up as a demi-rep!'

Eleanor made a sound of repressed fury. 'All you can reproach me for, my lord, is indiscretion, whereas you…' Her voice failed her. She could not even begin to put into words all the things that Kit had done wrong.

'What was I supposed to do?' she burst out. 'Sit

and wait for you? You might never have returned! At one point we even thought you dead!'

Kit's expression was bleak. 'And better off that way so that you could carry on a merry widow? You honour me, my dear!'

It was the last straw. With an infuriated squeak, Eleanor picked up the ugly clock from the mantelpiece and threw it at him. Kit fielded it with ease.

'Glaringly abroad, my dear! One wonders why you did not use it against Sir Charles if his attentions were so repugnant to you!'

There was a heavy silence. Eleanor pressed both hands hard to her mouth to prevent herself from crying. She could not believe how close she had come to losing her self-control, nor how furious and unhappy Kit was making her. She could not see beyond the wicked coil that had enveloped her. Kit's return had solved no problems for her; in fact it had generated nothing but trouble.

Kit rubbed his hand across the back of his neck. For the first time, Eleanor noticed that he looked weary.

'Maybe we are both in the wrong, Eleanor.' Kit's tone was heavy. 'May we not just sit down and discuss this sensibly? I know that I have been away for a space, but I sent you a letter as soon as I could, explaining what had happened. And then several more, after that. Surely you cannot deny it?'

The very patience of Kit's tone grated on Eleanor's nerves now, when all she wanted was to give way to impassioned recriminations. Perhaps if he had shown such calm forbearance when he had come in, matters might have been different. But he had not. And now…

She looked at him and wondered if she really knew him at all. Once, a year ago perhaps, she would have said that she knew Kit instinctively. There had been a recognition between them, sharp and exciting, as they had circled each other at *Ton* balls and snatched a dance or a conversation when her mother's back was turned. Kit Mostyn was the type of man that all the chaperones warned against and under the veneer of well-bred sophistication, Eleanor had sensed a certain degree of ruthlessness in him that had made her feel in danger yet protected at one and the same time. She had not understood it but it had been desperately romantic—or so she had thought.

Now, though, she realised that she was married to a stranger. A very good-looking stranger, she allowed, as she studied him. The Mostyns, like the Trevithicks, were generally accounted to be a good-looking family and Eleanor saw little to argue with in that assessment. Like his twin sister Charlotte, Kit was tall and fair, but where Charlotte's classical features were pleasingly feminine, Kit's face was strong and unforgettable, aristocratic arrogance softened only by a rakish smile that had made her heart beat faster. But he was not smiling now. The arrogance, Eleanor thought furiously, and not the charm, was decidedly to the fore.

She walked over to the fire and made a business of checking her cloak and gloves to see if they were yet dry. The steam was still rising from her dress. Eleanor felt as though she was going through the washing process still inside it. And strangely she was suddenly aware of how every damp fold clung to her figure, yet when she had been intent on preventing Sir Charles's seduction she had not even noticed it. But it was Kit who was watching her now, his smoky blue gaze appraising as it rested on her. Eleanor's nerves tightened with misery and anger.

She swallowed hard. 'Several letters!' she said incredulously. 'Thank you, my lord. I fear I never received them.'

Kit sighed again. It was clear that he simply did not believe her. Eleanor felt another hot layer of anger add to the volcano inside.

'Very well,' he said wearily. 'I am quite willing to explain what happened and where I have been…'

Eleanor clenched her fists to prevent herself from screaming. So now he wanted to explain—when it was too late! If he had arrived at Trevithick House one evening rather than catching her in flagrante in such a ridiculous situation, if he had been remorseful rather than accusatory, if she had not felt so wholly in the wrong and yet so furious with him… Eleanor shook her head. It was impossible to sit down and discuss matters quietly now.

Visions of opera singers flitted before her eyes and she tried to swallow the tears that threatened to close her throat. She did not want the humiliation of hearing Kit justify that a man was permitted to come and go as he pleased, to take his pleasure where and when he chose, whilst expecting a different standard of behaviour from his wife. She had heard all of that from her mother when she had been a débutante and had thought it so much nonsense—except that now it appeared to be true. She had had such romantic notions of marriage, whereas her husband evidently did not expect it to interfere with his existing way of life.

Eleanor pressed her hands together. Her pride would never permit her to tell Kit her true feelings— how she had waited for him, heartbroken; how her mother had made matters irredeemably worse by broadcasting intimate details of her situation to the *Ton*; how she had been reviled and made a laughing-stock, her hasty marriage and even swifter abandonment the *on dit* on everyone's lips. It was Kit who had left her at the mercy of every rake in London then made matters worse by apparently parading his amours elsewhere. And deeper than all of these things was the secret suffering that made it impossible for her ever to forgive him his desertion.

Explanations… There were some that she would never make to him. And Kit was clearly incapable of expressing any kind of remorse. He had not apologised, not at all, and with every minute that went by Eleanor resolved that she would not, *could not*, move to make matters right when he clearly did not care. She turned away and hunched a shoulder against him.

'You do not need to explain yourself to me, my lord! You may do as you please!'

Kit was now looking positively thunderous. A little thrill of pleasure went through Eleanor at her ability to provoke him. She knew it was childish but just at the moment it was all she had.

'Eleanor, I *want* to explain...'

Eleanor smiled. Even thwarting him in this small matter made her feel perversely better. It might be contrary but it was satisfying.

'There is no need for explanations, my lord,' she said coolly. 'I think it would be better if we pretended that it had never happened!'

'Confound it, Eleanor, do you simply not care?' Kit sounded exasperated now. 'Not ten minutes ago you were castigating me for leaving you! I thought you would at least wish to know the reason why!'

Eleanor fabricated a delicate shrug. 'It was the suddenness of your reappearance that shocked me, my lord, rather than anything else. I have no particular desire for us to become drawn into descriptions of what each has been doing. That would be most tiresome! Far better to let the matter drop!'

There was a pause. She saw a strange expression steal across Kit's face but she did not understand it. He ran a hand through his dishevelled fair hair and sighed heavily.

'I understand you, I suppose! And for all my anger earlier I shall ask no questions of you. Truth to tell, I really do not want to know.'

Eleanor frowned a little. She was not quite sure what he meant.

'Oh, I was not intending to tell you anything of my exploits anyway, my lord!' she said brightly. 'I have managed quite well on my own! I have had the status of a married lady after all, without all the tedious responsibilities of tending to a husband!' She paused as she heard Kit swear, and finished sweetly: 'Now that you are back we shall be a thoroughly modern couple—you have your interests and I have mine—'

'And plenty of them—'

Eleanor ignored him. 'And we may present a charming façade to the *Ton*—'

'It sounds delightful,' Kit said, with an edge to his voice.

Eleanor essayed a bright smile, though in fact she knew the tears were not far away. For all that she had manoeuvred the conversation in this direction, it was not what she truly wanted. If only he had swept her into his arms and told her he loved her, everything else, even apologies and explanations, could have waited. She had imagined a reunion with Kit a hundred times, and it had never been like this. This cold stranger, with an angry light in his dark blue eyes, was not a man she could reach.

She told herself sternly that she had been brought up to understand the concept of duty in marriage and so did not expect a husband to show her an unsuitable affection, the way that her brother Marcus did so unfashionably with his wife Beth. Her parents had preserved just such a chilly outward show, and whilst she had sometimes thought that love might be more fun, she had learned that that was not so. Nevertheless, something was hurting her and she did not intend to give Kit the satisfaction of knowing it.

'After all, I hardly expect you to hang on my sleeve

in a tediously slavish way!' she finished lightly. 'You shall go your way—indeed, you already have done!—and I shall go mine—'

'As you also appear to have done,' Kit concluded dryly.

They looked at each other in silence, and then Eleanor shrugged. 'So there we have it, my lord! What happens now?'

'We go up to our chamber, I believe,' Kit said slowly. A mocking smile touched his mouth. 'As you are so determined to maintain a pretence of normality, my lady wife, I do believe we should start practising straight away!'

Chapter Two

'This is ridiculous, my lord,' Eleanor said in an outraged whisper as Kit, the candle clasped in one hand and his other firmly gripping her elbow, steered them up the rickety stairs to the bedchamber above. 'Why can we not simply go back to London tonight?'

'I do not care to do so,' her husband said coolly. 'It is dark and I cannot risk an accident to the wife I have so recently found again…'

Eleanor made a humphing sound. 'I cannot believe that such matters can weigh with you, my lord! And if you think that I will get one minute of sleep in this flea pit—'

She broke off. It was not the fleas that were troubling her but the thought of sharing a chamber with Kit. She glanced at him apprehensively. His face was set, dark and brooding, and he did not look at her. Eleanor's stomach did a little flip.

'You may stay awake if you please,' Kit said indifferently. 'I assure you that I am tired from galloping across country to find you and will no doubt sleep as soon as my head touches the pillow. Ah, a charming room...' He pushed the bedroom door open.

'The scene of your seduction, I imagine!'

Eleanor wrenched her arm free of his grip. 'Enough, sir! I do not wish to hear another word from you on that subject! If you think that it has been pleasant for me to suffer Sir Charles's attentions and then to be subject to your scorn as well...' She stopped, sniffed hard and pressed a hand to her mouth. Now she was going to cry. She knew she should not have said anything.

Kit was watching her. He passed her a handkerchief as she angrily dashed her tears away.

'I beg your pardon,' he said expressionlessly. 'You will perhaps feel better once you have had some rest.'

Eleanor glared at him. 'If you think that I will have a moment's rest whilst you are here you are far and far out! Can you not sleep in the parlour or somewhere?'

'Or somewhere?' Kit raised his brows. 'Somewhere away from you, I infer?'

'Precisely!' Eleanor scrunched the handkerchief into an angry ball.

Kit shook his head. 'I fear I cannot leave you unprotected, my love...'

'Fiddle!' Eleanor marched across to the bed and looked at it unfavourably. The curtains were full of dust and the bedclothes none to clean. 'There is no one here to be a danger to me...'

Except for you. Scarcely had the thought formed when she realised that Kit had read her mind and she blushed to the roots of her hair. He smiled gently, coming across to take the crumpled handkerchief from her hand. His touch was warm.

'There is the landlord. He looks a villainous fellow...'

'You are absurd.' Eleanor found that her voice came out as a whisper. Kit was standing close now, his hand resting in hers. She found herself unable to move away, unable to look away from that shadowed blue gaze.

'Your dress is still damp.' Kit's voice was as husky as hers. 'You should not catch a chill...'

Suddenly Eleanor was back in the house in Upper Grosvenor Street, remembering with exquisite pain the only occasion on which they had made love. The night before their marriage. And the morning... She ached at the sweetness of the memories and recoiled at the naïve trust of the girl she had been.

'I can manage very well on my own, my lord,' she said, almost steadily, taking her hand from his and stepping back. 'You will oblige me by sleeping in the armchair if the parlour does not suit.'

Kit looked at her in silence for a long moment, then he inclined his head. 'As you wish, Eleanor. Good night.'

Before she realised what he intended he had raised a hand and touched her cheek. The feather-light touch shivered down her spine and made her tremble.

'Good night, my lord,' she said, with constraint.

After Kit had gone out she locked the door, removed her damp dress and lay down on the bed, curled into a ball. She did not cry, but lay staring dry-eyed into the darkness. And she tried to tell herself that she was glad he had left her alone.

Kit Mostyn closed the parlour door, moved over to the sofa and sat down. The fire was dying down now and the room was chill. The dinner plates had not been removed and sat on the table, the food congealing, and the smell of beef still in the air. There was also a slippery patch of blancmange just inside the parlour door.

Kit reached for the brandy bottle, poured a generous measure into a glass, and then paused. Truth to tell, he did not really want a drink, but the temptation to drown his sorrows was very strong.

The springs of the sofa dug into him. It was going to be an uncomfortable night, hard on the body but even harder on the mind. Which was why the brandy was so tempting. He could simply forget it all. Except it would all be waiting for him when he awoke...

Kit pushed the glass away and lay down, wincing as a spring burst and stabbed him in the ribs. Eleanor. His mind winced in much the same way as his body had just done, but he forced himself to think about her. It was only five months, yet she had changed so much. Previously she had had an artless self-confidence that had been the product of a privileged and sheltered upbringing. She had been bright and innocent and sweet. Now... Kit sighed. Now Eleanor had a shell of brittle sophistication and he was not entirely sure what was hidden beneath.

Kit shifted on the sofa as he tried to get more comfortable. The candles were burning down now and the old inn creaked. He wondered if Eleanor was asleep yet.

He thought about her and about the rumours that had assaulted him ever since he had returned to England, and about finding her in a cheap inn taking dinner with Sir Charles Paulet. He had been so angry to see all the rumours apparently confirmed. Angry and jealous. His innocent Eleanor, who had evidently not spent the waiting time alone.

Yet she had insisted that she was there under duress and there was the evidence of the blancmange... Kit turned his head and the arm of the sofa dug painfully into his neck. Perhaps it was true—but then what of the others; what of Grosvenor and Probyn and Darke?

Most telling of all was Eleanor's fearful reaction when he had suggested that they should sit down and discuss matters calmly. Kit frowned. He knew that he should have explained himself much sooner, that he would have done so had his jealous anger not intervened. Yet when he had tried she had shied away from it. What had she said—*'I have no particular desire for us to become drawn into descriptions of what each has been doing'*. He was all too afraid that he knew the reason why. There must be compelling reasons why Eleanor did not wish him to enquire too closely into what she had been doing in the past five months.

A huge, heavy sadness filled Kit's heart. She need not worry—he would never force explanations from her, put her to the blush. Nor would he press her to accept his account of what had happened to him and thereby risk prompting any unfortunate disclosures from her. It seemed they were trapped within the modern marriage that Eleanor had decreed, each going their separate ways. It was not at all what he had hoped for when he had returned.

By the time that the carriage rolled into Montague Street the next day, Eleanor's nerves were at screaming point. She had slept very little the previous night, had rejoined Kit for a poor breakfast of stale rolls and weak tea and had spent the journey mainly in silence, pretending to an interest in the countryside that she simply did not possess. It was raining again, and it seemed only appropriate. Kit had been as silent as she on the journey—Eleanor thought that he looked tired and he had seemed withdrawn. All in all it was enough to make her retreat even further into herself and to reflect that her life from now on would be a pattern card of superficial contentment. She and Kit would preserve a surface calm, and no one would know that underneath it her feelings were still aching. Least of all her husband. And one day, perhaps, she would feel better.

Eleanor could well remember her mother, the Dowager Viscountess of Trevithick, instilling in her day after day that a lady never gave way to any vulgar display of feeling and particularly not in public, but when the carriage steps were lowered and Kit helped her down, her composure was put to the test almost immediately.

'But this is not Trevithick House!'

She saw Kit smile. 'No. Naturally I would expect my wife to live with me in the house that I have rented for the Season!'

Eleanor stared. 'But my clothes—all my possessions…'

Kit took her arm, urging her up the steps, out of the rain. 'They were sent round from Trevithick House yesterday.'

Eleanor was outraged at this apparent conspiracy. 'But I don't want to stay here with you! Surely Marcus—'

'Your brother,' Kit said, with a certain grim humour, 'whilst disapproving heartily of the whole matter, was not prepared to come between husband and wife! Come now, my dear, we are getting wet and achieving very little standing here…'

Eleanor allowed him to help her up the steps and through the door of the neat town house. The butler came to meet them; Eleanor recognised his face and flinched away. How could she fail to recognise Carrick, whom she had last seen fetching a hansom to take her back to Trevithick House five months before? She had been pale and exhausted from crying over Kit's disappearance and Carrick's face had mirrored the pity and concern he felt for her. Now, however, he was smiling.

'Welcome home, my lady. I will show you to your room.'

Eleanor raised her chin, horrified to realise that she was almost crying again, uncertain if it was because of the unlooked-for warmth of his welcome or for other reasons. This was ridiculous. She was turning into a watering-pot and could not bear to be so feeble. This rented house, comfortable and welcoming as it looked, was not her home and she did not want to be here, especially not with Kit. She managed a shaky smile—for the benefit of the servants.

'Thank you, Carrick.'

The butler looked gratified that she had remembered his name. Eleanor felt even worse. She followed him across the hall and up the staircase, very aware that Kit was bringing up the rear. She wanted to tell him to go away. Instead she ignored him. It was the best that she could do.

The house was small but extremely well appointed. Eleanor could not fail to notice that the carpet was a thick, rich red, the banisters polished to a deep mahogany gleam. There were fresh flowers on the windowsill and the smell of beeswax in the air. It was charming and she could not fault it. It was simply that she did not want to be there.

Her suite of rooms consisted of a large, airy bedroom and an adjoining dressing room decorated in cream, gold and palest pink. A small fire burned cheerfully in the grate though the May morning was promising to be warm.

Carrick bowed. 'I will send your maid to you, my lady—'

'In a little while, Carrick.' It was Kit who answered, before Eleanor could even thank the butler. 'There are some matters that Lady Mostyn and I have to discuss first.'

The butler bowed silently and withdrew. Eleanor straightened up, marshalling her forces. She looked at her husband as he lounged in the doorway.

'Must we speak now, my lord?' she asked, just managing to achieve the bored tone she strove for. 'I am unconscionably tired and want nothing more than some hot water and a luncheon tray. Then I think I shall sleep. I fear that I had very little rest last night.'

Kit strolled forward into the room, swinging the door carelessly closed behind him.

'It will not take long, my dear,' he said, effortlessly matching her *sang-froid*. 'I simply wanted to mention that I understand there is to be a ball at Trevithick House in a couple of days and we shall attend.' His smile deepened. 'It will be the perfect occasion to demonstrate our reconciliation!'

Eleanor grimaced. The Trevithick ball had been planned for some months but now it threatened to turn into more of an ordeal than ever.

'I am not sure that I wish to attend...'

Kit wandered over to the window. 'If you are as intent on presenting a good face to the *Ton* as you implied last night, you will have to be there.' His tone was sardonic. 'People will talk otherwise. Moreover, we shall have to be seen to pay at least a little attention to each other!'

Eleanor sighed. 'This is all very difficult...'

'It is indeed.' Kit's voice betrayed his tension. 'But

I am tolerably certain that we shall pull through—provided that we do not ask each other any difficult questions, of course!' He looked at her thoughtfully. 'Do you think that is sufficient understanding between us?'

Eleanor clutched her reticule to her as though it was a lifeline. Her heart was beating fast and she felt panic course through her.

'Lud, my lord, we do not need an understanding!' she said, in a brittle tone. 'We are married, after all! That should be understanding enough.'

Kit's expression closed. 'Very well. In that case I will just add that I do not expect to have to fight my way past every rake in the *Ton* in order to claim a dance with my wife! It may be unfashionable in me to expect it, but you will behave with circumspection, my dear. Is that understood?'

Eleanor narrowed her eyes. 'I shall behave precisely as well as you do, my lord.'

Their gazes, dark blue and dark brown, met and locked, then Kit inclined his head. 'Capital! Then we may preserve that excellent pretence that you alluded to so charmingly last night. Neither too warm, nor too cold! Delightfully mediocre, in fact.'

Just for a moment Eleanor thought that she had detected something else in his voice other than a bland lack of concern, a hint of bitterness, perhaps, which was gone so swiftly that she decided she must have been mistaken. She looked at him uncertainly. He was still looking at her, with a mixture of speculation and amusement.

'Was there anything else, my lord?'

'Just one more thing,' Kit murmured. His gaze drifted from her face, which was becoming pinker all the while under his prolonged scrutiny, down her slender figure and back again. His eyes lingered, disturbingly, on her mouth. Eleanor stiffened.

'I wished to disabuse you of any notion you might have of a marriage of convenience,' Kit said slowly. 'All this talk of going your own way and I going mine might lead you to imagine…erroneously…that ours would be a marriage in name only.'

Eleanor stared at him. Her face, so flushed a moment previously, was now drained of colour. Her heart fluttered and she felt a little faint.

'But I… You… We cannot…'

'No?' Kit had come closer to her, unsettlingly close. 'It would not be the first time.'

'No,' Eleanor snapped, moving away abruptly in order to conceal her nervousness, 'only the third! It is out of the question, my lord! *You* may disabuse yourself that there is any likelihood of our marriage becoming a true one! I married you for your name and your protection, and just because I made a bad bargain I need not pay any more for it!'

Kit nodded thoughtfully. Eleanor was disconcerted to see that he did not look remotely convinced.

'It is a point of view, certainly. But not one that I can share. Maybe it is old-fashioned in me to wish for a true marriage—and a family. However, that is how I feel.'

A family! Eleanor shivered convulsively. She

walked across the room to her pretty little dressing-table, simply to put some distance between them. Kit's proximity was too disturbing and his words even more so. She started to fiddle with some of the pots on the tabletop and kept her face averted.

'I believe we are at an impasse, my lord,' she said. 'I cannot agree with you.'

Kit smiled a little mockingly. 'I dare say it will take you a little time to grow used to the idea, Eleanor. And since I have no wish to force my attentions on an unwilling woman, you are quite safe—for the time being.'

Eleanor doubted it—not the truth of his words but the strength of her own determination. Already he had come dangerously close to undermining her resolve, or rather, she had been in danger from herself. It seemed that she could dislike Kit intensely—hate him for the way he had behaved to her, she told herself fiercely—and yet feel a confusing mixture of emotions that owed nothing to hatred. She shivered.

Kit raised her hand to his lips and she snatched it away, but not before his touch had sent a curious shiver along her nerve endings. Eleanor flushed with annoyance. She did not intend to give him the impression that he still had any power over her feelings.

'I will send your maid to you, my dear,' he said, and sauntered out of the room leaving Eleanor to let her breath out on a long sigh.

She heard his voice in the corridor, speaking to Carrick, then his footsteps died away and she was alone.

Two minutes later she was sitting on the end of the bed, staring into space, when the door opened and Lucy, her maid from Trevithick House, came in with an ewer of water. Eleanor thought that the girl looked excited. Goodness only knew the stories that were circulating in the servants' quarters.

'Oh milady! Is this not grand! The master returned and the two of you together again…'

Eleanor sighed. So that was the story—some highly coloured romance, no doubt encouraged by Kit to give the impression of a happy reunion! She knew that she should be grateful, appearance mattering above all, but it felt hollow and a sham.

Lucy was still chattering as she emptied the water into the bowl for Eleanor to wash her face.

'They say that his lordship has been abroad for a space, ma'am…'

Eleanor nodded listlessly, not troubling to reply. What could she add? *He was on the Continent with his opera singers.* She started to unfasten her spencer.

'In Ireland, ma'am…'

Eleanor frowned, her fingers stilling on the buttons.

'On government business, I understand…' Lucy nodded importantly. 'Bromidge the first footman said that his lordship has done such work before, in France, for the War, ma'am…'

'Nonsense!' Eleanor said sharply, slipping the damp spencer from her shoulders and sighing with relief. She started to unpin her hair and Lucy came to help her. 'I am sure that Lord Mostyn has been doing no such thing, and if he had it would be a secret…'

In the mirror her eyes met those of the maid.
Lucy's eyes were as round as saucers. She gave a
little conspiratorial nod.

'Oh no, of course he hasn't been abroad or...or
doing any such thing, ma'am!'

Eleanor sighed again. So now they were both involved in some imaginary conspiracy of silence to do
with Kit's absence. This was getting foolish. She really must tell him not to spin such tales to the servants.

To distract Lucy's attention, she pointed to a door
at the opposite end of the bedroom. 'This is really a
very pleasant house, but what is through that door,
Lucy?'

'That's his lordship's dressing-room, ma'am,' the
maid said, picking up the hairbrush again. 'His suite
of rooms is next door, and then the guest suite. It's
ever so pretty, ma'am, furnished in blue and gold...'

Eleanor was not listening. She had hurried across
to the connecting door, only just managing to stop
herself opening it through a sudden, belated realisation that she was now in her shift and Kit might well
be on the other side.

'His lordship's dressing-room! But I had no idea
he was so close...'

The maid smiled. Indeed it looked to Eleanor as
though she almost winked, but thought better of it at
the last moment.

'Oh yes, ma'am! This is a most convenient house,
if you take my meaning! Well-situated rooms—' She

broke off as she caught Eleanor's quelling look. 'Yes, ma'am, and may I fetch you anything else?'

'Just a carpenter to fix a large bolt upon the door!' Eleanor said brightly, happy to see that she had wiped the complacent smile from the girl's face at last. 'And if you cannot find one, Lucy, bring me a hammer and nails! I will do the job myself!'

'Truly, Kit, what do you expect? A hero's welcome?'

It was seldom that Lord Mostyn had to face the combined disapprobation of both his sister and his cousin, who were the only people on the face of the earth who could make him feel as though he were back in the nursery. He now reflected wryly that he had rather face Marshal Soult in the Peninsula again than take on the combined forces of his relatives. Not that anyone knew he had been in the Peninsula. That had been when he was supposed to be working for the East India Company, and before that... Kit sighed, and sat back, accepting the cup of tea that Charlotte passed him. She gave him a severe frown at the same time. Kit offered her a weak smile in return.

'You look radiant now that you are a married woman again, sis—'

'Gammon!'

'And Beth...' Kit manfully braved the glare that his cousin was directing his way '...increasing already! You are to be congratulated...'

'Pray spare us, Kit!' Beth said shortly. 'You cannot

be glad to see either of us married into the Trevithick family, but since you were not here to advise us you must just accept the consequences!'

Kit raised his brows. 'Would you have accepted my advice, Beth?'

'Certainly not! Especially with the example that you have set us!'

It showed all the signs of degenerating into a nursery tea party. Kit sipped his tea and wished he were at his club. He had hoped that his sister and cousin would be pleased to see him, fall on his neck with tears of joy, and provide the welcome that Eleanor had so singularly failed to do. He shifted uncomfortably. He was already grimly aware that he had no right to expect a warm reception from his wife and the fact that her coldness had hurt him was just too bad. He would learn to live with it.

To be fair to Charlotte and Beth, they had greeted him very warmly when he had first arrived at Charlotte's town house that morning. Now, however, they were over their initial relief and pleasure and were full of questions—and recriminations.

'How could you do that to poor Eleanor!' Charlotte was saying, strongly for her. 'To marry her and leave her all in the one day! To marry her in the first place so precipitately…'

'To *seduce* her in the first place!' Beth put in, eyes flashing. 'Yes, Kit, I know that Eleanor ran away to you, but you could have exercised some restraint…'

Kit gave her a speaking look. Beth looked at him,

looked down at her own swelling figure and after a moment, burst into a peal of laughter.

'Oh, very well, I know I cannot upbraid you when my own behaviour has not been above reproach, but what an odious wretch you are to remind me, Kit! And I shall have you know that I am most respectably married now, and even if the tabbies count the months they can go hang—'

'Beth!' Charlotte said warningly. 'You become ever more unbridled in your speech!' She passed her brother a biscuit. 'As for you, Kit, you know you have no defence. Your treatment of Eleanor has been truly dreadful!'

Kit sighed. He dipped the biscuit into his tea—it immediately broke off and sank to the bottom of the cup. It seemed all too apt.

'I never intended to treat Eleanor so shabbily but matters fell out that way. I am not at liberty to explain…'

He shifted uncomfortably. They were watching him with scepticism and it made Kit feel both guilty and annoyed. He did not like the sensation of feeling in the wrong—and he felt it most strongly.

'It was a difficulty relating to business that kept me away so long…'

'Oh, please…' Beth murmured, putting her teacup down with a disgusted clink of china.

'I am sorry that I cannot be more precise…'

He thought he heard Beth say something that sounded like: 'Pshaw!'

'It is not important for you to explain to us, Kit,'

Charlotte said gently. 'Eleanor is the one who requires an explanation—and an apology. I feel sure that you are able to take her into your confidence.'

Kit shrugged, hiding his frustration beneath a nonchalance he was far from feeling. 'I have tried to offer Eleanor an explanation, sis! She would not let me speak. She has decreed a marriage of convenience and she says that she has been enjoying herself hugely as a married woman without the constraints of a husband!'

Kit cleared his throat and looked away from his sister's penetrating eye. He had no wish to allude any more precisely to his wife's disgrace and he hoped that he had not given away too much already. But perhaps Charlotte and Beth already knew all about Eleanor's behaviour. It seemed that the whole of the *Ton* knew.

Charlotte and Beth exchanged glances over the teacups.

'Oh dear,' Beth said. 'Eleanor has taken this every whit as badly as I would have expected.'

'She is very young and has all the Trevithick pride,' Charlotte agreed. 'Besides, she has suffered a great deal. It is no wonder she is so adamant.'

Kit looked at them, mystified. They appeared to him to be speaking in riddles.

'It seems quite simple to me. Eleanor is not interested in explanations...'

'Nonsense!' Beth said robustly. 'She is hiding her hurt behind that confounded pride, Kit! I'll wager she is positively expiring to know! If Marcus disappeared for five months without a word, the *first* thing that I would wish to know is where he had been—'

'And the *second* would be who he had been with!' Charlotte finished, nodding. 'That would be after he had apologised, of course! Kit, I hope that the very first thing that you said to Eleanor was how sorry you were and how much you had missed her…'

Kit could feel the guilty expression spreading across his face. 'Well… There was the matter of Paulet to deal with first…'

Charlotte sighed heavily. 'Oh Kit—no! Tell me you did not blame Eleanor for her situation!'

Kit made a hopeless gesture. 'I tried to explain matters to her later when my temper had cooled, but—'

'Too late!' Beth said, in a disgusted tone. 'How like a man!'

There was a heavy silence.

'There have been rumours about you, you know, Kit,' Charlotte ventured. 'It has been most distressing for Eleanor.'

Kit looked up, his attention arrested. 'Rumours of what?'

'Rumours of actresses—or was it opera singers?' Charlotte looked vague. 'You know how these tales spring up! People were forever claiming to have sighted you abroad and Eleanor has heard every one of the stories! The gossips made sure of that!'

Kit scowled. This was getting worse and worse. His guilt settled into a lump in his stomach. So Eleanor had heard rumours about him and he had heard scandal about her… And if he was unsure whether *she* had been unfaithful, she must believe the same of him... What a confounded mess they had got themselves into!

'Those stories are not true!' he said coldly. 'And I have heard plenty of stories about Eleanor, if it comes to that! Muse to Sir Charles Paulet, mistress to Lord George Darke—'

'Poppycock! Club scandal!' Beth's silver eyes flashed. 'Eleanor is as virtuous as on the day you married her!'

Kit frowned at her. 'Beth, I admire you for defending Eleanor, but...' he shifted his shoulders uncomfortably '...she practically admitted to me that she had encouraged the attentions of other men! Oh, not in so many words...' he had heard Beth's exasperated sigh '...but why else would she refuse to discuss what had happened during the last few months? She is afraid to tell me the whole truth!'

He thought that his cousin looked as though she would explode and he almost backed away. Beth could be awesome when her anger was roused.

'Kit,' Beth said, with reasonable restraint, 'you are speaking nonsense!' She took a deep breath. 'We were not going to tell you this since we both agreed that it was Eleanor's place to speak to you, but...' she broke off at Charlotte's murmured objection '...no, Lottie, I cannot keep quiet! For some extraordinary reason Kit thinks himself the injured party, when poor Eleanor is only nineteen and has been reviled and laughed at and *ruined* through the careless way in which he abandoned her—' She ran out of breath and started again. 'And now Kit adds his own voice to the chorus of disapproval! Oh, it makes me so cross!'

'Yes,' Charlotte said, in her customary, more measured tones. 'Beth is correct, you know, Kit!'

Kit held a hand up in surrender. 'Perhaps I have misjudged the situation…'

Beth glared at him. 'You have, Kit! Indeed you have!'

'I am sorry.'

There was a startled silence.

'I beg your pardon?' Beth said faintly.

Kit gave her a glimmer of a smile. 'I know you think I can never apologise…'

'No, I know it…'

'Whatever the case…' Kit grimaced. 'I had no notion of any of this.' He looked away. 'I do not understand. How could Eleanor have been reviled when I was the one who deserted her?'

Beth raised her eyes to heaven.

Charlotte tutted. 'For all your supposed experience of the world, Kit, I sometimes think you the veriest babe in arms! Do you not know that it is always the woman's reputation that suffers? If you left her there must have been a reason—so goes the reckoning. In this case the favourite explanation is that you found her not to be virtuous… Which is where the rumours started!'

Kit groaned. 'I did not think… Was it so very bad for her?'

'Yes,' Beth said baldly. 'However, I believe she

might have borne it with fortitude had she but heard one word from you!'

Kit put his head in his hands. 'I sent her letters…'

'They never arrived.' Charlotte was definite. 'And though I agree with what Beth has said, what good a letter when it was you that Eleanor needed, Kit!'

'It might at least have made a small difference to how she felt.' Kit remembered the words he had written with something like pain. He had never penned a love letter before but his anguish had lent finesse to his words:

My dear love

Forgive me for leaving you so suddenly and without a word. I had no intention of this… Pray seek my sister's help until I may return and I swear it will not be for long… Forgive me, my love…

But it had been long, far longer than he had intended. Each day away from her had been purgatory, hoping that she had received his letters, that she would understand. And then he had come back, found his wife in a compromising situation with another man and had heard all the scandalous tales about her. He had been blinded by an astonishing jealousy that had swept all other thoughts from his head. She had not been pining without him. She had had the effrontery to stick her proud little nose in the air and declaim that they should have a thoroughly modern marriage.

Well, that was one idea of which he would just have to disabuse her!

He stood up. 'I believe that I must speak with my wife. We must untangle this muddle. I will *make* her listen to me!'

Charlotte smiled. 'No, Kit, I believe that would be disastrous! You should handle the situation with delicacy rather than go rushing in like a bull at a gate. You must set out to court your wife again and only when you have her trust can you embark on the necessary explanations.'

'Yes,' Beth added, with a mischievous grin, 'and then you must *seduce* your wife, Kit! Slowly and subtly. For a man of your reputation it should not be too difficult a matter!'

Kit gave her a rueful smile. 'With a lady of Eleanor's strength of mind I believe I shall have my work cut out. She will not forgive me easily.'

'Good!' Beth said severely.

When Kit had gone out, the two Trevithick ladies looked at each other in silence for a moment.

'I hope, Lottie, that you did not think me too harsh with your brother?' Beth asked, hesitantly for her. 'I am afraid that I did lose my temper a little.'

Charlotte smiled ruefully. 'No, no, Beth, you said nothing Kit did not deserve! Indeed, I believe he got away lightly and we certainly gave him something to think on. I was only afraid that you were going to say something about…'

'About the baby?' Beth said slowly. 'No. Only Eleanor can tell him about that.'

'Do you think she will?' Charlotte asked.

Beth looked sad. 'I do not know, Lottie. I do not know.'

Had Kit but known it, his wife was having no easier an interview that he was himself. On discovering that her husband had gone to take tea with his sister in Upper Grosvenor Street, Eleanor had decided that she also had some calls to make. It would not do to be seen to be sitting around at home waiting for him. The difficulty was where to go. During the Season she had been taken under Beth and Marcus's wing and depended very much upon them for society. Though they had not been able to prevent the outrageous gossip about her amongst the *Ton*, they had been steadfast in their support and Eleanor had even felt comfortable enough to joke that Marcus would have called out every man who insulted her, except that he did not have enough time to deal with them all.

Now, however, she felt a reluctance to go to Trevithick House. Beth would probably be with Charlotte and Kit, and even if she were not... Eleanor sighed. Beth was Kit's cousin, after all, and Eleanor did not wish to put her in an awkward conflict of loyalties. She also shrank from sharing her feelings with anyone when she felt so sore and confused.

Instead she went to Bedford Square, where the Dowager Viscountess of Trevithick had taken a small mews house and was happily ensconced in ripping to shreds the character of her family and acquaintance, much to the enjoyment of her small audience of like-minded matrons. They were all assembled: Lady Pomfret, sharp and fat, Mrs Belton with a thin face like vinegar, and sundry other ladies large and small, with the common interest of malice and scandal. Eleanor had always secretly called her mother's gossiping friends the Trevithick Tabbies and had given them a wide berth during the Season. Now she came forward into the circle, already regretting the impulse that had driven her into their company and almost half-inclined to flee.

'Eleanor, my dear!' Lady Pomfret, her mother's bosom bow, edged along the sofa to make room for her. 'How lovely to see you again! You have been avoiding us, you naughty puss! Squeeze in here, my love, and tell us all about that *wicked* husband of yours! He has not left you again, I presume?'

Someone else tittered. The Dowager Viscountess grunted her approval of the sally and leant forward to drain her glass of laudanum, her massive figure creaking like a ship in a storm. Her bonnet was awry on her greying curls and her face was curiously flushed, her eyes sunken and bloodshot in the folds of her face. Eleanor wondered, with a stab of pity, whether her mother realised quite the figure she cut.

Lady Trevithick gestured impatiently to Eleanor to refill the glass before she sat down, and after a moment Eleanor moved across to the sideboard and poured from the bottle concealed in the corner. She made sure the glass was full—Lady Trevithick would only send her back to top it up if it was not. Eleanor sighed. Her mother had become increasing dependent on her laudanum in the last few years, taking it to mitigate the pains of bad headaches, or so she said. She handed the glass to her mother, who swallowed most of it immediately.

'Bad blood in the Mostyn family,' the Dowager said, glaring malevolently at her daughter from under her heavy brows. 'Bad *Ton*. Always were a bunch of pirates and scoundrels!'

The group murmured its agreement. Eleanor shifted slightly on the sofa. She accepted a cup of tea and picked at a piece of fruit cake.

'Is Lord Mostyn happy to be back, my dear?' Mrs Belton enquired, picking biscuit crumbs from her dress and watching Eleanor covertly under the guise of the manoeuvre. 'I had heard that he was having such a high time of it abroad!'

'He has been kept occupied with business these past five months, ma'am,' Eleanor said, wondering why she was bothering to defend Kit when she was so cross with him herself.

'Business was it?' Lady Pomfret cackled. 'I hear he is very adept at that sort of business!'

Eleanor flushed. These harpies, who considered themselves so very well bred, were more vulgar than anyone she knew.

'Kit has been in Ireland,' she said coldly. 'He has told me all about it!'

Mrs Belton's painted eyebrows swooped up. 'Ireland, was it? I heard it was the Continent! I could positively swear that he was seen in Italy…'

'They seek him here, they seek him there,' Lady Pomfret murmured. 'Dearest Eleanor sought him quite everywhere, did you not, my love? But then, you do not seem to be repining! I heard that Sir Charles Paulet has written an ode to your ankles!'

'Oh!' The ladies plied their fans.

'Sir Charles does indeed have a vivid imagination,' Eleanor agreed frostily. She turned to her mother.

'Pray, Mama, has my Aunt Trevithick written to say when she will be arriving in town?'

Lady Trevithick nodded, and paused from stuffing bonbons into her mouth. 'She arrives in a couple of weeks.' Her gaze swept around the circle of curious faces. 'My late husband, God rest his soul, has an eccentric sister who sees fit to come up to London. I am sure we shall make her most welcome, for all that she is quite unpresentable!'

'We shall show her how to go on.' Lady Pomfret nodded condescendingly.

'Explain to her the ways of town.' Mrs Belton simpered.

Eleanor felt a sudden lift of spirits. The prospect of this group of cats attempting to give Lady Salome Trevithick some town bronze was enough to cheer anyone who knew that eccentric spinster. She rose to her feet.

'Well, I must be going home. We are engaged to dine with the Fanshawes tonight and there is the Trevithick ball the day after tomorrow…'

'Oh indeed!' Lady Pomfret beamed. 'I can scarce wait…'

'And you need to make sure that your husband is still with us,' Mrs Belton observed, smiling sweetly. 'How terrible if he had disappeared again. Dear Eleanor, such a pleasure to see you! I am so glad that you are not in the least cast down by that dreadful man.'

'Dreadful man—dreadful behaviour!' Lady Pomfret echoed. 'All men are beasts, dear Eleanor!'

Eleanor bent dutifully to kiss her mother's cheek. 'Goodbye, Mama. I will see you this evening.'

Lady Trevithick grunted. She pressed the sticky glass into Eleanor's hand. 'Fetch me another before you go, girl. And make sure that no one sees you.'

This was clearly impossible, for all eyes were upon her. Eleanor refilled the laudanum again, noting that Mrs Belton dug Lady Pomfret in the ribs as the Dowager Viscountess reached greedily for the glass.

'We will see you at the ball, Eleanor dear!' carolled Lady Pomfret. 'Be sure to hold on to that wicked husband of yours when he tries to stray away! Or at least persuade him to be more circumspect next time. Discretion, my dear. Discretion is all!'

Chapter Three

Eleanor had lied. There was no dinner engagement for that night, and as the coach clattered home she remembered that Lord and Lady Fanshawe were in fact out of town, and thought that no doubt Lady Pomfret would discover this for herself and would quiz her about it. The time stretched emptily before her. Would Kit be home for dinner or would he dine at his club? Would he return at all that night? If he did so, would they have anything to say to each other or would they sit staring into space, occasionally making desperate remarks on the decoration of the room or the flavour of the food? Eleanor had observed that many married couples, of long standing or otherwise, had absolutely no conversation with one another and spent their entire time seeking more congenial company. She had not wanted that to happen to her.

The house was quiet and Carrick respectfully informed her that Lord Mostyn was out but was expected back for dinner. There were two posies of flowers waiting for her in the hall; the first were pink rosebuds tied with ribbon, and the second were huge stripy orange lilies, their stamens covered in thick pollen, lolling open in a way that Eleanor could only consider most vulgar. She looked at the rosebud posy and her heart lifted slightly. Perhaps that was from Kit—tasteful, understated, a small token of admiration that might grow into something more meaningful, were she to permit it... There was a note nestling between the stems. Eleanor felt a sudden rush of anticipation and pulled it out, scratching her fingers on the thorns on the process.

The sweetest rose
That ever grows
Amidst the snows
Is mine to...

The final word was scored through, as though the poet had had some difficulty with his rhyme and could not be bothered to rewrite his message. Beneath was scrawled:

'I live in hope, sweet Eleanor, that you will still be mine,' followed by the flourish of Sir Charles Paulet's signature.

Eleanor felt a vicious stab of disappointment, stronger by far than the irritation engendered by Sir Charles's obtuse persistence. Of course Kit would not be sending her flowers—how could she have been so foolish? She was cross with herself for even wanting it.

The rosebuds had no scent and she was tempted to ask Carrick to throw them away, but she loved flowers and could not bear to waste them. Sending Lucy to put them in water, she turned her attention to the lilies. They really were dreadfully brash, like a Cyprian tricked out to catch a new protector. Again there was a card. Eleanor opened it with some trepidation. There were only five words:

'The night of the ball?'

Eleanor clutched the card to her chest as though she had already been caught out in an illicit act. She did not recognise the writing but in her heart she knew these could only be from the man who had been pursuing her for some time, the most notorious rakehell in London...

'Oh, ma'am!' Lucy had reappeared and was eyeing the lolling lilies with a mixture of admiration and doubt. 'How...um...striking! Are they from his lordship?'

'No!' Eleanor snapped, still heart sore. 'Married people do not send each other flowers, Lucy!'

Lucy's eyes opened wide. 'Flowers of another sort! Oh ma'am, they look very common...'

'Excessively!' Eleanor said crossly. 'I cannot conceive what sort of man would think these appropriate to me...'

'Well, there is Lord George Darke, ma'am,' Lucy said obligingly. 'He is forever pestering you and I have heard tell that he is the most dreadful rake! Indeed, before his lordship returned I did wonder if you would succumb to his charms, but what the master would say now...'

'Be quiet, you foolish girl!' Eleanor frowned ferociously at her. 'Take those ugly flowers and put them in the darkest corner of the house! No, put them in the cellar—'

She broke off as the street door opened and Kit came in. It was raining a little outside and she saw that his hair was dusted with tiny drops that sparkled in the light like diamonds. He stripped off his gloves and handed them with his coat to Carrick, with a quick word of thanks. He came across to her and gave her a cool kiss on the cheek. Eleanor jumped away. She knew it was only for the benefit of the servants but it threw her into confusion.

'Good evening, my love,' Kit said casually. His gaze fell on the lilies. 'Dear me, what ugly flowers! One would hope for better taste from your admirers!'

Eleanor knew it was true but she was still furious that Kit would not wish to send her flowers himself, yet still criticised those who did. She turned to Lucy.

'Bring the flowers up to my bedroom once they are in water please, Lucy…'

Lucy dropped a flustered curtsey. 'But ma'am, I thought you wished them to be placed in the cellar…'

Eleanor saw a twinkle come into Kit's eyes. She sighed sharply. 'Just do as I ask, please, Lucy! And quickly! I need you to help me dress for dinner!'

'You will surely be sneezing all night with those flowers in your room,' Kit observed. 'The pollen is most potent!' His keen blue gaze travelled over her and stopped at chest level. Eleanor started to blush, then realised that she was still clutching the card in her hand.

'And who is this admirer with so sound a taste in some things and not in others?' Kit enquired gently.

It was a moment of some delicacy. Eleanor clutched the card all the harder.

'I do not know,' she stuttered, knowing that she was reddening to the roots of her hair. 'The card does not say…'

Kit raised a disbelieving eyebrow. Lucy bobbed another curtsey.

'Oh ma'am, I thought it was Lord George—'

'Lucy!' Eleanor almost screeched. 'Get you gone with those lilies! Now! Throw them out of the house for all I care!'

As Lucy sped away, Kit started to laugh. 'If you are to indulge your penchant for romantic intrigue, my love, you will have to change your maid! That girl is incapable of artifice! I will see you at dinner.'

He raised a hand in casual farewell and started up the stairs.

Eleanor glared after him. She was mortified to feel in the wrong again but worse than that was the evidence that Kit did not care one way or the other. If he had rung a peal over her for encouraging other admirers… She sighed. If he had rung a peal over her, that would have been wrong as well but at least it would have showed he cared. But perhaps that was not true anyway. Last night he had been furious, but with the fury of a man whose pride did not wish him to be seen to be cuckolded.

She traipsed slowly after him up the stairs. Well, if Kit did not care, there were others who would. She told herself that the admiration of a man such as Lord George Darke was balm in the face of such apparent indifference. And immediately her heart whispered that Lord George's feelings for her were counterfeit and not really what she wanted at all.

'Atishoo! Atishoo! Atishoo!' Eleanor sneezed three times, reached for her scrap of lace cambric, realised that it was not up to the task and gratefully accepted the handkerchief that Kit proffered.

The lilies had indeed been banished but their legacy still lingered. Eleanor felt as though her nose was twice the size it should be and her eyes had been watering for a full half hour.

She put her spoon down as a tear dropped into her soup bowl and looked at Kit through streaming eyes.

'If you so much as smile, my lord…'

Kit gave her a look of injured innocence from his very blue eyes. 'I would not dream of it, my dear, when you are suffering so! Are you sure that it is not that charming posy of rosebuds that is causing the problem?'

Eleanor's head snapped round. She had forgotten Sir Charles's gift, which had paled into insignificance beside its more florid cousin. Now, however, she saw with a sinking heart that Lucy had chosen the dining-table as a suitable place to display the flowers, and not just that but the foolish girl had left the card amongst the stems so that Sir Charles's hopeless ditty was displayed for all the world to see. She really would have to speak to the maid.

Kit gestured to the footman to take the soup away.

'Did you have a pleasant day today, my dear?' he enquired.

Eleanor stifled a yawn. 'Yes, thank you. Did you?'

'Yes, thank you.'

The next course arrived, an overcooked turbot with boiled potatoes. Eleanor suppressed a shudder. Kit raised his wineglass to her.

'Your good health, my love.'

Eleanor nodded politely. 'Thank you.'

The conversation languished.

Roast pheasant with cauliflower succeeded the turbot. After a few minutes of silent, valiant chewing, Eleanor put her fork down.

'Oh dear, I think I need to speak to cook about menus. I did not wish to interfere before I knew the standard of servants you had engaged, my lord, but…' she looked at her plate and wrinkled up her nose '…I think perhaps this might be improved…'

'As you wish, my dear,' Kit responded. 'The ordering of the household is, of course, your domain now that you are here…'

Eleanor bit her lip. She was tempted to send the footman for Kit's newspaper, so bored did he sound. When she had specified a modern marriage she had not thought that it might be quite so tedious. To have nothing in common with one's life partner, to exchange only the most banal of observations… She would be fit for bedlam within a week if she could not find something more interesting to say to Kit.

'Perhaps we might give a dinner party in a week or so,' she ventured.

Kit looked at his plate of food and looked at her quizzically. 'Perhaps we should leave it a little while longer, my love.'

Eleanor's shoulders slumped. 'Of course.'

'Though I do hear that the dinner party is the ideal way to conceal the fact that a husband and wife have so little to say to each other,' Kit continued. 'There are so many other people to talk to, after all. And then there are the balls and the concerts and the other entertainments... No wonder the Season is so popular! One need scarcely see one's spouse at all!'

Eleanor sighed. This echoed her own thoughts precisely—except that Kit did not seem to mind. He continued to chew his way through the pheasant, a bland smile on his face. Eleanor, piqued by his indifference, picked up her side plate, turned it over and examined the base.

'I see they have furnished us with the latest Wedgwood china, my lord. It is in very good taste. One can never be sure with a rented house...'

Kit looked around him vaguely. 'Yes indeed. I think the house has been furnished very well, though I do wonder if this room needs decorating. What do you think, my love? A colour scheme in pink and gold perhaps?'

Eleanor put her knife and fork down with a sharp snap and revised her view that she would be bored to death within the week. Two days would do the trick. She was tolerably certain that soon they would be addressing each other as Lord Mostyn and Lady Mostyn, in that odiously coy manner that she had observed being adopted to hide a lack of affection. She mentally surveyed her social diary. She had no engagements other than the Trevithick ball the night after next, but she would have to find something else to do or she would run quite mad in this stifling nothingness. She stood up.

'If you will excuse me, my lord, I think that I shall forgo the pleasure of a pudding. Pray do not hurry your port. I shall see you tomorrow.'

Kit stood up politely. 'Good night then, my dear. Sleep well.'

An hour later, Eleanor was sitting on her bed, a sheet of paper in front of her and an inkpot and candle resting on the table nearby. She put her pen down and held the paper up to the light, contemplating the list of activities that she had just finished.

It started with balls, routs, picnics, concerts and the like. Eleanor frowned a little. She had put them first because they were the most obvious of the Season's entertainments but even these were not without problem. She could not attend unescorted and, more to the point, she could not arrive uninvited. Previously all her invitations had come via Marcus and Beth, but now the mantelpiece was bare. Perhaps it would start to display those coveted cards once word of Kit's return spread. And then he would have to be prepared to escort her…

Eleanor moved on down the list. Exhibitions and talks. She was not sure about these, mostly because she did not know anything about them other than that there were a lot of them about. She could attend alone, but it would probably label her an eccentric. Perhaps that did not matter. It was better than sitting at home alone, or taking tea with the Trevithick Tabbies. She remembered that during her come-out, her mother had denounced such entertainments as the last resort of the uninvited, full of cits and mushrooms who could not gain entrance to more sought-after events.

So... Eleanor sighed. The circulating library. Eminently respectable, but she had never been a great reader. Which left the park—walking, driving or riding. She could not ride. She crossed that out.

Eleanor stared into space. When she had been a débutante there had been no difficulty in filling her days. In fact it seemed that she had the delightful problem of not having enough time for all the activities. There had been dancing lessons, of course, although she had not really needed them, and music lessons, and so many débutante balls and parties... It had been delightful... Well, it had not always been enjoyable because some of the other girls had been quite cattish, but it had mostly been fun. Whereas now she had a house to run and a stranger for a husband, and no fun unless she availed herself of the dubious and dangerous offers of the rakes of the *Ton*...

Shopping. That was fun and she could still do that. Eleanor picked up the pen, then put it down again. Shopping involved money, which meant an allowance and she did not have that any more. Marcus had settled some money on her at the start of the Season but that was almost gone and it would not be appropriate for her to apply to him for more. Which meant that she had to ask Kit... Eleanor sighed again. Still, there was always credit...

Feeling more restless than ever, Eleanor got up and walked over to the window. The street outside was busy with carriages and couples strolling, for the evening was still young. There would be balls and masquerades going on, and she was sitting in her bedroom like a child banished to the nursery. It was intolerable.

She ran down the stairs. The dining-room door was open but the room was empty. A half-eaten marasquino jelly was sliding off the plate. Eleanor could not help giggling. No doubt Kit had given up and gone out to his club. Which meant that his study was empty...

It was. Up until that moment Eleanor would have sworn that she had no intention of rummaging about in Kit's office to see if she could find any evidence of where he had spent the previous five months. In fact she would probably not have admitted, even to herself, that she wanted to know. Now that the opportunity was upon her she barely hesitated. She pulled the door closed behind her and went across to the desk.

At first her search turned up a disappointing lack of information. There were two or three letters relating to the renting of the house, plus a couple of bills from Schultz the tailors. Two of the drawers were empty. Another held only candles. Eleanor frowned. There was a day-old newspaper lying discarded by the armchair, a book on the table by the fire and pen and ink on the top of the desk. It seemed that her husband led an utterly blameless life.

There were no scented notes from opera singers or actresses, smelling of rose water and tied with pink ribbon. Eleanor was uncertain whether she had hoped to find one or not. In fact there were no personal notes of any kind, which was suspicious. Decidedly that was suspicious. Eleanor was sure this was unnatural and that these missives would be found elsewhere. Except that there was nowhere else…

Caught in a crack in the wood at the back of the very bottom drawer was a piece of paper. Eleanor had to kneel on the floor and peer right to the back of the drawer to see it, then work her fingers into the gap to pull it out. It was only a scrap, written in a flowing hand. Eleanor sat back on her heels and let her breath out on a sigh. That was definitely a woman's writing.

'St John at seven tonight. With all thanks—'

Eleanor came round the desk, trying to decipher the next line. It looked like a signature, but the paper was torn and frustratingly difficult to read. In the top right hand corner was another scribble that looked like the date but again she needed to scrutinise it in a good light…

There was a stealthy click as the study door closed. Eleanor spun round. She dropped the piece of paper and put her foot firmly on it, sweeping her skirts over the top.

'Can I help you, my dear?' Kit enquired. 'Are you looking for anything in particular?'

'Oh! No...' Eleanor knew that she sounded flustered and the realisation made her blush all the more. What mischance had prompted Kit to return from Whites so soon when she would have laid odds he would be there all evening? It was most unhelpful of him.

She made an airy gesture. 'Oh, I was just looking for pen and...and ink. I wished to write a letter to...' She stopped, utterly unable to think of anyone she might wish to correspond with.

Kit waited. After a second he said:

'No doubt the servants could have brought you all you needed to avoid you having to hunt around here in the dark. But now that you are here, my love, perhaps you would like to join me in a nightcap? Shall we go into the drawing-room?'

'Oh no!' Eleanor could not think up a way of picking up the scrap of paper without Kit seeing and she was determined that she was going to read it properly. St John at seven tonight... Could that have been an assignation? She looked up, suddenly remembering that Kit had asked her a question.

'Oh, let us sit here!' she said gaily. 'This room is so cosy, my lord, and I so seldom venture in here!' She edged over to the nearest armchair, pushing the paper a little with her foot and sweeping her skirt along as though it were a broom. Fortunately it was only a couple of steps to the armchair. If Kit would only turn his back...

Unfortunately Kit did not. He came over to help her sit down and then poured her a glass of Madeira, all without taking his eyes off her. Eleanor found it disconcerting and even more so because of her guilty secret. She could feel the piece of paper smooth beneath the sole of her slipper.

'Have you had a pleasant evening, my love?' Kit asked. His blue eyes twinkled. 'I hope that you have not been bored. No doubt we shall receive plenty more invitations soon.'

'I expect so,' Eleanor said half-heartedly. A few more evenings like this and she would be fit for Bedlam. She took a sip of Madeira and tried to concentrate.

'Of course, it is the way of things for a husband to go out to his club and a wife to sit in at home,' Kit said, straight-faced. 'I do hope that you were not expecting more in the way of excitement, my dear. A few dinner parties and a ball or two—those are the kind of entertainments suitable for you now that you are no longer a débutante.'

'I suppose so,' Eleanor said. Her débutante days did indeed seem far away. 'Though surely I may be able to go visiting sometimes…'

'Not alone in the evenings,' Kit said sharply. 'You would be a prey to every rake in town—again!' He got up to refill his glass. Eleanor started to bend down surreptitiously to retrieve the paper. Kit turned back. Eleanor straightened up quickly.

'No indeed…' Kit continued '…a little needlework

or reading, perhaps... It will do you no harm to give the impression of virtue!'

Eleanor bristled. For all her quarrel with Kit she had never previously considered him a self-important man, yet here he was showing all the signs of turning into the most odiously pompous of husbands!

'I am sure it is not a question of an *impression* of virtue, my lord—' She began hotly, but Kit held up his hand.

'My dear...' His tone was condescending, 'the whole *Ton* will have seen your somewhat questionable behaviour in the past, so I venture to suggest that an impression of virtue is precisely what you wish to cultivate! The likes of Darke and Paulet must learn not to send their pathetic little floral tributes to this house—'

Eleanor made an infuriated noise. Under most circumstances she would have agreed with him but this irritatingly patronising tone was too much to bear.

'Upon my word, my lord, I had no idea that you were such a killjoy!' she said furiously. 'I may not go out, I may not entertain, I may do nothing more amusing than embroidery—why, I declare I shall be dead of boredom within a week!'

'Not if you learn a little decorum, my dear,' Kit commented.

Eleanor leaped to her feet. 'I have heard enough! I may be lacking in decorum but at least I am not pompous and arrogant! Allow me to say, my lord, that living with you is the most tiresome thing imaginable—boring, tedious and utterly without enjoyment! Good night!'

'Good night, my love,' Kit murmured as she shot past him out of the room. His smile lingered as he heard her angry footsteps beating a quick pit-a-pat across the tiles of the hall. He got up, stretched lazily and moved across to where Eleanor had been sitting. The small scrap of paper was still there by the leg of the chair. Kit bent to pick it up, read it and smiled again. He tucked it into his waistcoat pocket.

He sat down again and reached for his book, glancing at the clock as he did so. If he knew Eleanor at all he would wager that she would come back when she realised. He did not believe that she had the temperament for a long game. He gave it ten minutes.

It took only seven.

There was a flicker of movement outside the study door and Kit put the book down again, opened the door quickly and caught his wife's arm before she could hurry away again.

'Whatever is the matter, my dear Eleanor? Did you forget something earlier?'

He saw her gaze flash to the carpet before it returned to his face with what she no doubt thought was a guileless expression. Kit tried not to laugh. To see Eleanor try to dissemble was highly amusing. She evidently had no talent for deceit at all. The thought warmed him.

'No... Yes... I...'

'This perhaps?' Kit reached into his pocket and extracted the scrap of paper. He was rewarded by a vivid blush. Eleanor's eyes widened.

'Oh, no! But…' She peeked at him. 'Did you know I was hiding that all the time we were talking?'

Kit's lips twitched. At least she had not underestimated him. 'I knew you were hiding something! You are not good at deception, my dear!'

Eleanor's blush deepened. 'And did you deliberately set out to make me cross so that I would forget it?'

'That too!'

'Well, I call that very cruel of you, Kit.' Eleanor sounded piteous. 'I just saw the little piece of paper on the carpet when I came in for the…er…the pen and ink! I confess I was curious…'

'Spinning me another tale, my love?' Kit said cheerfully. 'Why not confess you have been rummaging through my drawers? Would you care to tell me why?'

Eleanor's lips pursed. 'Oh…well…'

'Perhaps you were trying to discover what I had been doing during my time away? Would you like me to tell you?'

A stormy look came into Eleanor's eyes. 'No! I have told you that it is of no interest to me, sir!'

'Very well.' Kit smiled to himself. That was manifestly untrue but it seemed he would have to give her more time. That was no hardship, for he was starting to enjoy himself.

'Good night then, my lord.' Eleanor was looking

at him hesitantly, surprised, perhaps that he was about to let her go so easily. Kit put out a hand.

'A moment, Eleanor…'

'My lord?'

She was standing close enough for him to smell her perfume. It was a very subtle mix of rose and jasmine, faint but sweet as Eleanor herself. Kit felt his senses tighten.

'Do you truly think me pompous and boring?'

She cast her eyes down in maidenly confusion. 'Oh no! But you were deliberately saying those things to provoke me, my lord!'

'Very true. And is our life together very tedious and lacking in excitement? I imagine it could be much different…'

This time she did not look away, but held his gaze with her own. He saw innocence and confusion in her eyes and it was unbearably tempting. He leant closer and touched his lips to hers. Her eyelashes fluttered as she closed her eyes, her lips softened, full and sweet. Every predatory instinct Kit possessed was pushing him to take her in his arms and plunder her mouth with the ravenous hunger that had possessed him ever since he had seen her again.

He drew back.

He heard her sigh quietly and could have sworn that it was with frustration. He hoped so.

'Good night, Eleanor.' He held the door open for her and after a moment she went out of the room, pausing to look back at him as she crossed the hall.

He watched her all the way up the stairs and she looked back at least twice more.

Kit smiled as he closed the study door softly. So Eleanor was curious about his absence even though she was denying it. That augured well. And she had not pulled away when he had kissed her. And she had addressed him by his given name. Only once, perhaps, but entirely naturally. Kit picked up his unfinished drink and took a swallow. It would take time to win back her trust but he was confident that he could do it.

Chapter Four

The following day was fine. Eleanor woke to sunlight, the sounds of the birds and the faint calls of the vendors who were already setting up their stalls in the street outside. For a moment she lay still, feeling vaguely happy. Last night... Last night Kit had kissed her—if that tiniest touch of the lips could really be called a kiss—and it had been very pleasant. Very pleasant indeed. Eleanor frowned. That was not what she had intended. That would not do at all. She was angry with Kit and wished to keep him at arm's length. The happy feeling drained away.

When she went down to breakfast she discovered that Kit had already left the house for some unspecified destination. The remaining scraps of Eleanor's cheerfulness now disappeared in a manner she could not but admit was contrary. She had wanted to avoid Kit rather than seek him out. Yet...

She called Lucy, put on her bonnet and went out. From the extensive list of entertainments that she had put together the previous night she chose the circulating library. It did not hold her interest for long, though she chose two books, one Miss Burney's *Evelina* and the other a well-worn copy of a book called *Tristram Shandy*.

From the library she went to look at the shops, with Lucy still respectably in tow. This proved to be a mistake, however. With her nose pressed to the window and no money in her reticule, Eleanor felt deprived and cross, though she struggled hard with herself against the feeling.

No one called in the afternoon. Eleanor sat in the garden and read *Tristram Shandy* and rather enjoyed it. As the day wore on she went in to speak to Cook about menus for the rest of the week and was happy to approve the list for dinner that night. She went up to change early, filled with a happy anticipation of Kit's company, which she assured herself was only because she had been alone all day. In the event she could have saved herself the excitement, for Kit sent an apology explaining that he was dining with a business acquaintance and did not know when he would be back. Eleanor sat alone at the big table with her book propped in front of her, pushed the food around her plate and retired early.

She had been reading in her room for another hour when she started to feel restless again and decided to go back downstairs. This time she had no intention of rummaging through Kit's drawers but decided to play the piano. The music-room was cold, for no fire had been laid and this was the north side of the house. Shivering a little, Eleanor opened the piano lid and sat down on the stool, placing her candles on the piano lid. Then she realised the next problem—there was no music. But in fact that was not a problem. She had not excelled in many things—her needlework was no more than adequate, her watercolour painting very poor and her singing painful to the ear of a listener—but she loved music and dancing. She resolved to play from memory.

At first her fingers stumbled a little over the notes, for she had not played for over five months and was out of practice. She chose a couple of Bach cantatas to help her regain her skill, and the smooth, slow cadences were soothing to her spirit. Then she tried something a little more lively—a minuet by Louis Boccherini that she had heard at a concert the previous year and had committed to memory. Finally she picked a haunting tune by Beethoven that had been popular with the débutantes because of its romantic overtones and poured all her feelings into it.

The candlelight guttered as the last notes died away and Eleanor shivered in the draught from the doorway. She had been playing from memory, eyes closed, but now she opened them and blinked a little. Kit was standing by the empty fireplace, his tall figure casting a long shadow. He did not speak at once.

Eleanor got clumsily to her feet and closed the piano lid with an abrupt click, almost trapping her fingers in her haste to go. She felt obscurely as though she had been caught doing something wrong—again.

'I did not realise that you had returned—' She

began, then stopped because that made her sound even more guilty although she had nothing to be guilty for.

Kit came forward into the circle of light thrown by the candles. His voice was low. 'That was beautiful, Eleanor. I had no idea you played so well.'

Eleanor looked at him, then away swiftly. 'Thank you.' She knew she sounded stilted. All her frustrations came rushing back. 'It is not surprising that you did not know. I never had the opportunity to play for you, did I?'

'No,' Kit said slowly. 'I imagine that there is a great deal that we do not know about each other.'

They looked at each other very steadily. 'Almost everything,' Eleanor said. She shivered. 'Excuse me, I must go. It is cold in here.'

Kit took her hand in his, which was not precisely what she had intended.

'You are frozen! Come into the study and have a glass of wine to warm you.'

He picked up the candlestick and offered his other arm to Eleanor, who accepted reluctantly. After the chill of the music-room the study was warm, with a welcome fire glowing in the grate. A glass of port stood on the table beside Kit's chair; a book was turned spine up on the seat. Evidently Kit had been reading and had got up when he had heard her playing.

Eleanor took the other chair before the fire.

'Sherry, ratafia?' Kit raised his brows.

Eleanor smiled. 'Thank you. I will have a glass of port with you.'

Kit smiled and inclined his head, filling a glass for her and topping up his own. He put the book aside and sat down.

'So how did you learn to play without music?'

Eleanor took a sip of port and savoured the taste. She knew it was not a lady's drink, at least not a drink that respectable ladies took, but it was extremely nice.

'I just found that I possessed the talent,' she said candidly. 'I had been playing the pianoforte for years, but one evening when I was about fifteen my parents held a concert and I heard a piece that I did not recognise. I tried to commit it to memory and the next morning I went down and played it.' She laughed. 'Everyone was so surprised! Oh, I made a few mistakes, but I soon mastered it. And of course I practised and practised.' She saw that Kit was watching her with a disturbingly intent look in his eye. 'All débutantes must have an accomplishment, be it singing, or playing, or drawing,' she finished brightly.

Kit nodded. 'I suppose so. Only yours is rather unusual.'

Eleanor shifted a little uncomfortably. She downed the rest of her port in a single draught.

'Thank you, I am warm now. I will leave you to your book.'

'A moment.' Kit put out a hand and touched the back of her wrist lightly. Eleanor tried not to flinch.

The slight touch felt as though it had burned her, making her catch her breath. The study was warm, small, intimate.

'You said earlier that we knew so little of each other and you were right,' Kit said slowly. 'How would it be if we spent a little time—like this—just talking on innocuous topics. There could be no harm in that, surely?'

Eleanor sat and looked at him. It sounded harmless. In fact, it sounded very pleasant. Here was a way to avoid the loneliness that had frightened her earlier, whilst in no way threatening the comfortable surface calm of their marriage. She gave a tentative nod.

'Well… I suppose…that sounds quite enjoyable…'

Kit smiled slightly. 'I think so too. Perhaps tomorrow you could tell me of your other interests?'

'Tomorrow it will be your turn!' Eleanor said pertly. Her face fell a little. 'But there is the ball, and we shall have no time…'

'I am sure we can make time,' Kit said gently.

Eleanor got up. She suddenly felt quite tired. Then she remembered about the allowance, and lingered.

'Kit…' she could feel herself blushing a little '…there are some items that I need to buy, a few trifling purchases…'

Kit nodded. 'We shall go shopping tomorrow.'

'Oh!' Eleanor frowned a little. 'But there is no need for you to come! They are only small things, underwear…'

Kit looked at her quizzically and somehow it made her feel even more self-conscious. 'Of course if you wish to come that would be very pleasant, but...I only wanted to save you the trouble, and if you were to make me an allowance instead, then you could go to your club instead of squiring me about town...'

'Eleanor,' Kit said softly, 'I should be delighted to accompany you.'

There seemed little else to say. Eleanor looked at him, a little at a loss. 'Then that would be most agreeable...'

Kit got up to hold the door for her. 'In the morning?'

Eleanor glanced up at him. 'Um... Yes, thank you.'

Kit took her hand and pressed a kiss on the back. Eleanor felt it all the way down to her toes. When she reached the bottom of the stairs she glanced back and saw that Kit was still standing in the doorway watching her. It made her feel strange. She imagined that she could feel his gaze following her all the way up the stairs, raising a little tingle of awareness on the nape of her neck. Once in her bedroom, she called for Lucy to help her undress and endured her chatter with far more patience than before. She did not expect to sleep well and would have been astonished to discover that she had fallen asleep as soon as her head touched the pillow.

'The amber scarf would become you exceedingly, my love, and the rose pink too,' Kit said judiciously.

They were seated on the striped satin sofa in one of Bond Street's most elegant—and prodigiously expensive—mantua-makers, and Eleanor was bewildered by the fact that she had just purchased a walking-dress in bronze, a ball-gown in gold and a dashing pelisse in a deep crimson velvet, despite the fact that she had set out requiring one pair of gloves, some silk stockings and possibly, just possibly, a new bonnet. It was Kit's bad influence, she told herself—he had suggested purchases with a prodigality that had made her eyes open wide and had made the shop's proprietor, a lady who was as well-upholstered as her gilt sofa, beam with pleasure. And Eleanor was forced to admit that shopping with her husband had been so very much more pleasant that going out with her maid.

'I will take the amber,' Eleanor said cautiously, 'and perhaps a pair of gloves in the pink—'

She broke off as she saw Kit exchange a nod of complicity with the proprietor. No doubt both scarves would find their way into her wardrobe and she could scarce complain, for they were excessively pretty.

'That really was quite unnecessarily generous of you, my lord,' she said, once they were out on the street, sped on their way by the heartfelt good wishes of the shop owner. 'I have no need of additional dresses and as for the scarves, I can hardly wear two at once! It really was quite unwarranted extravagance—' She broke off at the spark of amusement in Kit's eye.

'Why, what is it?'

'I do believe that you are a secret puritan, my love,' Kit said ruefully. 'It is another aspect of your character that I would never have guessed! How many gentlemen have to *force* their wives to buy dresses…' He gave her a droll look. 'I can see I shall have to watch you to prevent you sending them back!'

Eleanor laughed. 'Oh, I am not so much a puritan as that, my lord, and they are all very pretty.' She sighed. 'I only required some stockings, however…'

Kit looked down at her. There was a wicked smile curving his lips. 'Then by all means let us go and buy you some, my love…'

'However, I think that I shall send Lucy to purchase them for me!' Eleanor finished swiftly. The thought of Kit sorting through silk stockings with her made her feel quite faint. 'I am a little fatigued and would like to go home now.'

Kit shot her an amused look but he did not demur. They strolled along the pavement, through the crush of shoppers. It was a fine morning and Bond Street was busy.

'So now I know you are a secret puritan who plays the piano like an angel,' Kit said thoughtfully. 'What a curious mixture you are, my dear, and I wonder what else there is to learn?'

Eleanor smiled up at him. 'It is your turn,' she reminded him.

Kit looked thoughtful. 'Well… I prefer living in the country to living in town, I detest mock turtle soup and I was bullied shamelessly by my cousin and sister when I was a boy!'

'Oh for shame!' Eleanor burst out laughing. 'That cannot be true! Charlotte and Beth would do no such thing!'

Kit grinned. 'I assure you that being the only boy at the mercy of those two girls was no pleasure. Charlotte, being the elder twin, would order me about, and Beth, being younger than the two of us, would whine to join in. But since you do not like my disclosures, tell me what you already know of me instead.'

Eleanor's eyes sparkled. This was much easier than she had thought, for once she started to think of it there were plenty of things she remembered about Kit from her come-out Season. Perhaps he was not so much of a stranger as she had thought.

'You like the plays of Mr Sheridan but not those of Mr Shakespeare,' she began. 'As a boy you used to steal apples for cider—I am sorry I do not recall the correct term…'

'Scrumping,' Kit said obligingly.

'Yes—you would go out with the village boys to raid the orchards!' Eleanor laughed. 'I remember you telling me about it one evening when we sat out a dance together. And speaking of dancing, I also know that you are very kind, for when Lord Grey scorned poor little Miss Harvey at Almacks that time and referred to her as a cit, you asked her to dance—'

'When I would have preferred to stand up with

you!' Kit finished. He grimaced. 'I suppose that was kind…'

'Excessively so, and you know it. You did it to spare her blushes.' Eleanor paused, head on one side. 'Unless I mistake, of course, and you were cherishing a secret *tendre* for her!'

Kit smiled down at her. 'I think not! I had room in my heart for only one secret passion…'

There was an odd pause. They looked at each other. Eleanor was silent, utterly unaware of the crowds that ebbed and flowed around them. Suddenly she was aware of Kit in the most curious detail; the sheen of his skin in the sunlight and the tawny gold of his hair, the smooth material of his sleeve beneath her fingers and the strength of his arm beneath that, the fresh air scent of him and the warmth of the smile that was creeping into those blue eyes as he looked down at her…

'Eleanor! And Kit! I am so glad to see you! I was hoping to call on you soon—'

Eleanor jumped and tore her gaze away from Kit, knowing instinctively that he too had been snatched from whatever intense preoccupation had captured them. She blinked a little in the sunshine.

'Beth! Marcus! How lovely! Are you—' Eleanor broke off. Her brother had given her a brief smile, but when Kit had held his hand out, Marcus had ignored it as though Kit simply were not there. Now Eleanor watched as her brother turned to Beth a little abruptly.

'If you are ready, my dear…'

The colour flamed to Eleanor's face. Although Marcus had acknowledged her, she was as indignant as if he had cut her dead. How dared he ignore Kit in such a public manner! She felt Kit stiffen beside her and shot a quick look at him. She could tell that he was furious. His expression was set, his blue eyes hard. Eleanor saw his hand fall back to his side, saw Marcus cast him a look of comprehensive dislike. She was mortified—this was all on her account and she could not bear it. Eleanor trembled, thinking that in another moment her husband would be calling her brother out and they would all be engrossed in the most appalling scandal imaginable.

It was Beth who rescued the situation whilst the rest of them stood about like waxworks. She reached up to kiss Kit's cheek, then turned to Eleanor as though there was nothing wrong in the world.

'I was hoping to catch you for a quiet coze, my love! Were you returning home? I confess I have been shopping and am quite done up!'

'Oh yes!' Eleanor said hastily, not daring to look at Kit's unyielding face. 'By all means let us return to Montague Street! Kit, dearest...' she put a hand on her husband's arm '...you do not mind if I go back with Beth? I know that you have business at the gunsmith's...'

'Of course.' Kit covered her fingers with his own and Eleanor was inexpressibly relieved. He gave her a glimmer of a smile. 'I will see you later, my love. Good day, cos...' He bowed to Eleanor and Beth, ignored Marcus pointedly, and strode away.

'Marcus—' Beth began indignantly, but her husband merely sketched them a bow, turned on his heel and strode away—in the opposite direction to Kit.

'Men!' Beth said furiously. 'Of all the silly, childish behaviour...'

'And we are left to procure ourselves a hackney carriage!' Eleanor said mournfully. 'One or other of them could have had the chivalry to call one for us before they left!'

'Of course, it's all of a piece!' Beth said half an hour later, as she and Eleanor sat in the drawing-room of the house in Montague Street taking tea together. 'You know as well as I, my love, that Marcus can be the most tiresomely obstinate creature when he chooses. Goodness knows, I love him to distraction, but sometimes...' She broke off, stirring sugar vigorously into her cup. 'Well, I shall have to speak to him about it!'

Eleanor shuddered slightly. When it came to obstinacy, Beth could win prizes herself and Eleanor was sure the results of such a confrontation would be spectacular.

'It is all a little difficult,' she said carefully. 'I had no notion that Marcus would disapprove so...'

'It is not his place to approve or disapprove,' Beth said sharply, reaching for a piece of cake. 'It is a matter between yourself and Kit only. Oh, I am so cross! And so hungry! I am always hungry!'

'I expect that is because you are in a delicate condition,' Eleanor commiserated. 'Indeed, Beth, you should not allow Marcus to annoy you so. It will be bad for the baby!'

Beth sat back with a sigh. 'Let us hope the child is of a less stubborn disposition that its father. But never mind about that! What about you, dearest?' She fixed Eleanor with her perceptive silver gaze. 'I so wondered how you were getting on but thought that you might not wish to see me.'

'Because Kit is your cousin and you felt you had to defend him?' Eleanor asked. She gave a rueful laugh. 'Oh, Beth, this is getting so complicated!'

Beth patted her hand. 'It need not be. We are friends, Eleanor, as well as sisters-in-law and,' she laughed, 'cousins-in-law if you will. If you wish to talk to me I should be pleased but if you wish me to attend to my own affairs then pray tell me so!'

Eleanor laughed too. Deep down she had known that Beth would stand her friend whatever the situation, but it was reassuring to have the matter confirmed.

'To be frank, I should be glad of a confidante,' she said, 'but I do not wish to make matters awkward for you, Beth…'

Beth shrugged, scattering cake crumbs. 'Oh, do not regard it. I know I am a sad rattle and I rush in where angels fear to tread, but if you do not wish me to tell anyone your secrets, dear Eleanor, then of course—I shall not!'

Eleanor only just managed to restrain herself from hugging her. 'I know! I trust you. After all, you hold the biggest secret of them all.'

Beth's smile faded. 'You have not told Kit, then? Perhaps it is too soon…'

Eleanor pressed her hands together. Despite the warmth of the day, she felt the chill steal over her. It was always the same when she remembered those miserable months in Devon. She looked up and met Beth's gaze.

'I don't intend to tell Kit, Beth. Not ever! Oh…' she hurried on as she saw Beth's look deepen into concern '…I know we have spoken of this and you think that Kit should know about the baby, but…' she shook her head '…I could not bear to tell him! It would be too painful!'

'I see,' Beth said slowly. She leant forward and picked up her teacup. 'Of course you may change your mind. Trust takes time to grow…'

'I do not wish to trust Kit ever again!' Eleanor said, in a rush. Now that she had started to talk it felt as though all her feelings were rushing out in an unstoppable flood. She looked at her sister-in-law. 'Did Kit tell you that I had refused to listen to his excuses?'

'Well…' Beth said carefully.

'Oh do not scruple to be kind to me!' Eleanor said, feeling as though she wanted to burst into tears. 'Truth to tell, I know I am being contrary but I am doing it deliberately because it is the only way to defend myself! I have to keep Kit at arm's length, Beth, for once I start to let him even a little closer, where will it end?' She made a gesture of despair. 'First he will apologise and then he will tell me where he was for those five months and then I will forgive him and tell him what befell me and…' she gulped '…before I know it I will be in danger of falling in love with him all over again!'

'Well…' Beth said again. She looked up and fixed Eleanor with a serious look, the sort of look that made her sister-in-law's heart sink. 'Would that be so bad, Nell? I know that Kit deserted you but he is a good man and there were reasons…'

Eleanor put her hands over her ears. She remembered the affinity that she and Kit had achieved only hours earlier. She did not want that to happen again. 'I do not wish to hear!'

Beth smiled ruefully. 'Very well!'

There was a silence. Eleanor peeked at her. She knew her sister-in-law was exercising almost superhuman powers of self-control in order to keep quiet, and somehow that made Eleanor feel even fonder of her than before because she knew Beth found it so difficult. After a moment she said cautiously:

'Did Kit tell you where he had been, Beth?'

Beth gave her an old-fashioned look. 'I am not telling!'

Eleanor sighed. 'Please?'

Beth reached for another piece of cake. 'Oh, very well. No, he did not tell me! Charlotte and I felt that Kit should speak to you first, Eleanor, before the rest of us hear his tale. So if you persistently refuse to hear him then I suppose we shall all just have to go in ignorance!'

Eleanor hesitated. Beth looked at her shrewdly. 'Do you truly not want to know, Nell?'

Eleanor sighed. 'Of course I want to know! I am consumed with curiosity!'

They both laughed, Eleanor with a little embarrassment.

'Then…' Beth said meaningfully.

'But I shall *not* ask!' Eleanor said, with spirit. 'I have told you, Beth—I do not wish to like Kit any more…'

'What, any more than you do already?'

Eleanor sighed again. There went another of her secrets. 'Beth…'

Beth clapped her hands together. 'I knew it! You cannot help yourself!'

Eleanor blushed a little. 'I do like Kit, I admit it! I cannot seem to help it! Yet…' she sobered '…I am also so very angry with him, Beth! I cannot just forgive and forget!'

'Then speak to him!' Beth urged, leaning forward. 'Oh Nell, you cannot bottle it all up and pretend it never happened! Your resentment will fester and turn sour and…' she made a slight gesture '…what sort of existence is that? Please…'

Eleanor's heart was beating fast. She had to make Beth understand. She put her teacup down carefully.

'Beth, I cannot allow Kit too close,' she said baldly. 'He wants a family and will expect—in time—that we will resume…that things will be…oh, you know what I mean!' She made a gesture of exasperation. 'He does not want a marriage in name only…'

'I imagine not!'

'So…' Eleanor looked at her pleadingly. 'Surely you understand? I cannot go through that again! The thought of making love…' She shuddered. 'Oh, a part of me wishes reconciliation with Kit more than anything, for safety, for security… But then I remember…'

Beth sighed. 'Eleanor, because it happened once, it need not be the same again. And with Kit's love and support—'

'No!' Eleanor could feel a pain starting in her throat, the pain she always got when she remembered the horror of losing her child. 'I know there is no good reason for how I feel…'

'Of course there is!' Beth caught both her hands. 'The best reason! You were young and alone and you miscarried your baby! No wonder you are angry and upset…'

Eleanor clung to her. 'Then say you understand! If I allow myself to like Kit even a little, I am afraid of what will happen!' She freed herself and put her hands over her face.

She felt Beth's arms go around her as her sister-in-law hugged her tight. It was inexpressibly comforting. Eleanor gave a little sigh.

'Damnation! I hate being such a watering-pot!' She sat up. 'You should know, Beth, that though I envy you the affection you have in your marriage to

Marcus, in mine I intend nothing more than a luke-warm respect...'

'Oh, Eleanor!' Eleanor heard the laughter in Beth's voice as her sister-in-law let her go and sat back. She looked at her enquiringly.

'Beth? What have I said?'

Beth was shaking her head. 'Have you thought about Kit at all in this, my love?'

Eleanor frowned. Was Beth being deliberately ob-tuse? 'Constantly! I thought that you realised that that was the problem...'

Beth shook her head again. 'No, I mean, have you thought what Kit will do whilst you try to achieve some sort of lukewarm, makeshift marriage?' She laughed. 'I have known my cousin all my life and I would say that he is no more patient than the next man! Well...' Beth shrugged '...a little more patient than Marcus, perhaps, but in general terms—' She broke off.

Eleanor watched her with foreboding. She had the sudden feeling that she had miscalculated and that Beth was about to put her finger on the flaw in her reasoning.

'All the time that you are laying your plans, Nell...' Beth expanded carefully '...Kit will be mak-ing his. And believe me, they will not involve a mar-riage of convenience, or a compromise where you never speak to each other except to request the but-ter! So you must be prepared to oppose him. And which of you will be the stronger? Especially...' Beth fixed her with a stern regard and Eleanor felt herself shrink a little '…when at least a part of you is on the same side as Kit!'

Eleanor felt her heart sink. She knew Beth was right but she also knew she had to try. It was the only compromise that she was prepared to accept. The idea of making love, the thought of another pregnancy, the horror of another miscarriage… She shuddered violently.

'It is the only thing that I can do,' she said sadly. 'I am sorry, Beth, but I have no choice.'

Chapter Five

'Damnation!'

Eleanor peered at her reflection in the mirror, dropped her reticule on the floor with a thud and sank down on to her bed in a heap. She was already dressed for the ball and now she had decided that she would not attend after all. She was feeling very cross-grained. In fact, she was blue-devilled.

'Whatever is the matter, milady?' Lucy enquired mildly. She had been helping her mistress to dress and only a moment before had told her how very pretty she looked. And indeed, Eleanor thought now, she did look her best in her favourite dress, a simple silk slip with gold gauze that flattered her colouring and emphasised the slenderness of her figure. She had chosen the dress for two reasons—one was to give her courage at the first social occasion since Kit's return and the second… Eleanor snapped her fan closed and drummed it against her fingers. The second reason also featured Kit and here Eleanor frowned ferociously. Her pride had demanded that she look her best so that Kit admired her and now she was disgusted with her own behaviour. Remembering her conversation with Beth earlier, Eleanor sighed heavily. Kit's admiration—or lack of it—should be nothing to her. If she wished to keep her distance from Kit she should do nothing to encourage him.

'I am not going,' she said baldly.

Lucy continued with her placid tidying of the room. She picked up several discarded dresses and hung them away.

'I expect you're feeling nervous, ma'am,' she sympathised. 'You'll feel better when you have his lordship by your side…'

'No I shan't!' Eleanor said pettishly. 'I shall feel much worse! In fact the thought of going to this ball with Lord Mostyn makes me feel quite monstrous ill…'

'May I come in?'

Eleanor broke off sharply at the sound of Kit's voice. He was standing in the doorway, not the door to his dressing-room, which was still firmly fastened on Eleanor's side with a shiny new bolt, but the door to the landing. Eleanor scrambled to her feet, feeling foolish and annoyed to have been found slouching on her bed in so undignified a position. Had Kit heard her words? She could not tell. His face was impassive. She felt ashamed of herself.

'I have something for you,' Kit continued, coming forward into the room. He was carrying a flat package in his hand. He nodded a dismissal to Lucy who tripped out, a smile of romantic satisfaction on her face. It only added to Eleanor's irritation that her maid persisted in thinking that she and Kit were involved in some passionate reconciliation—despite the ostentatious bolt on the door.

'What is it?' she asked, knowing she sounded ungracious.

Kit seemed unperturbed. 'It is a surprise,' he said. 'Turn around to face the mirror and close your eyes.'

It was on the tip of Eleanor's tongue to refuse, but something in Kit's face made her comply with his request. She closed her eyes, then almost jumped as she felt Kit's fingers lightly touch her neck, warm against her skin. The sensation was in no way unpleasant but suddenly her skin seemed peculiarly sensitive to the brush of his hand and she had to force herself not to move away. She felt confused and light-headed, and it was a relief when Kit said:

'Open your eyes!'

Eleanor did so, and saw that she was wearing a delicately worked pendant necklace of diamonds and emeralds set in white gold, the exact colour of her dress. She stared, entranced.

'Oh, it is so pretty! But...' she turned her head to look at Kit '...surely these are the Mostyn diamonds? I have seen Beth wearing them...'

Kit was smiling at her in a way that only served to increase her confusion. 'They suit you very well,' he said slowly. 'I thought that they would.'

Eleanor stroked the stones of the necklace gently. The metal had felt cold at first but was starting to warm now as it lay against her skin. It was a beautiful necklace and Kit was right, its delicacy suited her well. Not for her the enormous parures of some of the matrons, the stiff encrustations of jewels that looked as though they were some sort of armour. She was so slender that she needed something equally light and ethereal.

'Beth wanted you to have them,' Kit said now, smiling at her reassuringly as Eleanor continued to look uncertain. 'They are family jewels intended to be worn by each Lady Mostyn. They are rightfully yours. Besides,' he grinned, 'maybe it is ungentlemanly of me to mention it, but Beth felt that she needed something slightly more…robust… to suit her figure!'

Eleanor was betrayed into a giggle. 'Well, she could carry off something more magnificent, whereas I do not have the…er…appropriate proportions…'

She glanced down at her own, small bust, looked up and realised that Kit was looking in the same direction. He raised a lazy eyebrow, the smile still on his lips.

'I have no complaint, Eleanor!'

Eleanor felt a huge wave of colour start at her feet and envelop her up to her hairline. She felt hot and embarrassed and, worse, she felt dizzy and confused. If Kit was always going to be able to make her feel such a troubling awareness, she was not sure that she could bear to live in such close proximity with him. To cover her embarrassment, she reached for her evening cloak and started to chatter brightly.

'Perhaps if Mama could be persuaded to give up

the Trevithick rubies, Beth would have a necklace worthy of her. They are not really Mama's to wear anyway, given that Papa was never the Earl. Have you seen the necklace, Kit? It is a magnificent piece but huge and barbaric and needs to be set off by an appropriate…' She stopped and waved her hands about mutely, realising that she was back on the same subject again.

'An appropriate décolletage?' Kit murmured. He had taken the cloak from her and was setting it about her, and Eleanor was aware of his hands on her shoulders, firm and strong. She pulled the cloak together to hide her own décolletage, which once again appeared to have become the focus of his eyes.

'Well, shall we go?' she enquired, a shade too brightly. 'We do not wish to miss any of the ball!'

'No indeed,' Kit said, a little wryly. 'It should be an occasion to remember!'

Eleanor eyed him a little warily. It had not occurred to her that Kit might have any concerns about the evening, yet when she thought about it she realised that his position was as awkward as her own. Not only was there the difficult water of family relationships to negotiate, but there was the unknown element of the reaction of the *Ton*. Society was so fickle and could outlaw one of their own at a stroke.

'I am sure you need have no concerns about your welcome from the family,' she said, as they seated themselves in the carriage. 'No matter what anyone is thinking, I am persuaded that their behaviour will be quite proper on the surface.'

'As your brother did this morning?' Kit enquired with sarcasm. 'You may feel it important to maintain a superficial façade, my dear, but I fear that Trevithick does not share your values!' There was such an undertone of bitterness in his voice that Eleanor put out an instinctive hand to him, then snatched it back, hoping that Kit had not seen. They completed the rest of the short journey to Trevithick House in silence.

'Marcus!' Eleanor hissed in her brother's ear two hours later, 'can you not behave with a little more discretion? Everyone is looking at us and if you persist in cutting Kit dead every time that you pass him they will have plenty more to gossip about! It was bad enough for you to behave so disgracefully earlier, but now it is outrageous!'

They were standing in the entrance to the main ballroom and were ostensibly watching the press of visitors who were pushing their way into the room with the eagerness, Marcus had said distastefully, of a crowd at a public hanging. Eleanor supposed that the popularity of the event was no great surprise—the Trevithick ball was one of the major events of the Season and in addition, society wished to indulge its curiosity. One family could provide a great deal of entertainment, after all, and just at the moment the Trevithicks were good value. There was the handsome Earl of Trevithick and his beautiful wife who would, it was whispered, produce a child after only *seven months* of marriage. Since no one knew exactly when the marriage had taken place they could not be completely sure, but they were counting. Then there was the bride's cousin Charlotte, a beautiful widow who had lived retired but had been snapped up by the Earl's cousin, Justin Trevithick, who had fallen in love with her at first sight. Justin himself was quite scandalous because he had been born out of wedlock. It was all a long time ago, but some of the dowagers had very long memories. And then there was Eleanor herself and the titillating tale of her desertion and apparent reconciliation... Eleanor sighed. Until that morning, she had not thought that Marcus would make a gift of things to the gossips.

'If you could just speak to Kit without looking as though you would like to hit him across the room...'

The Earl of Trevithick gave his sister a derisive look. 'Eleanor, that is precisely what I wish to do to your husband and I never saw fit to hide my feelings on the matter! Whether you wish to effect a reconciliation with Mostyn or tell him to go to hell, that is your concern and I will support you whatever you choose! However, you cannot expect me to *like* him after what he did...'

Eleanor clutched his sleeve, trying to smile at the same time at Lady Pomfret, who was hovering a short distance away. 'But Marcus, the scandal! Everyone will see...'

Marcus shrugged. 'Who cares? You refine too much upon such things, Eleanor!' A smile softened his face as he looked down at her. 'I only agreed to you staying with Mostyn because Beth persuaded me

I should not stand between you. Do not ask any more of me than that, I beg you!'

Eleanor sighed. She knew that Marcus, ever the protective elder brother, only wanted what was best for her, but he was making matters very difficult, whilst Beth and Charlotte, with connections on both sides, were trying to make peace. It was as though the Mostyn and Trevithick feud, so virulent for centuries and only recently laid to rest, had somehow reasserted itself. Except that it was not that simple any more.

She tried one last time. 'Marcus, I am trying to put a good face on this and you and Justin are undoing all my good work…'

Marcus quirked a brow. 'So Justin is shunning Mostyn as well, is he? Excellent!'

Eleanor sighed in exasperation. 'I believe you have put him up to it!' she said wrathfully. 'And Charlotte is deeply upset… Oh, it is too bad of the two of you! Why must you be so stubborn?'

Marcus grinned. 'It is the Trevithick pride, my dear Eleanor! Surely you know of it, for you possess it too!'

'Well, I do not see why you should be so proud of being proud!' Eleanor said, trying not to stamp her foot with frustration. 'It is childish and conceited and rude! Really, Marcus! I shall not stand up with you for the boulanger now!'

Marcus sketched her a bow, giving her an unrepentant grin. Eleanor found it was surprisingly difficult not to smile back. She was very fond of him for all that he infuriated her.

'Very well, dear sis, withdraw your promise to dance—if you wish to make a scandal!'

He strolled off and Eleanor could almost swear he was whistling softly under his breath.

Feeling irritated in the extreme, she sought the quiet of the conservatory, which had been decorated with little coloured lanterns and furnished with rustic benches to provide a restful place away from the noise of the ballroom. She had arranged to dance the next with Kit, but for the moment he was dancing a stately minuet with Beth and Eleanor was glad to see that despite Marcus's poor example there were plenty of people who were prepared to acknowledge him.

Eleanor sat down. It was most infuriating that she, with the greatest grievance, was the one who was defending Kit against Marcus's intransigence. She hoped that Beth might exert some influence but she thought it unlikely. Marcus could be damnably stubborn. The whole family suffered from the trait.

A movement caught her eye in the most deeply shadowed part of the conservatory and for a moment Eleanor wondered if she had disturbed a tryst. It was not unlikely, for people would snatch whatever moment of privacy they were afforded. Then she realised that the lovers—if that was what they were—had not even noticed her presence, for they were continuing to talk in low, urgent whispers. She could overhear a very little:

'Do you have some for me? Oh please...'

There was a laugh. 'Not if you cannot pay for it, my lady…'

There was more pleading, even, Eleanor thought, the sound of a suppressed sob. She tried to keep still and quiet, hoping that the others would go out of the long doors at the other end of the conservatory without realising that she was there. It was impossible for her to escape without being noticed and she had no wish to move now and give away the fact that she had been there a little while—she was in a most difficult position.

'Here, take this then…' She heard a scrabbling sound, then a sigh of satisfaction. 'Ah, at last…'

'Thank you, my lady.' The man spoke a little louder now. Eleanor knew somehow that this was not a pair of lovers—the woman's desperation was of another sort and the man's tone more mocking than affectionate. She heard a step, fortunately away at the other end of the room, then the creak of one of the rustic benches as the woman moved into the lantern light and sat down. Eleanor could see that she was alone now, tilting a glass to her lips, closing her eyes. Eleanor stared, and felt the cold freeze her to the marrow. No young lover, this. It was the Dowager Lady Trevithick.

Eleanor leapt to her feet and hurried down the conservatory without pausing to think. Ever since her mother had made such a terrible fuss over her elopement, she had kept away from her as much as was practical, allowing the Dowager's anger to cool, avoiding the worst of her diatribes. They had never been on intimate terms, for Lady Trevithick was too cold and distant to have endeared herself to any of her children, but now Eleanor could think of nothing but that her mother must be ill, or in trouble, and needed her help. She reached Lady Trevithick just as the Dowager, with a little, furtive gesture, slipped something into her reticule and hauled herself to her feet, smiling at her daughter with a type of cunning triumph that was as puzzling as it was unpleasant. In the pale light of the coloured lanterns her eyes seemed unnaturally bright and her bonnet was askew. She was panting slightly.

'Mama?' Eleanor looked at her closely. 'What are you doing here? Are you feeling unwell? Are you fatigued?'

Lady Trevithick beamed at her daughter. 'Not at all! I am in plump currant! Never better! Delightful evening, is it not? Lend me your arm, girl, for I think I shall go to the card room for a round of vingt-et-un…'

Eleanor automatically extended her arm and the Dowager leant heavily on it as they walked with painful slowness towards the conservatory door and out into the ballroom. The crowd was thinning a little now but it was too late for Eleanor to identify her mother's companion of a few moments before. She hesitated to ask, knowing it was inviting a crushing set down, but her curiosity was strong.

'That gentleman, mama—the one who was just leaving…'

Lady Trevithick's claw-like hand dug into Eleanor's arm with bruising force. Eleanor winced.

'Mama! You're hurting me…'

'Did you see him?' Lady Trevithick hissed. 'Did you hear?'

Eleanor looked at her in puzzled incomprehension. 'No… That is, I was just coming in as he left you…'

'Ah…' The cruel grip on her arm relaxed just a little. Eleanor looked down, where the Dowager's hand still clutched her. Her mother's fingers were encrusted with diamonds and rubies, and round her throat hung the Trevithick rubies, the gleaming stones almost lost amongst the deep lines and folds of the Dowager's neck. Rings, necklace… Eleanor frowned. There was something missing. The ruby bracelet that matched the magnificent necklace had gone. Her mother's wrist was quite bare. In an instant Eleanor remembered the mysterious conversation in the conservatory, the payment… She bit her lip.

'I was talking to Kemble, my dear,' her mother said sweetly, smiling. 'You must remember Lord Kemble—you jilted him! He helped me to a seat so that I could rest. So thoughtful a man! I know that you have no taste for him, my dear, but I have always rather liked him!' She blinked at her daughter gently, her dark eyes unfocused. 'It would have been so much better had you married him, Eleanor, so much easier… My debts…'

'Mama,' Eleanor said again, deeply worried now. 'Are you sure you are quite well? Indeed you look most ill…'

The Dowager swayed like a giant tree in the wind. Eleanor tightened her grip on her mother's arm to help her stay upright and felt something sharp press against her—the bottle in her mother's reticule.

'I feel just the thing,' the Dowager murmured vaguely. 'I shall go and play a hand of cards and who knows, I may win! Money to pay my debts—now there's the thing!'

She loosened her grip on Eleanor's arm and raised a hand in unsteady salutation. 'Good night, my dear!'

Eleanor watched the Dowager wend her unsteady way towards the door of the card-room and did not know whether to feel glad or sorry when she saw the joint cohorts of Lady Pomfret and Mrs Belton converge on her from either side and carry her over the threshold. No doubt they would fleece her and then her mother would be in even greater debt. But to whom did she owe money? Lord Kemble? And if so, for what? Eleanor looked at her mother's voluminous figure as the Trevithick Tabbies carried her off and in her mind's eye could still see the tell-tale bulge of the bottle in the reticule and the tell-tale absence of the ruby bracelet from her wrist.

'Eleanor? Is anything wrong?'

Eleanor turned sharply to see that Kit had come up to her, unnoticed. He gave her a searching look. 'You seem a little discomposed, my dear. Is aught amiss?'

Eleanor painted a bright smile on her face. 'Why no, my lord, not precisely.' She took his proffered arm and they started to walk slowly around the edge of the floor. 'Everything is quite perfect if one discounts Mama's peculiar behaviour, and Marcus's bad manners...'

Kit's expression hardened. 'As far as your brother is concerned, he is only behaving as I would do if someone had acted so shabbily to Charlotte. In my heart I find I cannot blame him!'

This was not what Eleanor had expected to hear. She looked at him, a little taken aback. 'Oh, well—but that does not excuse him! Of all the childish things...'

Kit shrugged. He drew her a little closer to him. It felt very pleasant and Eleanor allowed herself to relax.

'I fear Marcus is too stubborn...'

'It is good of you to take my part against him but it is a trait that I understand,' Kit said with a smile. 'Is it not a charge that could be levelled at the Mostyns as much as the Trevithicks?'

'Yes, but Marcus should learn when it is appropriate to be more tolerant! Surely if I can behave with dignity...'

'Ah, but that is all for show, is it not?' Kit's expression, as it rested on her face, was quizzical. Eleanor flushed.

'Yes, but... No, not precisely. I mean I would be pleased if we could be friends...'

'Friends,' Kit smiled suddenly at her. 'That sounds most pleasant, albeit a little colourless. But perhaps we could start with that. Yes, I should like that too.'

Eleanor looked at him uncertainly. 'Are you teasing me, Kit?'

'Not at all. I am happy to accept whatever you are prepared to give.'

Eleanor looked up into his face. Behind the light tone she could hear something more serious and it made her pulse jump. She tore her gaze away from his and spoke quickly.

'Then that is settled. It would be more comfortable, I think, and a friendship need make no unnecessary demands upon us...'

She risked a look at his face and saw that he was smiling, saw the leap of something in his eyes that made her own body leap in response. This was moving a little too quickly for her. She found that she was breathless.

'My lord...'

'Evening, Mostyn. I wish I could say that I am glad to see you back! Lady Mostyn, I have come to claim our cotillion...'

Eleanor jumped again and the colour flooded her face. 'Lord George...'

Lord George Darke had come upon them whilst she had been quite intent on Kit and now she did not know whether to be glad or sorry. In a rush she remembered the pouting lilies and the card, heavy with promise. She was not at all sure she wished to go with him.

Kit bowed, not troubling to hide his dislike of the other man. 'I am no more pleased to see you, Darke, than you are to see me.'

The two men measured one another for a moment, then Darke gave Kit an insolent bow and turned to offer his hand to Eleanor, and Kit walked away. Eleanor saw him stop to ask another lady for a dance—Miss Eversleigh, the Toast of the Season. Kit was wasting no time. The sight of him taking the girl's hand gave Eleanor a curious pang. She turned away.

Lord George was smiling at her. His grey eyes did not waver from her face, and his smile was intimate, charming, for her alone. He was reputed the most dangerous rake in London, fair as an angel but with a reputation so black Eleanor thought it could not possibly be true. Or so she hoped. She had heard tell that he wasted no time on the naïve débutantes of the *Ton*, that his interest was solely in widows or jaded married ladies whose boredom he alleviated with skill and finesse. Eleanor assumed that most of these ladies had experience to match Darke's own. She, on the other hand, had far more in common with the innocent débutantes and she was uncertain that she could cope. So far their skirmishes had been relatively harmless— a dance here and there, a few compliments that she should have repressed but had not, no doubt leading him to believe that she was fair game. Now she sensed that Darke meant business and oddly, it seemed that Kit's presence made him even more determined. He was pressing her hand in the most odiously familiar manner.

'Lady Mostyn, I have been waiting all evening for the pleasure of a dance with you…'

Despite herself, Eleanor could not repress a shiver of nervousness. Although she was in a crowded ballroom, she felt quite alone. Kit, having demanded that she show no favour to the rakes of the *Ton* had immediately abandoned her with the most dangerous one of all! And without a backward glance! Eleanor stole a look in his direction and saw that her husband was smiling down at Miss Eversleigh, bending close to her as he whispered something in her ear. The girl went into a peal of laughter and Eleanor felt out of proportion cross.

Darke saw her frown and his smile deepened, his fingers tightening on hers. Eleanor felt uncomfortable. She pulled her hand free and stepped away from him. He did not seem disconcerted, merely amused, as though he credited her with playing a game far cleverer than anything she had ever intended. She moved further away. He followed.

'Dear Lady Mostyn, do you care to dance or would you prefer to go somewhere more…private?'

Eleanor looked into those dissipated grey eyes and hesitated. It was imperative that she made it clear to him that she would not become one of his flirts, but it was difficult to see how to do this without drawing further attention. She had never been alone with him, except for the spurious privacy provided by a drive in the park, and knew better than to step aside with him now. She glanced around; plenty of people were watching them, which would make it even more foolish. Then she realised that Darke had interpreted this as calculation on her part and was smiling gently. He leant closer, taking her arm, his breath stirring the tendrils of hair about her face.

'Eleanor, if only you could be persuaded to look with kindness on me…'

Eleanor gave him a haughty glance. 'My name, sir?'

'Very well, Lady Mostyn. I understand that we must preserve the proprieties now that your husband is returned.' Darke's smile was predatory. Eleanor could tell that he thought she was still toying with him. She felt vaguely panicked.

'It is a pity,' Darke continued, 'that Mostyn chose to return when he did. But with discretion we can manage the situation…'

With a shock Eleanor realised just what it was he was suggesting. She raised her chin.

'I think that you mistake, my lord. My husband—'

'Yes, I understand,' Darke murmured. 'But it will be a greater challenge this way.'

Eleanor gave him a look of disgust. In a flash she saw herself as he did—a lady with a slightly soiled reputation who would be just another conquest, although her seduction would be sweeter for Darke because he would have taken her from under the nose of her husband. She felt sick.

'I repeat, you misunderstand me, my lord! There is no more to say!'

Darke's eyes swept over her with amused comprehension. 'You should not fear just because Mostyn is back! Nor suffer a belated bout of loyalty! What do you imagine that he has been doing whilst he was away, Eleanor? I hear that the winters are very pleasant in Italy, particularly if one has a little opera singer to warm one's bed!'

Eleanor pressed her hands together. 'I know all about my husband's absence, my lord,' she said steadily, looking him straight in the eye. 'He has told me all—'

Darke gave a crack of laughter. 'And you believed him? My dear, you are more foolish than I had thought!' His tone was spiteful. 'It is simply that you have no stomach for the game any more, is it not, sweet Eleanor? Assure you, you'd find me more than a match for Mostyn—'

'Excuse me if I wrest my wife away from you now, Darke. You should have enjoyed the dance while you could.'

Eleanor heard Kit's voice with inexpressible relief. She turned to him. 'There you are, my dear! Would you take me home now? I fear I am rather fatigued!'

'Certainly,' Kit said with aplomb. He offered her his arm and gave Darke the slightest and most insulting of bows.

'Do not even think about approaching my wife in future, Darke,' he said smoothly. 'She has made it quite plain that she does not wish to speak to you and I wish it even less. So unless you would care to meet me over this…' He let the sentence fade away. 'No, I thought not. Eleanor my dear, if you are quite ready…'

Eleanor swept past the curious guests as though they were not present, but by the time they reached the entrance hall she was shaking with shock and reaction. Kit took her cloak from the hovering footman and wrapped it around her, and she drew its folds closer for comfort. They went out to the carriage.

'A word of advice for future reference, my love.' Kit's voice was light. 'When you choose to divest yourself of your next admirer, pray do so in more private circumstances! That is if it is your expressed wish to present a façade to the *Ton* rather than make yourself an entertainment for them! I imagine people have not been so diverted by a public disagreement in an age!'

Eleanor's temper gave way. 'If *you* had not left me alone with Lord George the problem would not have arisen, my lord! Upon my word, I cannot do right for doing wrong!'

Kit laughed. He was sitting across from her and in the shadowed interior of the carriage Eleanor could not discern his expression. He sounded quite indifferent, however, and somehow that made Eleanor even more cross.

'I am sorry, my dear,' Kit said easily, 'but how was I to know that you wished to discourage Darke? I assumed that it was an indication of you going your own way, as mentioned the other night…'

'Piffle!' Eleanor said crossly. 'Nonsense, my lord! I was trying to get rid of Lord George just as I was trying to deter Sir Charles the other night! Why must you wilfully misunderstand me?'

'I am sorry,' Kit said mildly. Eleanor could hear the undertone of amusement still in his voice. 'You did indeed make it quite clear—to the entire room—

that you wished to discourage Darke! So are there any other admirers whose pretensions you would like me to…er…depress, my love?'

Eleanor looked at him suspiciously. She was sure he was laughing at her and the matter did not seem in the least amusing to her.

'Yes, my lord! All of them!'

'Dear me,' Kit said gently, 'and will there be that many? You have been unconscionably popular, my dear!'

Eleanor gave an exasperated squeak. 'How many times must I tell you that it is none of my doing, my lord! If you will believe all the scandal you hear in the Clubs…'

'Yes, I do apologise,' Kit murmured. 'And as I was not here to protect you before, the least I can do is to look after you now. You will find me the most attentive of husbands, I promise you.'

Eleanor shifted on the seat. She felt a little mollified. 'Thank you, my lord. If you can pretend to a certain degree of possessiveness…'

'No indeed…' there was a smile in Kit's voice '…I shall be quite genuinely protective, I assure you, my love. All in the interests of our…ah…friendship, of course!'

'Of course,' Eleanor echoed. She frowned a little, feeling slightly confused. Did that mean that Kit really cared or that he did not? She was not going to risk asking him. She wished it did not matter to her.

Chapter Six

The singer came to the end of her aria and Eleanor applauded politely, as did the rest of the company. Lady Seaton was so very proud to have persuaded so famous an opera singer as La Perla to perform at her musicale, but it was not to Eleanor's taste. She preferred country airs and slightly less rarefied songs—such heavy emotion seemed too much for the drawing-room, especially a drawing-room as crowded as Lady Seaton's.

'Are you enjoying the music, my love?' Kit asked, a twinkle in his eye. He was sitting beside her and Eleanor was tolerably sure that he had been asleep during the performance, if that were possible whilst La Perla was forcing out those top notes. She smiled at him prettily.

'La Perla is a consummate performer, I believe, my lord! It is my fault not hers that the music is not really to my taste!'

Kit laughed. 'I think we are all in need of some-

thing to revive us after that! Shall I fetch you a glass
of lemonade, Eleanor?'

Eleanor nodded. 'Thank you, my lord. That would
be most pleasant.'

She watched him go, a little mischievous smile on
her lips. Despite protestations to the contrary, she had
to admit that it was very pleasant to have her husband
dance attendance upon her. They had spent the best
part of the previous week together, driving in the
park, attending the theatre, dancing together at all the
balls… Eleanor sighed. It had been delightful. Better
still, it had been safe. Certainly there was nothing for
her to fear, for they had slipped into the easiest and
most undemanding of friendships.

Eleanor wrinkled up her nose. And yet… Perhaps
it was not entirely a simple friendship, for she had
the oddest feeling that Kit was waiting for something,
holding back, biding his time… She flicked her fan
open. She felt as though she was being courted, but
so gently that it was scarcely noticeable. But perhaps
she was imagining it. With so much unspoken between them it would be impossible…

Beth was waving at her from across the aisle.
Eleanor smiled back. That evening they had avoided
the embarrassment of Marcus, Kit and Justin coming
to blows by arriving at different times so that they sat
as far away from each other as possible. Fortunately
the Dowager Lady Trevithick was also present and
made such a fuss of sitting down and fidgeting around
after the music had started that she drew all attention.
Eleanor acknowledged that it was hardly a permanent

solution but it saved face in public. She made a mental note to speak to Beth about the feud as soon as she could. The whole business was becoming tiresome, like a schoolboys' game. She would almost swear that the men were enjoying it.

Eleanor waited until Kit had disappeared into the refreshment-room then made her way over to where Beth, Charlotte and the Dowager Lady Trevithick were sitting. After the flurry of greetings, Charlotte said mischievously:

'Do you think that one of us should go to keep and eye on matters in the refreshment-room? Marcus and Justin are in there and it would be most unfortunate if there were pistols over the lemonade!'

'Oh, let us both go!' Beth said hastily. She gave Eleanor a speaking look. 'I apologise for leaving you, dearest, but I am sure you will enjoy a comfortable coze with your mama. I will call on you tomorrow if I may.'

'Of course,' Eleanor murmured. She was not so sure that she would enjoy a tête-à-tête with Lady Trevithick, who had turned so strangely unpredictable of late. At the moment her mother was rocking backwards and forwards and humming a little under her breath, but as she caught Eleanor's eye she sat bolt upright and snapped: 'What are you staring at, girl? Didn't I teach you it was rude to stare? Never catch a husband if you look him straight in the eye!'

Eleanor blinked. It did not seem possible that her mother had forgotten she was already married. 'Yes, Mama. I was only concerned because you did not seem quite yourself tonight. Are you enjoying the music?'

Lady Trevithick made a vague gesture that knocked her diamond tiara askew. 'Ridiculous wailing noise! Wish I'd stayed at home!' She took a deep swallow of her lemonade. 'Pooh! Insipid stuff! Get me a glass of ratafia, there's a good girl!'

Eleanor looked around, hoping that Kit would be coming back so that she could escape with him. Unfortunately he was nowhere in sight. Instead a smooth voice said:

'Ladies, a glass of wine? Allow me…'

Lord Kemble had paused beside them, proffering two glasses and his obsequious smile. Lady Trevithick grabbed a glass so hastily that she almost spilled it. 'Kemble! Good man!'

Eleanor took the other glass rather more reluctantly. She did not care for ratafia and she cared even less for Lord Kemble, who now showed every sign of lingering by her side, a look of unwholesome admiration in his eyes. Eleanor looked around again a little desperately for Kit. How long could it possibly take to fetch a glass of lemonade?

'If you are looking for your husband, my dear, I fear he has found metal more attractive in the refreshment-room,' Kemble murmured, bending close to her ear. 'La Perla, you know. Mostyn is…renewing their acquaintance, I suppose you could say…I hear that they were quite…intimate…in Italy this winter…'

Eleanor caught her breath as a sharp pain seemed

to stab her just below her breastbone. So this was the opera singer whom rumour had so persistently linked to Kit, and he had the effrontery to escort her to a performance by his mistress! A consummate performer indeed! Eleanor blushed scarlet. She hardly needed to tell Kit what he must know already!

Kemble was looking odiously pleased with himself. 'You did not know? Oh, dear me…'

Eleanor looked him straight in the eye. 'You are speaking nonsense, my lord, and you know it! Furthermore it is nonsense that I do not care for—'

'Nonsense!' Lady Trevithick agreed, unexpectedly. 'Mostyn's been in Ireland, not Italy, don't you know! Heard it from the servants!' She thrust her wineglass at Eleanor. 'Hold my glass, there's a good girl. I need something from my reticule!'

Eleanor looked in some consternation from her mother to Lord Kemble, who was not smiling any more. 'There you are, my lord!' she said clearly. 'Ireland, not Italy. A simple mistake to make if one is not accomplished in geography…'

Kemble flushed. 'Very well, Lady Mostyn. I stand corrected…' He looked with ill-concealed contempt at the Dowager, who had grabbed her glass back and was gulping the ratafia down.

'I would watch Lady Trevithick most carefully, if I were you,' he added spitefully. 'She is making a fool of herself for the entertainment of the whole company! Good evening, Lady Mostyn.'

He straightened up and strolled off, and Eleanor blushed bright red and drank several mouthfuls of her ratafia to try to steady herself. It was true—Lady Trevithick was becoming so very odd and unpredictable that one had to wonder just what she would do next. Eleanor could see any number of their acquaintance sniggering and watching with avid curiosity as her mother calmly took all her personal possessions out of her reticule, placed them on the chair beside her, then started to put them all back again. She was humming again and seemed quite happy. Eleanor felt an acute embarrassment mixed with a sudden protective loyalty that made her want to denounce them all for spiteful scandalmongers.

'Mama!' She hissed urgently, trying to help Lady Trevithick push her combs, handkerchiefs and laudanum bottle back into the reticule, 'are you sure that would not prefer to retire—'

Lady Trevithick carried on as though she had not heard.

'My bottle,' she murmured. 'It is empty of laudanum…'

A chill stole into Eleanor's heart. Surely her mother had not taken to dosing herself wherever she went?

'I believe you have some more at home, Mama,' she said calmly. 'Why not wait until you go back…'

'Ask Kemble for some more!' the Dowager said fretfully, clutching her purse to her breast. 'Tell him that I can pay this time!'

Eleanor took the purse gently from her mother's hand and placed it in the reticule, snapping it closed and handing it back.

'No, Mama. Look, Marcus is returning now and the

concert about to start again. If you are sure you are well enough to stay—' Once again she broke off in consternation. Lady Trevithick had fallen asleep.

Eleanor finished her ratafia and handed the glass back to a passing servant. No, she did not like the drink and lemonade would have been preferable. Which reminded her about Kit… She looked around, but he was still nowhere to be seen. With a sigh, Eleanor went back to her seat and wondered wasp-ishly whether La Perla would resume her performance or whether she would not be able to drag herself away from Kit's side. Could Kemble have been correct? The rumours had been so very persistent.

Someone slid into the seat that Kit had vacated and Eleanor turned, startled. It was Sir Charles Paulet, a lascivious gleam in his eye. Eleanor sighed sharply. The evening was fast becoming most tiresome.

'Good evening, Lady Mostyn. You are looking quite, quite radiant tonight, truly a sight for delight.'

Eleanor inclined her head coldly. 'Good evening, Sir Charles.'

Sir Charles tittered. 'I see that Lord Mostyn is en-tranced with La Perla—the Pearl of great price, or should I say great vice…'

Eleanor snapped her fan together with a force that broke two of the struts. 'Excuse me, Sir Charles. I find your verse does not agree with me tonight. In fact it does not agree with me *at all* and I wish to hear no more of it!'

She saw that Kit was finally returning with a glass of lemonade and felt even more annoyed. La Perla was strolling back to her place at the top of the room, her silken skirts swaying suggestively, an arch little smile on her lips. Eleanor felt hot and flustered and frumpish.

'Good evening, my lord,' she snapped as Kit came to stand beside her chair. 'I thought you must have gone to Gunters to procure my lemonade—or possibly made it yourself!'

Kit raised a quizzical eyebrow at this display of bad humour.

'I beg your pardon, my love, for keeping you waiting!'

Eleanor hunched her shoulder against him and turned away. She saw that Sir Charles was smiling and it made her even angrier. The whole evening was degenerating into a farce in which her husband paid court to his mistress, her brother behaved like a stiff-necked fool, her mother displayed her bizarre antics for all to see and Eleanor herself was beset with the attentions of tiresome admirers.

Kit took charge of the situation.

'Paulet,' he drawled, 'you must be remarkably slow of understanding for a man of letters! I am sure that I warned you not to pester my wife with your attentions again!'

Sir Charles scooted away and Kit took his seat and handed Eleanor her glass.

'Something seems to have upset you, my love,' he said with commiseration. 'Can I help at all?'

'It is nothing, my lord!' Eleanor said crossly. She was watching as La Perla, the smile still on her red lips, held court amongst a group of five eager men. 'In your brief but eventful absence I have had to contend with Lord Kemble and Sir Charles as well as a host of other irritations! Whilst you…' her annoyance finally got the better of her '…have been renewing your acquaintance with La Perla—or so I understand!'

Kit's amused gaze went from her face to La Perla and back again.

'Acquainted with La Perla?' There was puzzlement in his tone. 'Indeed I am not! I apologise for my absence but I was speaking to Charlotte whilst Justin's back was turned. I barely addressed the diva—although I felt obliged to compliment her on her singing since she was standing next to me just now.'

'Don't seek to gammon me, sir,' Eleanor snapped. 'There are those who say you knew her in Italy…'

'I have not been to Italy recently,' Kit said. His gaze was very steady. 'What is this, Eleanor?'

Eleanor was starting to feel uncertain and a little silly. 'It was Sir Charles,' she admitted. 'And Lord Kemble. They were intimating that you… That the lady was a friend of yours…'

'Ah…' A smile curled Kit's lips. 'Our inestimable friend, Sir Charles! Always stirring up trouble! And in rhyming couplets to boot!'

Eleanor smothered a giggle. 'I am sorry.' She looked up, met Kit's eyes and fell silent. There was a curious feeling inside her now that the indignation had gone. She felt foolish for rising to the provocation, and she knew she had made it easy for those who had deliberately tried to upset her. But that was because she lacked confidence in Kit's affection and also…

'The rumours have been very persistent,' she said, blushing a little, 'and I did not know… You had not told me…'

Kit held her gaze very deliberately. 'I thought that we had agreed that you did not want to know?'

'Yes…' Eleanor fidgeted with the beading on her evening bag. She looked up unhappily and saw that Kit was still watching her. It made her feel curiously breathless.

'I was jealous!' She blurted out. The colour rushed to her face and she dropped her gaze at once, unable to believe what she had done. To confess such a thing, and in public! Why, anyone could have heard and now Kit only needed to laugh at her to shrivel her confidence completely.

He took one of her hands in his. His touch was casual but warm and it filled her with a curious tingling.

'Eleanor…' his voice was low, in her ear '…you have no cause for jealousy. Upon my honour, you never did.'

Their eyes met again, the deep blue of Kit's capturing and trapping hers. Eleanor took a shaky breath. 'Oh… Why did I say that?'

She saw Kit smile and it did strange things to her insides, making her dizzy.

'Friends can say anything to each other,' he said, tucking her hand through his arm. 'Old friends, good friends…'

Eleanor felt slightly disappointed but was not sure why. This friendship of theirs was becoming a little confusing and perhaps it was not exactly what she wanted after all. She struggled to sort out her feelings but was conscious of nothing but a rather peculiar languor coming over her. The room was full and very warm and now that the concert was starting again, La Perla was insisting on all the lights being doused because she preferred to sing by candlelight. Eleanor relaxed sleepily. They had been to a ball the night before and it had been a long day, but that hardly accounted for this strange feeling, which was a mixture of acute awareness and lassitude. She was very conscious of Kit next to her; her skin seemed to prickle where his arm brushed hers, and she imagined that she could feel the warmth of his body and told herself that she was becoming foolish.

She was, however, feeling very heated and was not at all sure why. At first she tried to fan herself but her hot cheeks seemed to radiate ever more heat. Then the room started to spin around very slowly. Eleanor sat up straighter, puzzled and alarmed. These were surely not the effects of thwarted love, nor did she feel particularly unwell, but she did feel rather giddy…

Her head brushed Kit's shoulder and she left it there. That was nice. That felt very comfortable after all the upsets of the evening. She closed her eyes briefly.

'Eleanor!'

Kit's whisper stirred the tendrils of hair by her ear. Eleanor opened her eyes reluctantly.

'What is it?'

'Are you ill?' Kit's face was very close, his expression concerned. Eleanor made an effort and turned her head. The room seemed very dark, the candlelight fluttering. The diva was still wailing, but her voice appeared to come from a long way away. Eleanor smiled.

'No indeed, I am quite comfortable, thank you.'

She saw Kit frown. 'Then why are you sleeping in the middle of a recital? People will see…'

'Let them.' Eleanor remembered Marcus's words when she had taken him to task at the ball. She smiled slightly to herself. Marcus knew a thing or two! Why worry what other people thought… She yawned and allowed her head to sink back on to Kit's shoulder. She felt as though she was sliding very gently down. Soon she would be resting in his lap but really it did not matter. She felt just as she had done five years ago, when she had tasted her mother's laudanum to see what it was like and had not realised that a small dose was all that was needed. Then she had slept for a whole day, but the initial feeling had been most pleasant.

'Excuse me, my wife is feeling unwell…'

'No I am not—'

Eleanor realised indignantly that she had been woken again. She struggled upright. She did not feel unwell—in fact she felt very happy. Kit had an arm around her and was steering her down the aisle between the chairs. Her feet seemed to be working independently of her mind. Fortunately. Behind them the opera singer's voice rose and fell like a peal of bells. Eleanor winced.

'She is giving me the headache…'

'Hush!' Kit spoke quickly, but there was an undertone of amusement in his voice that Eleanor could hear and it made her smile again. She could see quite well although the room was still revolving slowly and she could even keep her eyes open with an effort but it was pleasant to feel Kit's arm around her nevertheless. She leant against him a little more heavily and he obliged by tightening his grip.

They were in the entrance hall and Kit was requesting the carriage, quickly. He bundled her up the steps and sat down. Eleanor came to rest on his knee. She put her arms about his neck—to steady herself— and turned her face against his throat.

'Eleanor, you are foxed.' Kit's voice came sharply out of the darkness. 'What have you been drinking and how can you be in such state as this?'

Eleanor sat bolt upright. 'I am not drunk! I did not even have the lemonade if you recall…'

'No…' Kit still sounded sharp '…you evidently had something else! What were you doing whilst I was gone?'

Eleanor brightened. 'Well, there was the ratafia that Lord Kemble gave me, but I only had one glass. I have drunk it before, you know, and never felt like this! But do not worry, Kit! I am quite happy…'

The light from the carriage lanterns skipped across

Kit's face. She could see that he was frowning heavily and she did so want to try to help him puzzle out the mystery.

'Laudanum!' she said helpfully, and winced as Kit took her by the shoulders in a grip that bruised. She slid off his knee and came to rest half-sitting, half-lying on the seat of the coach.

'Ouch! You are hurting me, Kit!'

Kit shook her slightly. Eleanor's head bounced. She almost giggled.

'Eleanor, have you been taking laudanum?'

'No!' Eleanor blinked owlishly at him. Really he could be quite slow sometimes. 'I meant that the only time I felt like this before was when I had sampled Mama's laudanum...'

'And have you been sampling it again this evening?' Kit demanded.

'No!' Eleanor felt most indignant. 'Mama was asking for some, but...'

She heard Kit sigh and snuggled closer to him. 'Unless it was in her glass of ratafia, of course! I do believe I may have given her the wrong glass after she had emptied her reticule...'

Kit took her chin in his hand and turned her face up to the faint light. Eleanor blinked, trying to focus on his face. It was difficult in the dark.

'Well, you have certainly had something!' Kit sounded decidedly snappish and Eleanor closed her eyes and put her head on his shoulder.

'I do not know why you are so very cross, Kit. I am not cross, I am happy.' She wriggled a little. 'Everything happened whilst I was waiting for you to disentangle yourself from La Perla. And although I am happy to hear that she is not your mistress…' Eleanor gave a little hiccup '…her singing gave me an earache…'

'A most remarkable *alter ego* seems to emerge at times like this,' Kit observed. He pulled her closer, so that she was resting again on his lap. 'It is as though you have partaken of several strong drinks! Have you much experience with alcohol, Eleanor?'

Eleanor smiled against his neck. 'Certainly not, for Mama never let me drink anything other than tea and lemonade during my Season.' She hesitated. 'I confess that at the start of this year I did try a few glasses of punch, for I thought it would be fun to become a fast matron…'

'Did you? Why was that?'

'Oh, because they were calling me the abandoned bride and I thought it would be so much more fun to be know as the *fast* Lady Mostyn!' She felt Kit's arms stiffen about her and said kindly: 'Do not worry, Kit, for I am quite over that now. It did not suit my nature to be promiscuous, you see, for I worry far too much about the opinion of the world!' She was struck by another thought. 'Also I suppose it would not have been the right thing to do, as I was married to you. And I know you believed me unchaste but that is quite untrue, which is why I was so very glad to find that La Perla was not your mistress…'

Eleanor struggled a little, feeling glad to have got that off her chest but aware that there was a little more for complete honesty. 'Of course, there were a few men who tried to snatch a kiss…'

Kit's arms tightened again and it felt wonderfully protective. 'Let them try now!'

Eleanor smiled. This was all very satisfactory. She liked being Kit's friend.

'I am sorry, Eleanor.' Kit's mouth was pressed against her hair. She was dimly aware that there was an odd wrench in his voice. 'I never intended for matters to go so awry…'

'That is perfectly all right, Kit,' Eleanor said magnanimously. She was feeling remarkably happy and full of generosity towards the entire world. She wriggled, and felt Kit shift beneath her. 'Oh, I am sorry if it is uncomfortable for you!'

'It is, but not in the way that you mean,' Kit said dryly. 'However, as we have such a excellent opportunity, perhaps we might continue to find out a little more about each other.'

'Mmm!' Eleanor nodded. It had been a little like a parlour game as she and Kit had discussed their likes and dislikes, their interests and their hopes a little more each day. She had enjoyed it and it had been quite innocent. Eleanor vaguely remembered that she was supposed to be keeping Kit at arm's length for some reason that escaped her just at the moment. She looked down. He was not precisely at arm's length now, but as he was so warm and safe and friendly she did not really mind.

'You start!' she said.

'Very well, then. I have a question for you.' Kit's voice was warm. 'Do you believe in love, Eleanor?'

Love! Eleanor wrinkled her brow. She knew she had all sorts of ideas about love normally but just at the moment she felt so extraordinarily sleepy that she could not remember them.

'That is a difficult question,' she said cautiously. 'What do you think, Kit?'

Kit laughed. 'A skilful answer… What do I think? Well yes, I believe in love!'

'Truly?' Eleanor was entranced. She rubbed her cheek against the smooth coolness of his shirtfront. 'That is nice!'

'Yes…' She thought that Kit was trying not to laugh. 'It would be even nicer if you were to agree with me!'

'Yes,' Eleanor said dreamily, 'and I do believe that there must be something in what you say, Kit! For there is Marcus and Beth and Charlotte and Justin to prove your case! And though it may not be fashionable to love one's spouse it is rather pleasant to see…'

'Pleasant!' Kit's lips brushed her cheek lightly and Eleanor found herself shivering. 'That is one word for it, I suppose. A rather dull word—like friendship…'

'I do not think friendship dull!' Eleanor said, stung. 'It is the sweetest thing, for without Beth and Charlotte I should be quite lost…'

'And without me?'

'Oh well…' Eleanor smiled. 'You are quite different.'

'Better? Or worse?'

'Different!' Eleanor played with the intricate folds of his neck-cloth. 'I believe that you are fishing for compliments!'

'You may be right.' Kit sounded rueful. 'I doubt I shall receive any from you tonight though.'

Eleanor paused. She had succeeded in undoing the neck-cloth's starchy folds and felt quite inordinately pleased with herself. She also felt very light-headed, dizzy almost. This was an interesting experience but one she was not sure she wished to repeat.

'I do not know...' She put her head on one side. 'You are prodigious handsome, Kit, and it is pleasant to know that other ladies envy me your company. And you are really very kind to me and...'

'And?'

'And I think you quite an attractive man!' Eleanor finished triumphantly. 'There! So you see I can flatter you after all!'

'So you can.' Kit touched her cheek, very lightly, and Eleanor was perplexed to feel her dizziness increase. Something odd was happening, separating her mind from her increasingly wayward body. Whilst her thoughts were busily spinning off into space, her body appeared to be pressing itself closer to Kit, sweetly, confidingly wrapping itself around him...

'We are home,' Kit said dryly, and Eleanor realised that they were indeed turning into Montague Street and drawing up outside the house. She allowed Kit to help her down and the cool evening air outside the carriage doused her like a cold bath. She staggered a little and clutched Kit's arm.

'Oh! I beg your pardon. I shall not be taking any laudanum again, accidentally or not...'

'A wise decision,' Kit murmured. He swept her easily into his arms. 'Come along. I will take you upstairs.'

Carrick's jaw dropped when he saw Eleanor in Kit's arms, but he recovered himself quickly. Lucy, who had been stoking the fire in Eleanor's bedroom, and turning the bed down, was not so reticent.

'Oh sir, oh madam! How romantic!'

'No it is not!' Eleanor carolled, over Kit's shoulder. 'I am three parts disguised, I fear, Lucy, though from medicine and not strong drink!'

'Good night!' Kit said, shutting the door in the maid's startled face. 'I will call you if I need you!'

He placed Eleanor gently on the bed. She stretched luxuriously, arms above her head. It had been a most pleasant experience but she was aware that she was more than a little adrift and it would probably be better to go to sleep. She blinked sleepily at Kit. He was standing by the side of the bed looking down on her and in the pale light of the fire she could see that the lines of his face were tense. She wriggled a little and his gaze came up to her face and Eleanor saw the vivid flash of desire in his eyes before their expression was veiled again. She giggled.

'Oh dear, I am sorry! Am I behaving very badly? Do you wish to make love to me, Kit?'

She saw the flicker of a smile touch his mouth. 'Yes, but I believe I may be able to resist you! Although...' his gaze flickered over her face and rested

on her lips for a second before he wrenched it away
'...you are very lovely, Eleanor.'

Eleanor smiled sleepily. She felt warm and very
happy. 'Thank you. If you would like to make love
to me I do not mind...'

Kit smiled again. 'I would hope for slightly more
enthusiasm on your part when the time does serve,
my love. It would be better if you went to sleep now.'

There was no reply. Eleanor's eyelashes flickered,
and then she gave a little sigh and turned her head
against the pillow. She was still smiling.

Kit let out the breath that he had been holding and
sat down gingerly on the side of the bed. There was
a strange feeling in his stomach, similar to the guilt
and pain he had felt when Beth had torn a strip off
him—similar, but far more poignant. Eleanor looked
so very young and vulnerable lying there, her dress
just sliding from one shoulder to expose the slope of
her breast, her hair tumbled across the pillow in
strands of darkest mahogany and glossy black. Damn
it, he had never meant to hurt her so. When she had
confided about being the abandoned bride he had
thought his heart would break.

Kit leant back against the bedpost and looked at
her. Her face was untroubled in sleep, creamy pale,
black lashes against the curve of her cheek.

'Do you wish to make love to me, Kit?'

Kit smiled despite himself. Of all the artless questions... They had made love only twice before he had
gone away and it had been everything that he had
always wanted and had told himself did not exist;

sweetness, tenderness, intense pleasure. He had not experienced such a thing in any of his dealings with the bored wives of the *Ton* or the Cyprians whose legendary skill was supposed to grant such enjoyment. Eleanor's innocence had erased and supplanted all of that as though it had never existed. And she had cried a little in his arms and told him that she loved him…

But she did not remember that now. Tonight she was adrift with laudanum, and although it had shown a completely different side to her nature he was hardly ungentlemanly enough to take advantage. She would hate him for it in the morning and besides, there were too many matters unsettled between them…

Kit shifted, uncomfortable with both his thoughts and his state of arousal. He had ached to make love to Eleanor for the past week but this was scarcely the right time.

He put out a hand and brushed the hair away from Eleanor's face. It slid through his fingers, soft and silky. Her skin was warm to the touch. Kit stood up abruptly. Any more of this self-indulgence and he would be starting to undress her—whilst reassuring himself that it was only to make her more comfortable, to help her to sleep more easily. The idea was so appealing that he backed away hastily. Once he had started he would have to finish and disrobe her completely. It would not do to call the maid in when Eleanor was in her chemise—he did not wish to appear the sort of man who ogled his wife whist she was unconscious.

Bad-tempered and frustrated, Kit marched across to the door and flung it open. The corridor was suspiciously empty, although he suspected that Lucy would listen at doors if only to find out whether the longed-for reconciliation had been achieved. Not tonight, Kit thought grimly. Tonight the only union that would take place would be between himself and the brandy bottle at Whites. It was decidedly second best but it would just have to do.

Matters were not progressing happily between the Mostyn and Trevithick families elsewhere either. On returning from the musicale, Charlotte Trevithick had cornered her husband in the library. Her natural delicacy had prevented her from raising a personal issue in public but she wished to take Justin to task for his treatment of her twin. Charlotte's blue gaze, identical to her brother's, was stormy as she confronted him and she was twisting her hands together.

'Oh Justin, must you be so nonsensical? You cut Kit dead a dozen times tonight and you have no right to do so! You have been ignoring him ever since he returned! If Eleanor can be civil to her husband, who are you to criticise?'

Justin was looking mutinous. Fair-haired and green-eyed, he was different in appearance from the rest of his family but, as Charlotte had discovered, he had his own share of stubbornness. When she had first met him his easy-going nature had seemed in contrast to his cousin, the Earl—now she realised that they had certain infuriating characteristics the same.

'I am sorry, Charlotte…' Justin took her hands in his, which only served to make matters more difficult for his wife '…I understand that you feel a loyalty to Mostyn as your brother—indeed, it would be odd if you did not, but equally you must see that I have a loyalty to my family—'

'A loyalty to do what?' Charlotte snatched her hands away before Justin's touch could undermine her feelings of indignation. 'The decision is with Eleanor, and if she can stomach my brother as a husband then it is not for you or for Marcus to gainsay! This is pure folly and it only makes matters more difficult for Eleanor! People will talk—they are doing so already—and I have to say that you and your cousin are doing no more than making a cake of yourselves, yes, and making your family a laughing-stock!'

Justin ran a hand through his hair. His mouth was set in an obstinate line. 'I cannot approve of what Mostyn has done. Eleanor may choose to forgive him. I do not.'

'Oh!' Charlotte clenched her fists with aggravation. 'And does it matter nothing to you that you are making *me* unhappy? Does Marcus not care that Beth is made distraught by his behaviour?'

Justin put out a hand and pulled her resisting body close. '*Does* it make you unhappy, my love?'

Charlotte looked at him from beneath her lashes. 'Prodigiously!'

'Then I am sorry for it, but I cannot compromise

my principles. Now, kiss me to show that there are no bad feelings between us…'

Charlotte wrenched herself from his grip and stood back. 'Kiss you! I think not, sir! Nor shall I speak to you again until this whole, wretched matter is resolved!'

Justin frowned. 'You will not speak to me at all?'

'No! Until you come to your senses!'

Justin scratched his head. 'Charlotte, this is foolish! Can we not simply talk about it?'

There was no reply. Charlotte gathered up the skirts of her dress, gave him a speaking look over her shoulder and swept out of the room and up to bed.

Beth, Countess of Trevithick, was sitting before her mirror in her shift and brushing out her hair. It had also been a most trying evening and she was prepared to lay the blame completely at Marcus's door. At this point in her thoughts, the connecting door to her husband's suite of rooms opened and Marcus came through. He was wearing a brocade dressing-gown with, Beth would wager, nothing underneath, and as always the sight of him made her catch her breath and caused her heart to beat a little faster. Tonight, however, she was in no mood to be nice to him.

She waited until he was standing behind her then met his eyes directly in the glass.

'Marcus, how long do you intend to persist in this ridiculous behaviour towards Kit? You put me quite out of patience with you!'

Marcus laughed. 'Why, as long as I please, my

love! Your cousin should not think that he can return to be gathered into the bosom of the family! His behaviour has been inexcusable!'

'That is for Kit to resolve with Eleanor,' Beth said coldly, trying to ignore the shiver of pleasure that went through her as Marcus raised one hand and slowly stroked her bare arm beneath the short sleeve of the shift.

'I agree…' Marcus bent to kiss her neck. 'But as head of the family I have certain obligations and one is to make my disapproval plain…'

'Pompous poppycock!' Beth exclaimed, pulling her head away. 'Besides, Marcus, you are upsetting me…'

'Am I, my love…?' Marcus's lips moved to the soft skin of her throat. His hands were on her shoulders again, sliding the shift downwards. 'Let me make it up to you…'

Beth got to her feet, only to find that that brought her into even closer proximity with her husband. His arms went around her—she tried to pull away. The shift was already around her waist.

'Marcus, this is serious—'

'I know…' He had bent to kiss her breasts now and Beth almost groaned with frustration—and pleasure. It was becoming increasingly difficult to think.

'Marcus,' she whispered, 'if you do not end this ridiculous feud I shall not speak to you again!'

That caused him to pause for a whole five seconds. Beth held her breath. Marcus bent his head to hers, kissing her lips gently.

'We do not need to speak, love, at least not for now...'

Later, much later, cursing herself for her lack of determination, Beth looked at her sleeping husband and decided that something had to be done. Sterner steps should be taken to achieve her goal. And she had just had the very idea of how to do it.

Chapter Seven

'I am dreadfully sorry, my lord.' Eleanor tilted her parasol against the sunlight in an attempt to prevent herself from squinting. They were walking in the garden after breakfast and it seemed a very bright morning, unnaturally sunny, but perhaps that was merely because her head ached a little. When she had awoken she had had an imperfect memory of the night before, but she knew that it involved a mistaken dose of laudanum and that somewhere along the line she had made a complete cake of herself. She seemed to recall that Kit had been terribly kind to her, which somehow made her feel much worse. She peered at him from beneath the brim of her hat.

Kit was not squinting in the sunlight. He looked immaculately elegant to Eleanor's eyes, making her feel ever so slightly grubby. His hair was a tawny gold, ruffled by the slight wind, and his eyes a deep, dark blue. Eleanor gave an involuntary sigh.

'I am so very sorry, my lord,' she said again. 'I did

not intend to become unruly last night, or embarrass you in public…'

Kit's fingers, long and strong interlocked with hers. He was smiling.

'I confess it was a change to see you less…self-possessed,' he said. 'You need not apologise though, Eleanor. I found the whole experience highly instructive.'

Eleanor frowned. This sounded ominous, particularly as she could remember so little herself. She allowed Kit to take her arm and they walked down the terrace steps and on to the path that led across the lawn. The air was cool and refreshing.

'Instructive? Did you? But, surely…'

Kit smiled down at her. 'You said things that I am sure you would not have mentioned under normal circumstances. It was particularly interesting.'

Eleanor frowned a little harder. This sounded even worse than she had thought. 'I did? Such as…what, my lord?'

'Oh…' Kit's smile had a wicked edge '…that you wished to be a fast matron but that you found you did not care for it after all! That you had too much regard for the opinion of society but that in future you would not care so much…'

Eleanor pressed her hands to her cheeks. She had the dreadful suspicion that this was the least of the things that she had said. There had been something about stolen kisses…

'Did I mention…other men, my lord?'

'You did!' Kit eyed her blushing embarrassment

with good humour. 'I cannot tell you how glad I am that one small misunderstanding is resolved between us!'

Eleanor eyed him suspiciously. 'And that is…'

'That though we were apart from each other for too long, neither of us was tempted to avail ourselves of the charms of others. I confess I am glad that we may now both disregard the gossip!'

'Oh!' Eleanor let out a small breath of relief. 'It is a somewhat delicate topic…'

'But one that I am glad we have broached.' Kit smiled broadly. 'Now that that is taken care of, we may perhaps progress to resolving other matters—all in good time, of course, and in the interests of our friendship!'

Eleanor felt as though the ground was slipping from beneath her feet. On the surface Kit's suggestion seemed like a good idea—once they had resolved the past they might come to an easier understanding, and there were still plenty of issues between them that required resolution. Yet there was something treacherous lurking beneath the surface here. Each confidence brought them closer, inevitably, dangerously closer to each other. One thing led to another. Which reminded her of the previous night…

An image flashed through Eleanor's mind, a vivid picture of herself lying back on the big four poster bed—she could see the canopy above her head, and she could remember how she had stretched long and luxuriously and asked Kit… The colour rushed into her cheeks. She had asked Kit if he would like to make love to her, had invited him—twice! And he had turned her down…

'Ohhhh!'

'Are you feeling unwell this morning, my love?' Kit enquired solicitously, the twinkle still in his eye. 'It might have been expected. Come, sit down over here.' He led her to the garden seat that had been placed in the middle of the lawn, beneath a canopy of green. It was shadowed and cool and Eleanor sat down and folded her parasol, relieved to be out of the direct sun.

'Kit…' she spoke hesitantly, uncertain if she really wanted to know the answer '…is it true or did I just imagine asking you last night if you would make love to me?'

There was a pause whilst she waited for him to come to her rescue, to assure her that she had asked nothing of him at all. Kit grinned. He looked insufferably pleased with himself. 'No, you did not imagine it, Eleanor.'

Eleanor's blush deepened. 'Ohhhh… But you did not…'

Kit sobered. 'No. It would scarcely have been the right occasion.'

Eleanor took a deep breath. 'I think that I must thank you, my lord. You could have taken advantage of me—and yet you did not.'

Their eyes met and held. Kit was still smiling very faintly and there was something else in his expression that made Eleanor's stomach drop away. She sat quite still, transfixed, and Kit leaned forward and kissed her very gently.

Eleanor's lips clung softly to his. She immediately knew that she did not want to pull away. The sensation was so very sweet, the touch of his lips so tender, demanding nothing but giving everything. Eleanor moved a little closer along the seat. She wanted more than this tentative caress and the knowledge of her own desires shocked her briefly. But there was no danger—the kiss was no more than the lightest of touches. It was up to her to make more of it if she wished.

She did wish. She found that she wished it quite desperately. She parted her lips beneath Kit's and was instantly gratified to feel the change in him, the demand that lay beneath his iron control. His tongue touched hers, exploring her mouth, slowly and sensuously, evoking a response that made her tremble. She felt languid and melting, yet unbearably excited at one and the same time. She knew that Kit was still exerting a frustrating self-control and suddenly it seemed imperative to make him lose it. She pressed closer to him and Kit broke off the kiss. Eleanor let out a sigh of pure annoyance.

'Oh!'

'I am sorry, my love.' Kit was breathing a little unevenly, the only sign that he had been disturbed at all. 'Charlotte and Beth are coming across the lawn, and with them—yes, Carrick with the morning tea tray!'

Eleanor spun around. Beth had said that she would

call, and on most occasions Eleanor would have been more than delighted to see her, but now... She shivered as the sensual warmth ebbed from her blood. To think that she had not been unduly concerned about her developing friendship with Kit! Had she been wilfully blind or just deluding herself...

Kit stood up, bending to brush his lips against her cheek in a gesture that sent another echo of passion fizzing along Eleanor's nerves.

'I will leave you with Beth and Charlotte now, but I will see you later, my love.'

'Very well,' Eleanor agreed shakily. She watched as he strolled across the lawn, pausing to kiss his sister and cousin and exchange a few words on the way. Carrick brought the tea over and Eleanor dragged her gaze away from Kit's tall figure. It was odd—she found it incredibly difficult to look away from him. She started to think about the kiss, then hastily sought to distract herself by rearranging the chairs and table and helping Carrick with the cups.

'Eleanor! How are you this morning?'

Beth, resplendent in a silver and white striped dress, bustled over and bent to hug her sister-in-law. 'I wondered what had happened to you at the musicale last night!' she reproached. 'I thought that you might not be feeling quite the thing, or it could just have been the caterwauling of the terrible singer...'

'It was dreadful, was it not,' Charlotte agreed, with a shudder. 'It gave me the most appalling headache...'

'You are both dreadfully uncultured!' Eleanor

scolded, tongue in cheek. She was feeling quite kindly disposed towards the diva now that she knew Kit had no interest in her. 'Why, everyone knows that La Perla is the most sought-after opera singer in Italy—in more than one sense!'

Eleanor saw Carrick blush to his ears and blink very rapidly, a sure sign that the butler was discomfited. Really, he was a dreadful old puritan.

'Thank you, Carrick,' she said hastily. 'We shall call you if we require anything else.'

'Poor Carrick,' Beth said as the butler withdrew, 'he is so easily shocked! Why, you would have thought that he was inured to such things after witnessing my behaviour…'

'And mine,' Eleanor said feelingly.

Charlotte touched her hand. 'So tell us what happened last night! Were you taken ill?'

'Oh!' Eleanor frowned a little. She felt strangely reluctant to admit to her mistake with the laudanum, more out of loyalty to her mother than because of her own shame. 'I had some ratafia and it did not agree with me.'

'Nasty stuff,' Beth commented. 'I tried the Negus…'

'Oh, you did not!'

'I did, and it was quite revolting! I shall stick to port in future!'

'For my part I had nothing but lemonade—' Charlotte said, drinking her tea.

'But then you are always so good!'

They all laughed.

'So Kit had to bring you home,' Beth said, wiping her eyes, 'and put you to bed, Eleanor?'

'Beth…' Eleanor said, blushing. 'Truth to tell, I remember very little of it! Kit and I are the best of friends, but it is just that—friendship!'

She did not miss the significant glance that flashed between her sister-in-law and cousin.

'I see,' Beth said slowly. 'And when we arrived just now you were kissing Kit goodbye—in a friendly manner?'

Eleanor blushed to the roots of her hair. Remembering the conversation she had had with Beth only a week ago, she thought suddenly how perspicacious her sister-in-law had been in thinking that Kit would not simply sit back and allow her to dictate their makeshift marriage.

'I did warn you!' Beth said shrewdly, eyeing the tell-tale rose-pink in Eleanor's cheeks.

'Pray do not put poor Nell to the blush, Beth!' Charlotte said, rescuing her. 'You are too inquisitive! I am sure it is nobody's business but their own…'

'Speaking of which…' Eleanor rushed in to change the subject '…what are we to do about this ridiculous feud that the men insist on indulging in? Why, it is Lady Knighton's rout tonight and I feel half-inclined to refuse just to avoid another foolish confrontation!'

'That is just what we were saying on the way here,' Charlotte said comfortably. She stirred sugar into her tea. 'I tried to reason with Justin after the musicale last night, but he was quite adamant. In the end I was obliged to tell him that I would not speak to him until he showed some sense!'

'Has it worked yet?' Beth enquired, leaning forward. She fanned herself. 'Goodness, but it is getting hot today! The rout will be a sad crush tonight.'

'No, it has not worked,' Charlotte said, a little disconsolately. 'I used to enjoy discussing matters with Justin—the papers, the politics, any matter that was worthy of debate, I suppose—but this morning he said that he may get sensible conversation at his club and if I choose to sulk that is my affair!'

Beth tutted.

'I hear that Marcus and Justin are speaking of having Kit blackballed from Whites,' Eleanor said hesitantly. 'I tried to speak to Kit of it last evening but he just said that it was a matter between the three of them.'

'Pshaw!' Charlotte took a piece of cake. 'Have you had any success in influencing Marcus, Beth? I know you mentioned you were planning to speak to him.'

Beth raised her eyebrows. 'Surely you jest, Lottie!' She went off into a peal of laughter. 'I too told Marcus last night that I would not speak to him if he persisted in such ridiculous behaviour and all he said was that we did not need to speak for what he had in mind!'

Charlotte spluttered into her tea. 'Fortunate that Carrick has gone, Beth! You would have shocked him to the core!'

'But what's to do?' Beth asked plaintively. 'If the

men will not listen to reason we might be set with this foolish feud for months—or years—to come!'

'I agree that we need to take some action,' Eleanor said glumly. 'But what?'

The three of them looked at each other. Charlotte blushed. 'I did think of something...' she said, after a moment.

Eleanor and Beth waited.

'You are looking very furtive, Lottie!' Beth accused. 'Why, whatever can this be...'

Charlotte cast her eyes down modestly. 'I thought that if we were to refuse our husbands their... marital rights...they might come to heel a little more quickly than if we simply refuse to speak to them!' She looked at them. 'It was just an idea...'

There was a silence.

'Lottie!' Beth said, shocked. 'That is the sort of idea that I would have!' She sat back in her chair, looking thoughtful. 'Not that the scheme does not have merit! If we feel secure enough that our husbands will not seek solace elsewhere...'

'I do not think there is the least chance of either of your husbands considering such a course!' Eleanor said stoutly and truthfully. 'Why, anyone can see that Justin adores you, Charlotte, and as for Marcus, he has been known as the most attentive husband in the *Ton* for the past few months! Besides, you are both newly wed and I do not believe that it will take very long...'

Beth's eyes sparkled. 'No indeed! Oh, to see Marcus's face...'

Charlotte smiled. 'It is a piquant thought,' she agreed. 'I do believe we may have some success…'

Eleanor sighed. 'I am sorry that I cannot contribute to the plan. My friendship with Kit…' she blushed delicately '…is scarcely on such terms…'

'I'll wager he would wish it so though, Nell!' Beth said slyly. 'So you may find yourself called upon to participate! Remember—no giving in until the feud is laid to rest, no matter the temptation, no matter the blandishments…'

'When do we start?' Charlotte enquired, popping a sugared almond into her mouth.

'Tonight!' Beth said.

On returning from Whites, Marcus Trevithick was pleased to discover his wife alone in the drawing-room and apparently deeply engrossed in a book. There were a couple of hours before they were due to depart for Lady Knighton's rout and Marcus, contemplating the delicate line of Beth's shoulder and the delicious curve of her breast, was certain that he knew just how to pass the time.

'Good evening, my love,' he said, bending to kiss her lingeringly. 'I am so glad to find you here and alone…'

Beth returned the kiss in full measure but she did not put her book down and Marcus found himself ever so slightly piqued. Beth's pregnancy had led to certain changes in their lovemaking but she had never been anything other than wholehearted in her enjoyment. He kissed her again, allowing his lips to drift along the line of her neck to the soft skin above the lacy edge of her dress. He slid one hand inside her bodice and cupped her breast.

A moment later he felt Beth shift slightly and opened his eyes. She was reading her book over his shoulder.

Marcus was outraged. He straightened up and fixed his wife with a glacial look. 'I am sorry, my dear— was I boring you?'

There was a guilty expression in Beth's eye. 'Oh no, indeed! It is just that I had reached a particularly exciting bit…'

Marcus took the book from her and looked at the spine. '*A Vindication of the Rights of Woman!* Beth—'

He did not miss the flash of amusement deep in her eyes. 'Yes, my love?'

Marcus dropped to his knee beside the sofa, took his wife's chin in his hand and turned her lips up to his. This time he was really trying. After a moment he felt her lips soften and cling to his, a tell-tale quiver going through her. Marcus felt a surge of triumph. A particularly exciting bit indeed!

He stole a hand beneath her skirts and started to stroke her leg above the silken edge of her stocking. Beth shifted obligingly, sighing beneath his mouth. Marcus's fingers crept to the inside of her thigh. His own arousal was acute now and as he stroked he allowed himself to think about pulling up her skirts and…

Beth straightened up.

'No!'

Marcus froze. He hauled himself up on to the sofa and sat down heavily, only to feel the sharp edge of the book digging into a tender part of his anatomy. He picked the book up and threw it across the room.

'Beth, what the hell is going on?'

Beth's eyelashes fluttered modestly. She looked rumpled and pretty and very, very desirable. Marcus groaned.

'I am sorry, my love,' his spouse said sweetly, 'but everything has its price! Until you settle this ridiculous feud you have with my cousin...'

Marcus leant over and seized her shoulders. 'Are you telling me that you will refuse to sleep with me until I acknowledge Kit Mostyn?'

Beth nodded. Her eyes were bright with mischief. 'Exactly, my love.'

Marcus sat back and looked at her for a long moment, his dark eyes narrowing on her face. 'Beth, you will never succeed!'

'Oh, yes I shall!' Beth said. She smoothed her skirts down modestly, cast him one provocative look over her shoulder and got up to retrieve her book. She sat down again at the end of the sofa the furthest away from him.

Marcus sat irresolute for several moments. Beth turned the page. She seemed engrossed.

'God damn it!' Her husband said furiously. He got up and went out of the room, slamming the door hard behind him. It was only when his footsteps had died away that Beth put the book down with a sigh of relief and went into a peal of laughter.

Eleanor had also fallen asleep that afternoon, her borrowed copy of *Tristram Shandy* sliding off her lap as she dozed against the sofa cushions. It was only when she heard voices in the hall that she roused herself, wondering if they had visitors. Then she recognised Kit's voice and wondered who was with him. She tiptoed to the drawing-room door and peered round, just in time to see Kit disappearing into the study with a gentleman that she did not recognise. Eleanor resumed her seat on the sofa and picked up the *Ladies' Magazine* but she barely glanced at it. She was curious to know to know the identity of her husband's mystery acquaintance.

Little more than a half hour later, the study door opened again and the gentlemen emerged. Eleanor wondered if Kit would bring the visitor in—he must know that she was at home, after all, and it would be courteous to introduce them. However Kit ushered the man to the door and saw him off personally. It was evident to Eleanor, watching through the half-open drawing-room door, that they were great good friends and further that the man was indeed a gentleman and a very good-looking one at that. She heard the front door close and at the same time a stray draught pulled the drawing-room door from her hand—she had been holding it steady so that she could see what was going on—and slammed it with enough force to bring the house down.

Eleanor whisked herself across the room and on to the sofa just as the door reopened to admit Kit. He was looking mildly concerned.

'Is everything all right, my dear?' he enquired. 'I heard the door slam and wondered if you had injured yourself.'

'Oh no!' Eleanor was feeling flustered and thought that it probably showed. 'I was asleep…'

'You are looking a little dishevelled, my love.' Kit's gaze, warm and ever-so-slightly disturbing, roamed over her and lingered on the curl of hair in the hollow of her neck. 'I was only concerned because I saw you standing behind the door and thought you might have trapped your fingers when it closed…'

'You saw me?' Eleanor was mortified. She felt herself colouring a deep rose-pink. 'Oh, Kit…'

'Do not worry!' Kit said cheerfully. 'I merely thought that you were curious about my visitor and were spying on me again! Really, my love, you have the most lively interest in my private affairs!'

Since this was exactly what Eleanor had been doing she found it difficult to demur, but she did her best.

'Yes, well, I was only wondering if you would bring your visitor to meet me, Kit, and I was worrying in case I looked untidy…'

'You look delightful, Eleanor,' Kit said, smiling. 'As for Harry, I would have introduced him but he had a pressing engagement elsewhere. You will meet him tonight at Lady Knighton's ball.'

'Harry?'

'Captain Henry Luttrell. He is an old comrade of

mine with whom I was recently in Ireland, but of course…' Kit checked himself '…you do not wish to know about that!'

Eleanor was trapped. She wished to know quite desperately and had been feeling like that for the best part of two weeks. She looked at Kit, who looked back at her, brows raised quizzically.

'Perhaps I would like…' Eleanor began hesitantly. 'That is, perhaps we are now at that stage in our reacquaintance when I might ask… As we are friends again now…'

'Oh, of course,' Kit said courteously. He gestured to the sofa. 'Shall we sit down together, then?'

Eleanor sat down, clasping her hands tightly in her lap. Now that the moment of truth was upon her, she felt nervous and vulnerable and not at all sure that she wanted to know. Yet they could not continue as they had been doing, with so much lying unspoken between them. Perhaps it would be better to know everything and have done with it.

Kit did not hurry into speech. He sat looking at her with the same searching directness she had grown accustomed to seeing in his gaze. She shifted uncomfortably.

'Perhaps it would be best to start by saying that I spent the five months that we were apart in Ireland,' Kit said, at length. 'I was never in Italy, and certainly not consorting with any opera singers, whatever the rumours!'

'Oh, I know that!' Eleanor's nervousness made her loquacious. 'It is the least well-kept secret in London!

Why, the servants have been telling me this age that you have been in Ireland *and* that you were about government business!'

Kit looked slightly winded. 'Have they? Good God! But how did they know?'

Eleanor almost giggled at his appalled expression. 'I do not know, Kit! Perhaps you are not as discreet as you think yourself!'

'Perhaps not!' Kit thrust a hand through his hair. 'It is a good job that the business is concluded and I am to take on no further work for Castlereagh, for it seems I am utterly incapable of keeping a secret!'

'That must mean that you were a spy, Kit.' Eleanor frowned. 'I confess that I do not like the idea!'

Kit laughed. 'Oh, I was no spy—never more than a glorified messenger boy, I assure you! It only came about in the first place because I travelled such a great deal! This last job was by way of a favour for Castlereagh, and a more mismanaged, farcical affair it could not have been!'

'Tell me!' Eleanor said, suddenly desperate to know.

Kit looked at her. She could read nothing in his face but a rather bleak unhappiness.

'The summons came on the very day that we were married,' he began. 'You may remember that I told you I had to attend to a matter of business—I went to the meeting place in the tavern, intending to explain that I had been married only that morning and wished to delay my departure.' He sighed, sitting back against the cushions. 'Unfortunately we had previously agreed that I should be knocked on the head in a tavern brawl—to cover my tracks, you understand! And I was, as soon as I walked in! By the time I was in any fit state to explain anything, I was ten miles out to sea in company with a gang of pressed men...' He sighed. 'It would have been comical had it not been so desperate.'

Eleanor stared at him. 'You mean that you never had the opportunity to explain our situation...'

'Precisely.' Kit's expression was bitter. 'When I finally woke up it was too late.'

There was a silence. Eleanor could feel Kit's gaze upon her but he did not say anything else, and a part of Eleanor recognised and appreciated the fact that he chosen to tell her everything so plainly. He had made no appeal to her emotions and she suspected that this was not because he did not care but because he felt it would be unfair to her. She shivered a little. Now that she knew, she could see how simply such an accident had occurred. How simple and how unlucky. She did not really know how to feel.

'I see. But you wrote to me to explain?'

Kit shifted slightly. 'I wrote several times. The first letter was sent as soon as I reached shore. I cannot conceive how my letters went astray. All the time I was hoping desperately that you had received them and would understand what had happened! I even suggested that you should seek Charlotte out so that you would not be alone—' He broke off, evidently not wishing to pursue that.

Eleanor shook her head. It was too late for recriminations now, too late to say that Charlotte had been away and instead she was forced to return to Trevithick House and the Dowager's vengeful accusations.

'Maybe your letters were lost, Kit,' she said. 'Where did you direct them?'

'To Trevithick House,' Kit said. 'I did not know where to find you, and I thought that at the least they would be waiting there for you, but...' He shrugged again. 'It is a mystery. But there is something more that I must tell you, Eleanor.'

Eleanor waited.

'My work itself took very little time. I was in a fever of impatience to return to you, but then something else occurred, something that kept me in Ireland far longer than I had intended. And that...' Kit paused '...is a matter that I fear I cannot disclose, Nell. It is not my secret to tell.' He took her hands in his, in a strong grasp. 'Please do not imagine that it is because I do not trust you. The reverse is true. But I gave my word of honour that I would not speak until the person concerned gave me their permission. I believe that the matter will be resolved soon, and when it is you will understand...' His gaze sought hers. 'Forgive me! It is a difficult matter...'

Eleanor wrinkled her brow. 'It is difficult for me too, Kit! If you do not tell me—'

'I know!' Kit's grip tightened on her hands. 'I have asked so much of you already and yet now I have to ask you to trust me further—for a little while longer. Can you do that, Nell?'

Eleanor did not look at him. She felt utterly bewildered. She had no doubt of the truth of what Kit had told her and she believed that whatever his secret, he must be keeping it for the most honourable of motives. Yet her heart cried out that it was not fair to ask more of her. The anger and bitterness his absence had created had not yet vanished and still she did not know the whole truth… The warm touch of his fingers in hers only served to confuse her further. She was not indifferent to him—she could not pretend that she was—and yet she did not want him to draw any closer to her. Any suggestion Kit might make for them to be married in more than name only had to be repudiated.

Eleanor shrank a little. 'Thank you for telling me this, Kit. I will think about what you have said—'

'Wait!' Kit held on to her when she would have pulled away. 'There is but one more thing, Eleanor!' He drew her resisting body closer until he had an arm about her. 'I should have said this long ago. I should have said it first! I am so very sorry for what happened. You must know now that it was never my intention to leave you, and I will never stop regretting it—'

'Oh, do not!' Eleanor could not bear any more.

'Say that at the least you believe that of me—'

'Of course! Of course I do!' Eleanor pulled away from him a little. 'But it is not so easy for me, Kit! I had a truly terrible time of it whilst you were away! Yes, I understand it was none of your intention and in time I am sure I can forgive—' Her voice broke. 'Pray do not ask any more of me for now!'

'Very well.' Kit loosened his grip and she stood up shakily. She could see the vivid disappointment in his face and the difficulty with which he mastered it. His tension was palpable.

'I must go and get ready,' she said uncertainly. 'We shall be late for the ball—'

'To hell with the ball and everything else!' Kit stood up. 'Eleanor…'

He swept her into his arms, holding her ruthlessly whilst his mouth plundered hers with merciless skill. Eleanor tried to free herself but he held her still. It was violent and frightening, yet beneath her fear, Eleanor felt the pull in her blood as her body answered his. When he finally let her go they were both breathing hard and she could not tear her gaze away from the compulsive heat of desire she saw in his eyes. He did not apologise for his actions.

'I must go,' she said again, shakily, and after a second Kit moved to hold the door for her with scrupulous courtesy.

Eleanor ran up the stairs, feeling the trembling in her legs at every step. Her thoughts were whirling and her senses scarcely less so, and uppermost in her mind was that she was going to have to be much more determined and strong-minded if she were to thwart Kit's intentions in the future. He was undermining her resolution at every step and what was worse was the fact that part of her did not care. Part of her wanted Kit's lovemaking very much, and it was only the memories and the fear that held her back.

Chapter Eight

'Marcus is in a very bad mood this evening,' Eleanor whispered to Beth, as they sat out a dance together at Lady Knighton's rout. 'Why, he snapped my head off when I asked how he was earlier, and when we danced the boulanger he spoke no more than half a dozen words! Whatever is the matter with him?'

Beth raised her eyebrows expressively and Eleanor smothered a laugh.

'Oh no! No wonder he is so cross-grained. He and Mama make a matched pair tonight.'

Beth shrugged lightly. 'I'll confess he was not best pleased when I refused him!'

'It has not made him relent yet,' Eleanor said. 'I saw Marcus turn his back very deliberately when Kit passed him in the card-room. You will just have to try harder!'

She looked across the room to where Kit was standing, deep in conversation with Henry Luttrell. She had been introduced to the dashing Captain now and had had two dances with him. Naturally they had made no mention of Kit's recent sojourn in Ireland, but it was uppermost in Eleanor's mind—along with the discussion, and the kiss that had followed.

Beth nudged her.

'Nell, do you know the gentleman Kit is speaking with? Is he an old friend?'

Eleanor laughed. 'I believe so,' she said, a twinkle in her eye. 'That is Captain Luttrell. But what are you planning, Beth?'

Beth got to her feet. 'I must go and speak to Kit— and his friend. That will give Marcus something else to think about!'

Eleanor shook her head, smiling slightly. 'I think you have upset him enough for one evening!'

Beth smiled. 'I have a waltz with Marcus the dance after next. It should provide the ideal opportunity to torment him a little further!'

She swept away, pausing to exchange a few ostentatious words with Kit as he came up with an iced sherbet for Eleanor. Eleanor bit her lip. She could see Marcus watching them with a face like a thundercloud, and when Henry Luttrell bowed charmingly over Beth's hand Eleanor thought her brother would explode. She devoutly hoped that Beth and Charlotte knew what they were doing with their ultimatum.

Kit slid into the seat next to her and handed her the glass. 'There you are, my love! I do not believe it much melted, though it is very hot tonight. Are you enjoying the ball?'

Eleanor dipped her spoon into the ice. 'It is quite

pleasant, my lord, although rather too hot for dancing. What do you think?'

Kit slid his arm along the back of her chair in a gesture that Eleanor found both proprietorial and rather pleasing. She was very conscious of his hand resting close to her shoulder. 'You know that I prefer the country to the town! I fear I find all these endless social events unconscionably boring!'

Eleanor giggled. 'Pray do not let the fashionable hostesses hear you, my lord! There are any number of people who make doing nothing a fine art form and would take offence at your words!'

Kit smiled at her. His gaze was warm as it rested on her face and Eleanor felt herself blushing a little.

'You should know that I would like nothing so much as to leave London for the country,' he said slowly. 'My aim is no grander than to live peaceably at Mostyn Hall with my family about me—children, perhaps... Maybe we could talk about it, Eleanor?'

Eleanor could feel his gaze intent on her, though she could not meet his eyes. She felt as though she was suffocating. Ever since Kit had kissed her earlier she had been pushing such thoughts away. She had wanted him then, wanted to feel his arms around her, wanted to forget all the bitterness between them. But there were some things that she simply could not give him... A stray breath of wind from the terrace made her shiver convulsively.

'I find that I rather enjoy the Season,' she said, in a brittle voice that did not sound her own. 'Surely there is no hurry to leave town!'

She saw Kit's gaze narrow too perceptive, too searching for comfort. She turned her face away, knowing with relief that Kit would not press her on this, at least not at the moment.

'I hear that Lady Knighton has engaged the services of a profile miniaturist tonight!' she said brightly. 'Shall we go and see his work?'

Kit got to his feet and offered her his arm politely. The easy intimacy that had been between them a moment before had vanished and Eleanor felt as though she was chatting to an acquaintance.

'They say he is very talented,' she rattled on, as they walked towards the room that had been set aside for the silhouettist. 'He cuts profiles from black card in a matter of minutes! They say he is a student of John Miers, who has his studios in the Strand—'

'I know the place,' Kit commented. 'Perhaps you should have your silhouette cut, Eleanor!'

Eleanor stole a glance at him. His face was closed and expressionless and her heart missed a beat from regret and pity rather than anything else. This was all so difficult! As soon as they had achieved their comfortable friendship it seemed that it had all been spoiled by the dangerous physical attraction that had flared between them. It was quite natural that Kit would assume they had reached a closer understanding and one that would lead in time to greater intimacy. Yet here was she, drawing back again, unwilling to take any further risk and quite incapable of explaining why…

The miniaturist had just finished a silhouette of

Charlotte Trevithick when they arrived and there was an awkward moment as Eleanor and Charlotte stood admiring his work whilst Kit and Justin gazed studiously in opposite directions. The silhouettist was an earnest young man with intense dark eyes and flowing black hair, who clearly took pleasure in their praise of his work. Once the compliments had run out there was an awkward silence until Justin recollected that he and Charlotte were dancing the next waltz together, and Eleanor sat down. The silhouettist snipped away to produce a likeness and handed it to her in a matter of minutes. She smiled as she looked at it. He had made her appear very pretty, right down to the tender sweep of her eyelashes across her cheek, and the stray curl that caressed her neck.

Kit leant over the back of her chair to take a look and Eleanor, glancing at him over her shoulder, saw the genuine pleasure in his eyes at he looked on her likeness. Her heart gave another small lurch.

'Why, that has captured you precisely, my love,' Kit said, 'although…' He tilted his head a little, 'I do believe that your nose is a shade too long! Yes, decidedly a little too long for perfection—'

'That is because it is!' Eleanor said firmly. She smiled her thanks to the miniaturist and tucked her hand through Kit's arm. 'You are too partial, my lord.'

'There is nothing wrong in that!' Kit protested. He placed the silhouette in his pocket. 'I shall keep this— as a tribute to your beauty, my love, and to the fact that the miniaturist was evidently as much struck by it as I am!'

Eleanor blushed, disclaimed and felt even worse. She could not think of anything to say to lighten the situation and yet she felt a fraud responding to Kit's compliments. Some time soon she would have to make her feelings plain. It would be dishonest not to do so.

'Kit! Eleanor!' Charlotte Trevithick was hurrying towards them, her pale face flushed with distress. She put a hand on Eleanor's arm. 'I have lost my pearl bracelet! Have you seen it anywhere? I thought I must have dropped it whilst I was having my profile taken, yet it is not there! Justin will be so displeased, for it was a wedding present! I cannot believe I have been so careless!'

She looked as though she were about to cry. Eleanor put an arm about her.

'Oh, Charlotte, I am so sorry! Where have you looked?'

'Everywhere!' Charlotte was inconsolable. 'I should not have worn it, for the clasp was loose, but it was so pretty and now it has gone…'

Some curious impulse made Eleanor glance across the room to where her mother was sitting with Beth and Marcus. The Dowager's chin was sunk on her chest and she was not speaking, but was rocking backwards and forwards gently to the strains of the music. There was one empty rout chair by her side.

'Charlotte, were you sitting with Mama just now?' she asked casually. 'I see that there is a spare chair…'

Charlotte nodded miserably. 'We were all sitting together, for Lady Trevithick has softened towards Justin since his marriage, you know! But I fear she is not in good spirits tonight—she has scarce spoken a word and Marcus is also very morose tonight, so it has been a most subdued party!'

'You did not drop your bracelet over by the chairs, then?' Eleanor asked. She was beginning to feel rather cold at the direction her thoughts were tending. The last time she had seen a bracelet disappear had been at the Trevithick ball, and she knew exactly what had happened there.

Charlotte brightened. 'Well, I did not think so, but I had not checked. Perhaps I should take a look…'

Eleanor gave Kit an apologetic smile. 'I shall accompany Charlotte to look for her bracelet, my lord, but will be but a minute. Perhaps it would be better…' she paused delicately, '…were you to wait for me here?'

Kit bowed ironically. 'I will hunt up some company in the card-room!'

Eleanor linked her arm through that of her sister-in-law and they strolled over to the party from Trevithick House. At close quarters Eleanor could see the truth of Charlotte's words that the group was as sad as a wet Monday—Marcus and Justin were conversing together but there was a deep frown on Marcus's brow and at his side Beth was sitting flicking her fan with mock-innocence. The Dowager sat like a grounded ship, massive and a little apart from the others.

'Nell!' Beth said with a warm smile, 'how lovely for you to join us. Is Kit not with you?'

That gained her a glare from Marcus. Justin looked extremely uncomfortable. Beth smiled sunnily.

'No,' Eleanor said, trying not to laugh, 'he has gone for a hand of whist.' She turned to her brother and cousin. 'So perhaps the gentlemen should avoid the card-room.'

Both Marcus and Justin had the grace to look embarrassed and Eleanor felt a little spurt of pleasure. She might not be able to employ Beth and Charlotte's tactics but she could at least show them up for their bad behaviour. She turned to her mother.

'Mama, I believe that Charlotte has dropped her bracelet somewhere around here, and I wondered if you had seen it? She has searched everywhere else but it is not to be found.'

The Dowager had ignored the previous conversation but now she stopped rocking, opened her little dark eyes and surveyed her daughter calmly.

'I do not think I have seen it. That pretty pearl bracelet, was it? What a great shame! You should be more careful, Charlotte dear.'

'Yes, ma'am!' Charlotte shot a guilty look at Justin. 'I cannot see how I came to lose it!'

Eleanor looked her mother straight in the eye. 'For my part I believe that some unscrupulous person has taken it! What do you think, Mama?'

There was an odd silence whilst the Dowager's eyes narrowed on her daughter's flushed face. The others were looking puzzled but did not say anything.

'Perhaps if we were to search…' the Dowager Lady Trevithick murmured. She leant forwards on the chair and its spindly legs trembled. Eleanor could hear her stays creaking under the strain.

'You look, Eleanor,' the Dowager instructed. 'Down on your knees, girl, beneath my chair!'

Eleanor flushed. When she had started this she had had no intention of drawing the gaze of the whole room, and now she began to wonder if her suspicions of her mother could be in any way justified. Just because one bracelet had disappeared under mysterious circumstances it did not logically follow that her mother was a jewel thief, stealing to support her penchant for laudanum. Eleanor, who had shied away from this idea from the first, was now desperate not to pursue it. It felt wrong to impute such criminal behaviour to her own mother and she could scarcely ask Lady Trevithick to turn out her reticule or accuse her in front of the assembled throng.

But there was no need. Lady Trevithick twitched her skirts, there was a little thud, and the bracelet rolled out from under the chair to rest at Eleanor's feet. She bent to pick it up.

'It was there all the time!' the Dowager murmured. 'Beneath my skirts! I am sorry, Charlotte dear, I did not notice! Perhaps if you were to be more careful…'

'Yes, ma'am,' Charlotte murmured submissively. She gave Eleanor a grateful smile and clipped the bracelet about her wrist. 'I shall have the catch mended immediately!'

Eleanor smiled back. She deliberately did not look

at her mother. She knew that it was only the combination of the Dowager's size and a lack of opportunity that meant that Charlotte's bracelet was not gracing Lord Kemble's pocket by now. No doubt her mother had been waiting for a chance to scoop the bracelet up when she was unobserved. Eleanor knew her mother had to be stopped—and that she had to stop covering up her behaviour…

She saw that Beth had picked up on her uneasiness, for her sister-in-law patted the seat beside her and deliberately broke the strained silence.

'Did I tell you that Lady Salome arrived this afternoon? She was too fatigued to join us this evening but asked me to tell you that she would call on you tomorrow…' The conversation eased into more comfortable channels and after a while Justin and Charlotte went off to dance, Lady Trevithick nodded off to sleep again and it was suddenly easy for Eleanor to imagine that nothing was wrong. Except, of course, that it was and she knew that she had to do something about it.

'Oh ma'am, was the ball so very glittering and romantic? Packed with handsome gentleman and beautiful ladies?' Lucy, her eyes sparkling, helped Eleanor out of the lilac dress and went to hang it in the wardrobe. 'Oh, how I wish I could have seen it!'

'No, it was not really,' Eleanor said on a yawn. She had been turning the problem of her mother's thefts over in her mind and come to no useful conclusions other than that she must speak to Marcus about it.

'To tell the truth, Lucy, it was a deadly dull affair and full of the same boring faces and tedious gossip! At this rate I shall be retiring to the country! I would rather stay at home and do my needlework.'

Lucy giggled. She gestured to the chair at the dressing-table. 'Oh, ma'am, I cannot believe that! If you would like to sit down, I shall brush your hair out. Do you wish to take your necklace off first?'

'No, please leave it for now.' Eleanor yawned again and sat down, her fingers touching the diamonds and emeralds at her throat. The Mostyn necklace glowed softly above the neckline of her chemise, shimmering against her creamy skin. Eleanor smiled. It was indeed a beautiful piece and the Dowager would never get her hands on it.

The maid started to unpin the flowers from Eleanor's hair and brush out the long, dark strands. 'Lord Mostyn looked so dotingly on you this evening, my lady.'

'Lucy, you may be in need of spectacles,' Eleanor said, a little wearily. The maid's romantic obsession was particularly hard to bear when her own feelings were in such turmoil. 'Pray do not imagine that my marriage is anything other than one of convenience! It is the way of the world to marry for money and position—'

'May I come in?'

Eleanor closed her eyes in mortification. She must remember to tell Lucy to shut the bedroom door prop-

erly, for here was Kit, standing in the doorway and
eyeing her with an interrogatory look that suggested
he had just heard her unflattering opinion of their
match. This was disturbing, but more unsettling still
was the fact that it was three in the morning and she
was in her shift and Kit—Eleanor swallowed hard.
Her husband was partially undressed, having removed
his jacket, waistcoat and neck-cloth, and he looked so
rakishly dishevelled that her heart started to beat a
quick pit-a-pat. She did not believe that the current
terms of their relationship quite allowed for this. Nor
should it. This was where she had to call a halt.

Lucy bobbed a curtsey and laid the hairbrush down,
and Eleanor caught her arm in an urgent grip.

'Lucy, wait! I need you to help me remove the
necklace—'

'I can help with that,' Kit murmured. There was a
wicked twinkle in his eye.

'And to brush my hair and to help me undress—'
Eleanor rushed on.

'I can help with that too.' Kit sauntered into the
room, holding the door open for the maid to depart.
Lucy, the romantic sparkle restored to her eye, sped
out and the door closed behind her.

Eleanor stood up. 'My lord! Why are you wander-
ing the corridors half-dressed and giving rise to servants' gossip…?'

'There is a bolt in place on the other door, my
love,' Kit said, gesturing to the communicating door,
'so I was obliged to approach this way! As for being

half-dressed, just be grateful that I am not in my dressing-gown!'

Eleanor was, but she did not wish to admit it. She sighed crossly.

'By what right are you in my bedroom in the first place, sir?'

'The right of a husband,' Kit said easily. He came towards her. 'You would not deny that, I think!'

Eleanor snatched up the hairbrush and held it to her breast.

Kit frowned. 'What do you intend to do with that, Eleanor? Brush me to death? You have no need to fear...' He took the brush from her clenched fingers and laid it down. 'I only wished to speak with you.'

'Can it not wait until the morning, my lord?' Eleanor said, a little faintly. Her defiance was weakening now that he was so close. 'It has been a difficult evening and I am tired and wish to retire...'

'In a moment. You need me to help with your necklace, remember? Turn around...'

Once again Eleanor closed her eyes as she felt him lift the heavy swatch of her hair over one shoulder so that he could reach the clasp. The air was cool on the nape of her neck. Kit's fingers were on the catch of the necklace; his touch grazed her skin, setting it alight. Oh, this was the most dreadful torture, but she had to withstand it. She did not want him to see that he could affect her so, for it would only encourage him to think he could ask for that little bit more.

She heard the clink as Kit laid the necklace down on the dressing-table, then his hands were on her shoulders again, warm and strong as they had been at the start of the evening when he helped her on with her cloak. Only then the action had been innocent. This time, her shoulders were bare. Eleanor shivered.

'There…' Kit's voice was a little husky. He was running strands of her hair through his fingers. 'Shall I brush your hair for you now?'

'No!' Eleanor snapped. She could feel the warmth spreading from his hands where they still rested on her shoulders, down her whole body, flushing her skin pink with desire, making her blood feel heavy in her veins.

'No,' she said again, trying to speak lightly. 'Boys always pull girls' hair. It is inbred from childhood.'

In the mirror she saw Kit smile slightly. He was rubbing his hands very gently up and down her upper arms, stroking, caressing. 'I could try to make amends for that,' he said softly.

His hands returned to her shoulders and the pressure increased slightly. Eleanor found herself sitting down again—she had to, for her knees would have crumpled otherwise. Kit picked up the brush. The long strokes were soothing and stimulating at the same time, from the crown of her head to the end of each thick brown curl. Eleanor's skin prickled with awareness. She closed her eyes briefly.

'I am sorry that you did not enjoy the ball,' Kit said gently. 'Perhaps in future matters will be easier. Now that we have reached an understanding…'

Eleanor bit her lip. Such a comfortable phrase hardly reflected her feelings at that moment.

'I am sure matters will improve,' she agreed, trying to strike the same bright note. 'I used to love the Season's balls and parties…'

'I remember…' Kit's voice was as soothing as the caress of the brush through her hair. 'And you dance so beautifully. It was always a pleasure to partner you…'

Eleanor looked at him in the mirror. His gaze was fixed on the reflection of her face and there was a turbulent heat in his eyes that made her feel quite light-headed. She had to put a stop to this.

'Enough, thank you…' She realised with horror that her voice had come out as a whisper and cleared her throat.

'Thank you,' she said again, not quite steadily. 'That will be quite sufficient.'

'That was nowhere near one hundred strokes…' She could hear the undertone of amusement in Kit's voice. 'I hope it is not because you are dissatisfied with my attentions…'

'No…' The word came out on a shaky sigh. Eleanor took a deep breath to steady herself and stood up. 'You are a more than competent ladies' maid, my lord,' she said, as coolly as she was able. 'So much so that one wonders where you have learned your skill! I believe that is quite enough of your attentions for one night!'

'Ah,' Kit flashed her a grin. 'I am dismissed! But as to my skill, there is no mystery, my sweet. It is simply that I am prepared to be patient when there is something that I want so very much…'

Their eyes met again in the mirror. Eleanor watched their reflection as once again, Kit lifted the heavy curtain of her hair to expose one bare shoulder. She willed her feet to move, to carry her away from this insidious danger, but she found she could not take a single step. She did not want to. She shivered convulsively as Kit bent his head and she felt his lips touch the sensitive skin below her ear, then drift down the line of her neck to the hollow above her collarbone. She could feel his breath against her skin, the warmth of his hands holding her still. She leaned back against him. If he had let her go she was certain she would have fallen.

'I think that you had better leave...' Eleanor's words came out with about half the certainty that was required to make them sound even remotely convincing. She closed her eyes, wrapped up in the sensual spell that held her, and even as she did so she was aware that it could be her undoing. By now she did not care. Kit was kissing the smooth curve of her shoulder and instinct was prompting her to turn to face him so that he could kiss her properly. She remembered their embrace in the drawing-room and suddenly she wanted it very much. She tried to turn round but he held her still against him, her back against his chest, one arm about her waist.

'I remember that you mentioned you needed help to undress...'

Kit's hand had gone to the ties of her chemise, unfastening them so that her bodice was loosened. Eleanor felt it fall open and made a small sound of despair mixed with wanting. She opened her eyes and the reflections in the mirror stole the last of her breath—her hair was a tousled fall of dark, heavy silk tossed over one shoulder whilst the pale skin of the other was stung pink with Kit's kisses. Her head was thrown back, her eyes bright with a desire she could not hide. The open chemise showed the soft swell of her breasts and the hollow between them, whilst Kit's head was bent as he trailed a line of tiny kisses down the side of her neck, so frustratingly light and tender.

Eleanor wriggled, and succeeded in turning within the shelter of his arms. She felt Kit's mouth resume its agonisingly slow exploration, drifting from the line of her collarbone to the hollow at the base of her throat. When his tongue traced the curves there she could not prevent the small groan that escaped her— Kit's hands tightened momentarily on her arms, then slid round to the small of her back, holding her arched against him. Eleanor could feel the hardness of his arousal against her body and it was inexpressibly exciting. She tried to pull him closer.

Kit drew back, so suddenly that Eleanor felt dizzy. She looked at him uncertainly. His eyes were dark with a desire that was a mirror for hers and he was breathing hard. His gaze flickered over her, lingering on her parted lips, then dropping to the neck of her chemise.

'I must leave,' he said slowly. 'I do not wish to break my promise to you and in another moment that is precisely what I shall do.'

For a minute Eleanor could not even remember

what that promise was, then a second later she realised that she was desperate for him to break it. She almost reached out to him, but he was already turning away from her, walking slowly towards the door.

Doubt crept into her heart, and confusion. The heat in her blood was cooling now and she folded her arms tightly across her chest, holding the chemise to her. At the door Kit turned, and his mouth twisted with wry amusement.

'Do not be afraid,' he said. 'I am gone.' He smiled at her. 'Good night, my love. Sleep well.'

The door closed softly behind him. Eleanor slid out of the chemise—an easy task now that it was so thoroughly undone—donned her nightdress and doused the candles but for the one beside her bed. She did not want to call Lucy back and she was certain that she would not sleep. She lay and stared up at the canopy above her head, listening to the sound of Kit moving about in the next bedroom, speaking to his valet in low tones. The sounds were oddly comforting but she wished that they were not.

She turned on to her side and hit her pillow with ineffectual anger. How close she had come to succumbing, and how soon it had happened! How easy Kit must have found it to seduce her! Eleanor rolled on to her back again. She was sure that Kit had set out to seduce her and she was only puzzled as to why he had stopped. Yes, they had had an agreement that he would not touch her against her will but he must have known from her response to him that she would not have objected…

Eleanor wriggled miserably, torn between confusion and unhappiness. Perhaps she knew the answer to that too, and at the thought, her body started to burn with humiliation rather than passion. Kit wanted her to want him. He wanted her to be frustrated with unconsummated desire, burning for his touch. As a strategy it had worked damnably well—it was still working, for beneath her mortification, Eleanor could feel a heat that was pure lust. She thumped her pillow with unrestrained force this time. Damn him! Damn him for his skill to arouse her and for his self-control in holding back! And damn her lack of self-control in still wanting him! The memory of their previous lovemaking still haunted her, overlaid with the excitement of the recent encounter. She was as likely to sleep now as she was to fly to the moon.

Eleanor clutched the pillow to her, putting both arms around it. It was only as she remembered the past, the natural outcome of making love, the desire Kit had for children, that the cold seeped into her bones, replacing the anger she felt with cold fear. She stared at the wavering candle flame. The house was quiet now; the sounds from Kit's room had gone. She felt lonely. To all intents and purposes she *was* alone, just as she had been in Devon when she had faced the appalling outcome of where her thoughtless passion with Kit had led her.

Eleanor turned her face into the pillow, breathing in its calming lavender scent and pressing its coolness to her hot cheeks. She could not bear such a thing to happen again. So she had to resist Kit's seductions. That was all there was to it. She would not let him so close again.

Chapter Nine

'Thank you so much for accompanying me, my dears!' Lady Salome Trevithick said, beaming at Kit and Eleanor as the town carriage conveyed them across London. 'I have so wanted to see the sights—why, it must be all of twenty years since I was last in town, and your mama, my dear Eleanor, was quite appalled at the thought of having to come with me to Westminster Abbey!'

Eleanor smiled. 'I believe that Mama's idea of sightseeing is to drive down Bond Street, ma'am! She does not have much energy for walking these days.'

'And I, alas, can only bear to go shopping twice a week at the outside!' Lady Salome said, sighing. 'We are most incompatible!'

Eleanor caught Kit's eye and could not help smiling. It was difficult to imagine finding someone who was compatible with the Dowager. Lady Salome, Eleanor's late father's sister, had arrived at the house in Montague Street just as they had been taking a late breakfast and Eleanor had been glad of the diversion.

When she had arisen late that morning, she had
vowed to treat Kit with a cool courtesy that would
distance her from the events of the previous night.
She had felt awkward and unsure how to go on. To
her dismay, however, just the sight of him had been
sufficient to make her feel all warm and disordered in
the nicest possible way, reminding her as it did of
exactly what had happened between them, and she
had been hard put to it to reply to his conversation
with any degree of sense. Kit had smiled at her, that
slow smile that threw her into even greater confusion,
then when the maid had gone out to fetch her breakfast, he had come across and kissed her with great
deliberation. And all before Eleanor had had the
chance to make it clear that any further intimacies
between them were quite out of the question. Fortunately the maid had then returned with some warm
rolls and honey, and before the meal had ended, Lady
Salome had arrived.

Now, sitting across the carriage from her husband,
Eleanor was aware that although Kit was discussing
the tombs of Westminster Abbey very knowledge-
ably, his main interest was focused on her. His blue
gaze moved over her thoughtfully, taking in the fashionable little hat perched on her dark curls, lingering
on her face, moving down her throat to the modest
neckline of her gown and on… It was enough to put
Eleanor to the blush. She felt as though he was trying
to learn her every feature.

Kit handed them both down from the carriage with
a very proper attention, holding Eleanor's hand for

longer than it was necessary. Lady Salome billowed ahead of them into the Abbey. Eleanor, who had not seen her aunt for several years, had forgotten the unusual dress sense that prompted Lady Salome to combine colours and styles with reckless abandon. Today she was wearing a scarlet evening gown with a royal blue spencer over the top and her head was crowned with some truly awesome ostrich feathers. The Abbey guide, coming to meet them at the door, recoiled slightly at the sight.

'I wish to see *everything*!' Lady Salome announced, surging up the nave. 'What a truly magnificent building! Tell me a little of the history, sir—' She turned to the guide, who seemed quite overwhelmed that for once there was a visitor who not only seemed fascinated but genuinely knowledgeable. They moved up the aisle towards the high altar and Kit offered his arm to Eleanor as they fell into step behind.

'I hope that you do not mind spending some time here,' he murmured in her ear. 'Lady Salome seems quite rapt and I have no heart to foreshorten her pleasure!'

'No indeed!' Eleanor was looking about her with undisguised interest. 'This may not be the sort of place one usually visits during the Season, but it is truly fascinating! Only look at those arches—and the ceiling! It is very beautiful, but a little cold...'

She shivered and Kit drew her closer to his side. Their footsteps echoed on the stone floor.

'And the shrine of Edward the Confessor!' Lady

Salome's voice floated back to them. 'Only regard the stone carving! It represents scenes from the life of the Confessor himself, I believe.'

Eleanor stifled a little yawn. It was not that she was bored, but strangely the cold and the dark interior of the building were making her feel sleepy. They were the only visitors and it was very quiet. Then she had not slept very well last night, of course... She stole a glance up at Kit's face. He was looking straight ahead and his profile was as clear-cut as one of the tomb carvings. Only there was nothing particularly saintly about him. He turned his head and gave her a smile that both confirmed her opinion and made her heart skip a beat. If she had been confused the previous night, now she was even more at a loss. Cold resolution was no proof against Kit's determination, nor her own desires... Never had her body and mind been so thoroughly in opposition. She shivered again.

'Do you wish to go out into the sunshine?' Kit enquired. 'I believe that Lady Salome is intent on viewing the coronation chair, for she was horrified that the Westminster schoolboys had had the audacity to scratch their initials on it!'

Eleanor watched as Lady Salome, still talking volubly, disappeared from view behind a large pillar. Her voice, still talking nineteen to the dozen and quite drowning out the guide, echoed around the high ceiling and bounced back to them: 'Vandalism! Sheer wanton destruction! The youth of today...'

Eleanor laughed. 'Oh dear! It is fortunate those very youths are not now at Aunt Trevithick's mercy!'

She turned back to Kit. 'Perhaps we could wait here, my lord? I would not wish my aunt to think we had forsaken her!'

Kit pulled her round and into his arms. 'Perhaps I may keep you warm then, Eleanor?' His breath feathered across her cheek in the lightest of caresses. 'I wanted to speak to you about last night and I can wait no longer.'

'Pray, my lord, you cannot behave like this here— in a consecrated building!' Panic rose in Eleanor and she struggled to free herself. She was not sure if she was more afraid of someone seeing them, or of Kit's actions, or of her own responses. Kit did not let her go.

'What better place? I am not ashamed of the feelings I have for my own wife—'

Eleanor made a slight, protesting noise that was smothered as his mouth came down on hers. She put her hands up to his chest, determined to push him away, and somehow found herself passing her arms around his neck to draw him nearer instead. For a long heart-stopping, breathless interval they were pressed close and oblivious to all else.

Kit loosened his arms a little and they stood looking at one another. There was the same dazed and wondering look in his eyes that Eleanor was sure must be reflected in hers, and at the same time there was a hopeless confusion raging through her body, for she knew that without a doubt she was falling in love with her husband all over again, and there seemed no way to prevent it.

'Eleanor…' Kit said huskily. He put out a hand to brush a stray curl back from her cheek.

'There you are!' Lady Salome's voice echoed down the aisle behind them. 'I am so sorry for keeping you waiting all this time. I hope that you have not been bored?'

'Not at all, ma'am!' Kit said, smiling at Eleanor.

Lady Salome's bright, observant gaze moved from Kit to Eleanor and lingered there.

'Goodness me, but you look very flushed, my dear!' she said. 'It is suddenly very hot in here—I have noticed it myself! Let us go out into the fresh air and pray that you will cool down!' She linked arms with both of them and shepherded them outside. Eleanor felt rather like a small boat carried along inexorably in the wake of a much larger ship.

'I was hoping to visit St Paul's Cathedral,' Lady Salome continued, 'but I see that it is time for nuncheon. Perhaps some other time, if you would care to accompany me?'

Eleanor had a sudden, heated vision of Kit kissing her in every church across London.

'That would be very pleasant, ma'am!' she said, and her hand trembled a little in Kit's as he handed her back up into the carriage. She resumed her seat in the corner and looked out blindly as the familiar landmarks passed by.

She was falling in love with Kit again and she could deny it no longer. Perhaps her heart had never entirely abandoned its feelings for him. She did not know. All she knew was that the thought elated and terrified her at one and the same time, but whilst she knew that a reconciliation with Kit was what she wanted now, it simply was not fair to him. Not when he might never achieve the family he so desired. She leant her head against the back of the seat and closed her eyes, feigning tiredness. She needed to think. But in her heart of hearts she knew the answer.

'So, my dear,' Lady Salome said, when she and her niece were back in the dining-room in Montague Street and were partaking of a luncheon of cold meats and fruit, 'it seems to me that there is an unconscionable amount of sorting out needed in this family! How fortunate that I have come up from Devon for that very purpose, but I scarce know where to start!'

Eleanor looked up in some surprise. Kit had gone to his club and she had been quite looking forward to a coze with Lady Salome, who had always been by far the most entertaining and least stuffy of her aunts. She poured them both another cup of tea. Now indoors, Lady Salome had discarded her royal blue spencer and the outrageous ostrich plumes, and the red ball-gown could be seen in all its glory, as could the diamond jewellery that adorned it. Eleanor thought about Lady Trevithick—and wondered.

'Whatever can you mean, Aunt? You have been here but one day to observe us!'

Lady Salome's eyes twinkled. 'I *hear* things, you know, my dear! And it takes but a few hours in your brother's house know that all is not well…'

Eleanor passed her a cup. She frowned. 'All is well

with Marcus and Beth, surely? They are but new wed and very happy—'

Lady Salome raised an expressive eyebrow. 'Ah, marriage! Marriage! An honourable institution, as the Bible tells us! Yet how happy is a man when his wife refuses him entry to her bedroom no matter how he scratches at the door? And then there is your cousin Justin, who wears the expression of a man similarly afflicted. Both he and Marcus are decidedly cross and frustrated!' She saw Eleanor's scarlet face and patted her hand with her own, beringed one. 'I am sorry to put you to the blush, my dear, but I confess the matter intrigued me.'

'Oh dear!' Eleanor said faintly. She had quite forgotten her aunt's devastating combination of biblical quotations and outspoken sense.

'And then,' Lady Salome continued inexorably, 'there is the small matter of finding your mama in my room this morning about to relieve me of my favourite brooch...' She patted her ample bosom where the said piece of jewellery rested in all its splendour. 'A thief in the night! Or rather in the morning. She assured me that she had merely come to make sure that all my comforts had been secured...' Lady Salome crunched her fruit consideringly '...but I fear it was her own comfort she sought to achieve—by taking my diamonds. But then she is a slave to her laudanum, poor creature! We really must do something about that. And finally there is you, my dear...' Lady Salome tilted her head and looked thoughtfully at Eleanor.

Eleanor shifted uncomfortably, staring fixedly at the pattern on the carpet.

'I? I assure you, Aunt—'

'Oh, do not trouble to do that!' Lady Salome said blithely. 'It seems to me, Eleanor, my love, that you are mightily attracted to that husband of yours—and indeed, who would not be—but that you are not happy with your situation for some reason! Indeed, when I first met Christopher a few months ago and he was good enough to confide in me, I was struck by the difficult task he would have in regaining your love and trust—'

'Wait, wait!' Eleanor besought. Her head was spinning. 'You met Kit a few months ago, Aunt? He made no mention of it to me! I thought that you were meeting this morning for the first time!'

'Naturally, since I particularly asked him to let me speak to you before he explained,' Lady Salome said, smiling. 'A small deception, my dear, for which I apologise. Deceit is a bad thing, and I pray that I may redeem my soul from it, but in this case it was entirely necessary! Christopher had given me his word that he would tell no one of our previous meeting and I asked that he permit me to talk to you alone, so…' she made a slight gesture, 'here I am!'

Eleanor put her hands up to her cheeks. 'Aunt Trevithick, it seems that in a remarkably short time you know all our most closely guarded secrets!'

'I pride myself upon it, my love,' Lady Salome said complacently. 'One cannot spend as much time as I have upon Fairhaven Island without observing human life in all its glory!'

Eleanor was shaking her head in disbelief. 'So you know that Kit and I are not yet reconciled and that Mama is a thief and that Marcus and Justin are being stupid about reinstigating the family feud—'

'Ah, so that is what it is about!' Lady Salome said triumphantly. 'I could not imagine that Beth and Charlotte were…ah…withholding their favours for anything other than a good reason! But that is very piquant, as you will see when you hear my tale! Yes, decidedly we shall come back to that tale!'

'And as for Mama, she is under the influence of her laudanum and has taken to stealing jewellery to pay—'

Lady Salome shook her head sorrowfully. 'A nasty problem, that one! But we shall see!'

'And what do you have to tell me about Kit?' Eleanor eyed her keenly. 'He said that he was not at liberty to tell me the whole tale, but I thought, I assumed, it was a matter of business rather than a family affair…'

'Never assume, my love!' Lady Salome threw up her hands. 'Soon I shall give you a full assurance of understanding! Saint Paul's letter to the Corinthians, Chapter…well, well, never mind.' Lady Salome sat back. 'A delicious lunch, my dear. I find it helps the thought processes miraculously. So…' She exhaled her breath on a long and thoughtful sigh.

'As for this silly feud, I do believe that Beth and Charlotte will triumph in a very short time!' She twinkled at Eleanor. 'Neither Justin not Marcus have the temperament for a long abstinence, not when temptation is under their noses. Indeed, it is rather fun, like a morality play! As for your mama…' she sobered '…that is a more intractable problem, I fear.'

'Mama has been taking laudanum for years,' Eleanor said thoughtfully. 'Everyone does! Lady Pomfret, and Lady Spence and Mrs Hetherington… There is no harm in it.'

Lady Salome shook her head sharply. 'There I must beg to differ, my dear! Laudanum is the most pernicious dose and sadly undermining to one's moral fibre. Oh, I know that it eases the pain of the toothache or the bad head, but when one starts to take it simply for the beneficial feeling, when one becomes dependent upon it… Then it cannot be a good thing!'

'It is true that Mama doses herself up an unconscionable amount,' Eleanor admitted. 'And then her temper is uncertain and her health has been poor… But surely… I cannot believe that she is dependent…' She frowned, remembering the desperate look in Lady Trevithick's eye when she had realised that her bottle was empty at the musicale, her insistence that Kemble be asked to provide her with some more of the drug. Yet everyone took laudanum for their ills… Why, Eleanor thought incredulously, if she complained to the doctor of feeling out of spirits, no doubt he would prescribe it for her himself! Yet if Lady Salome was correct there was a far more insidious effect and Lady Trevithick was in its grip. She would do anything to satisfy her need for the drug…

'Mama does not purchase her laudanum from the apothecary in the normal way,' she said slowly. 'I believe that one of her acquaintance supplies her with it and that she pays him for the privilege. Though why she would need to do so...'

'Quantity,' Lady Salome said succinctly. 'You may know, my dear, that the chemists will only supply a small amount at a time, for they fear that some sad wretches will use it to end their lives! But your mama requires more than the usual dose and so she obtains it elsewhere—and pays for it with other peoples' jewellery!' Lady Salome patted her diamonds protectively. She looked almost offended.

'It is not the first time,' Eleanor admitted. 'I fear that a piece of the Trevithick ruby set is gone, as was Charlotte's bracelet at the ball the other night...' And she related the tale of the lost bracelet and her insistence that her mother return it, and all the other occasions on which she had observed Lady Trevithick under the laudanum's influence. It was a relief to tell someone without feeling disloyal; Lady Salome listened, and tutted and Eleanor felt a little less alone.

'We shall have to see what can be done,' Lady Salome said, at the end. 'Certainly this man Kemble must be stopped and your mama rescued from her difficulties. It is not so simple... I must think!'

'Yes, Aunt. Another cup of tea?' Eleanor was suddenly aware that they had covered two of the three family problems and would be progressing inevitably to her own situation if she were not careful, and whilst she was curious to know how Lady Salome had met with Kit in the first instance, she did not wish to expose her own feelings to that lady's unerring scrutiny.

'Thank you, my love.' Lady Salome watched her thoughtfully as Eleanor rang the bell and sent for a fresh pot and some cake. 'You will be wishing to know, I am sure, how I met with your husband...'

'Yes...' Eleanor said warily. 'I confess it is uppermost in my mind!'

Lady Salome smiled. 'You are aware, of course, that Christopher has undertaken some small... commissions...for Lord Castlereagh in the past?'

'Yes,' Eleanor said. 'Kit told me so last night. Before that I had no notion.'

'Of course.' Lady Salome twinkled at her. 'For the safety of the nation one would hope we all go unaware of these things! As to my own involvement in this story, I confess that I had no notion why Christopher was in Ireland in the first instance, but it was fortuitous for me that he was! When we met,' she settled her bulk lower in the chair as she prepared to tell the tale, 'it was in early February and I know that he was anxious to return to you as soon as possible, my dear. He said that he had already been away too long and intimated that it was the most ill-timed and mismanaged business imaginable... But that is for him to explain. Perhaps he has already done so...'

'Yes,' Eleanor said, frowning a little. 'The only information he withheld from me was the nature of the delay, but I understand now, dear Aunt, that this was on your account?'

'Quite right, my dear!' Lady Salome nodded energetically. 'I confess that I was in the most parlous straits when I met Christopher. There is no concealing it.' She sighed. 'You may know that your Uncle St John Trevithick had been summoned from Fairhaven to Exeter last autumn by the bishop, who was not at all happy with St John's behaviour?'

Eleanor nodded. Marcus had mentioned months ago that their uncle, St John Trevithick, who was the vicar of Fairhaven, had been called to Exeter on unspecified church business. Now it seemed that the matter was more ominous than had first appeared.

Lady Salome resumed: 'Well, it was to be expected that the bishop would get wind of St John's problems, I suppose! The drinking and the sleeping in the church services and those long-winded sermons… The islanders of Fairhaven used to find St John amusing, but I knew he could not carry on, though we were at pains to conceal it from the bishop for pride's sake if nothing else—' She broke off.

'Forgive me, child, I am rambling. In short, the bishop sent St John on a visit to Ireland in January. It was made quite clear that this was my brother's last chance, but alas and alack, he made the most appalling mull of it! He was late for appointments and missed services and was drunk and querulous…' Lady Salome sighed heavily and Eleanor could tell how much the memory of it still appalled her.

'When Christopher happened upon us in our lodgings I was at my wit's end, for St John had spent all our money on drink and I did not even have the funds to pay our rent or the return trip. You can imagine that when I saw a kinsman I was utterly relieved and begged for his help.'

Eleanor frowned. 'Forgive me, Aunt, but how did you know that Kit was kin of yours? Why, until recent times the Mostyn and Trevithick families were the most staunch enemies imaginable!'

Lady Salome gestured widely. 'Indeed, and it was most fortunate they were, for it was that that made me recognise the Mostyn name. And of course I knew that Beth was to wed Marcus…'

'Oh, of course…' The pieces slid into place in Eleanor's mind. When Lady Salome had left Fairhaven to join her brother in Exeter, Marcus and Beth had already been betrothed. She would have known that the marriage had gone ahead and that there was now a tenuous but real link between the previously warring families. No wonder Lady Salome had applied to Kit for help in her difficulties—and he had responded as any true kinsman would… Eleanor felt a sudden, warm sense of appreciation for Kit's honourable conduct.

'It took several weeks for Christopher to untangle the mess that St John had made,' Lady Salome said sadly, 'and although I sensed that he was chafing to return home, he was the perfect gentleman and never sought to leave us to our own devices. Eventually one evening, when matters were at a very low ebb for both of us, he confided in me the story of your marriage, child…' Lady Salome's eyes were sad. 'I confess that I was shocked—oh, not that the wedding had come about as it had, but that Christopher had been obliged to leave you so untimely, and here was I, delaying him still further…' For a moment Eleanor thought her Aunt was about to cry, but Lady Salome was made of sterner stuff. 'I urged him to leave us but he would not. It was then that he told me of the letters he had sent you and how he hoped that matters would come right in the end…' She sat up straighter. 'And here I am, hoping against hope that that will be the case!'

Eleanor put both hands around her teacup, drawing comfort from the warmth. Now that she knew the truth, it was impossible to reproach Kit for his conduct in staying away so long, for he had put Lady Salome's problems first, no matter the personal cost.

Lady Salome was hunting in her reticule for her handkerchief, and gave her nose a hearty blow.

'I am so very sorry, my dear child,' she said gruffly. 'You will see now why I found it imperative to speak to you and to explain matters! Indeed, I should have done so before our trip this morning, but I confess I was a little nervous, and needed time to prepare…'

A sudden thought struck Eleanor. 'When was it that you returned to England, Aunt? Did Kit travel with you?'

Lady Salome nodded. 'Yes, my love. We all travelled back together at the end of last month and St John and I went straight to the bishop in Exeter. St John did the only thing he could, and retired from his living, so in the future we will both be settled in Devon.'

Eleanor let out her breath in a silent sigh. So Kit

had been with Lady Salome until the end of April and then had returned to England, parting company with them and making his way up to London at last… She remembered the scrap of paper with 'St John at seven' written on it. An assignation indeed. She would never have guessed.

Lady Salome was looking much happier now, putting her handkerchief away with a briskly practical air, the tears now quite banished. She leaned forward and patted Eleanor's hand again.

'Pray do not hesitate to tell your husband that we have spoken, my love, for I know he cares for you deeply and I cannot but feel here…' Lady Salome pressed her hand to her breast in the general area of her heart '…that I am responsible for your estrangement! It was all so difficult! I swore Christopher to secrecy because I did not wish St John's disgrace to be known until he had resigned his living and I had the chance to tell your brother. As the head of the family Marcus had to be told first, but neither Christopher nor I really imagined the difficulties that would cause—'

'Marcus!' Eleanor cried. 'He cannot know that Kit helped you, Aunt, or he would never be pursuing this silly feud…'

Lady Salome's smile twinkled briefly. She got to her feet and embraced her niece fervently. 'No indeed! Your husband did not wish me to tell him, my dear! Some foolish matter to do with men and honour!'

Eleanor hugged her back. 'Oh, dear Aunt…' a

thought had suddenly popped into her head '…I understand now what you meant when you mentioned that it was piquant that Marcus was pursuing the family feud! For if he were to know of Kit's involvement in your affairs—'

'He would feel obliged to repay him, never mind to thank him!' Lady Salome finished, her eyes gleaming. 'Indeed, it is very bad of me not to enlighten your brother, my dear, and I am tempted to do so, for all I gave Christopher my word! For now I feel that Beth's solution is so much more…entertaining, so we shall see what happens! But be sure that the truth will out in the end! It always does, my love! It always does!'

Eleanor retired to bed that evening reflecting that it was typical that she had not been able to speak to Kit alone on the one occasion that she was desperate to do so. He had been tied up with his man of business that afternoon and had arrived home late, and as they were engaged to dine with a party at Lady Spence's there was no time to broach so serious a subject as Lady Salome's revelations before they left. At dinner she was seated as far away from Kit as possible and afterwards he had accepted Lord Spence's invitation to join him at Whites and Eleanor had returned home feeling tired and annoyed. It was not that she was expecting Kit to hang on her coat-tails, she told herself crossly, but it would have been pleasant for him to do so that particular evening when she had a special reason for needing him. She vowed to stay awake until he returned from Whites, then realised that to appear in his bedroom at that time of night would be somewhat equivocal, especially in view of the situation between them. Finally she retired to bed—Kit had still not returned—and fell into an uneasy sleep, only to awaken an unspecified amount of time later.

The house was quiet but for some reason she could not understand, Eleanor was wide awake. She slid out of bed and listened for sounds from Kit's room to see if she could ascertain whether he had returned, but there was no noise to guide her one way or the other. Eleanor reached for her dressing-robe. It was a plain no-nonsense affair, far removed from the light confections of silk and lace that Beth had purchased after her marriage to Marcus. Eleanor smiled to herself a little wryly; it seemed that she had moved from the innocent apparel of a débutante to the practical attire of a dowager with barely a pause in the middle. She tied the belt firmly. That was not precisely true, of course—there had been two nights of passion in between and even now the memory made her shiver, like a pleasurable spell that had not quite lost its power to charm. But that was the last thing that she should be thinking of at a time like this. Such pleasure must never be permitted to charm her again.

Eleanor slid back the bolt and turned the knob on the dressing-room door. The dressing-room itself was empty, as was the bedroom, although the candles were lit. Eleanor was about to turn around and go back to her own room, when the door opened and Kit came in, a candle in one hand and a glass of wine in the other.

Eleanor recoiled, clutching her dressing-gown under her chin. It was Kit who recovered himself first.

'Eleanor! Good evening! Could you not sleep?'

Eleanor came forward into the room slowly. 'No, I could not. That is, I wished to speak with you, Kit. It will not take long.' She drew herself up. 'Lady Salome has spoken to me and I now know the whole tale.'

'I see,' Kit said. 'Then there is no need to look as though you are about to run away again! Won't you sit down? Please?'

There had always been something about Kit's voice, Eleanor thought weakly, something persuasive, almost hypnotic, that made you agree to whatever he suggested before you had really thought about it. The timbre of his voice, low and mellow, was one of the first things that she had noticed about him. It had fascinated her, made her think all kinds of foolish things when he had spoken to her of love… And now it was set fair to undermine her defences before she had barely uttered a word. Yet it was too late to flee. Kit was placing a chair for her before the fire.

Eleanor sat down, curling up within the comforting bulk of the armchair, tucking her bare feet under her. Kit tossed another log on to the fire and made the flames hiss in the grate. Then he sat down. And looked at her. Eleanor's heart started to race. Here, in his bedroom, she felt so vulncrablc that she could barely keep her mind on the matter in hand.

'Lady Salome has spoken to me.' She blurted out again. 'I know what happened in Ireland!'

Kit smiled a little ruefully. 'I knew she was determined to tell you! And indeed, Nell, when I realised what a coil my promise to keep silent had put me into, I was sorely tempted to break it and tell you myself.' He looked rueful. 'When I offered my services to your aunt and uncle in Ireland, I did not think the matter would take so long. More than once I cursed the delay, but I could not break my word. It was damnably difficult!'

'You acted most honourably, Kit,' Eleanor said, a little gruffly.

Kit smiled reluctantly in return. He got up and came across to her, taking her hands in his. 'So now it is all over. Do you forgive me, Eleanor?'

Eleanor's smile faded. She felt a little cold. She knew what Kit wanted and she could not give it to him. Forgiveness, yes. Reconciliation…

'Of course I forgive you, Kit.' She made her voice as steady as she could. 'I am glad that we have reached an understanding, for it makes it so much easier for me to say…what I have to say.'

She stopped. Kit was still holding her hands and the warmth of his touch was disarming. Eleanor struggled to blot it out. She would not be able to do this if she allowed herself to weaken even slightly. And she had to do it. She could not allow even the possibility of a reconciliation and she knew that they had been moving towards it gently, inexorably…

She saw the wariness in Kit's eyes as he realised

that something was wrong. His grip on her hands tightened.

'Eleanor…'

Eleanor looked down at her lap. She could not meet his gaze.

'I think that our marriage should be annulled,' she said.

Chapter Ten

Kit relinquished her hands and stood up slowly. There was a strange, stunned look in his eyes, a mixture of disbelief and denial. He cleared his throat.

'Eleanor, I cannot believe that you really mean that!'

Eleanor clenched her fists. 'Oh but I do, Kit!' Her voice wavered slightly and did not have anywhere near the conviction it needed, but she ploughed on.

'I have been thinking on this for some time. It seems to me that our marriage was hasty in the extreme and that had we but exercised some sense in the first place, it would never have happened!' She took a quick glance at his face and looked away even more quickly. This was torture. Not only was she tearing herself apart but she was ripping Kit's feelings to pieces before her own eyes.

'No,' Kit said, and there was an angry edge to his voice now. 'At least do not pretend that we did not care for each other then, Eleanor!'

Eleanor tried to shrug. 'It was so, I suppose. At least, I thought that I cared for you—'

She saw Kit flinch and felt sick. For both their sakes she had to finish this quickly.

'And it is not that I do not care for you now...' Her voice wavered.

'Then what is it?' Kit's tone was harsh. 'For God's sake, Eleanor, tell me what has put this foolish notion into your head!' He took an angry turn about the room. 'Is it that you wish to punish me for leaving you? That even now, having heard my reasons and my apologies, you cannot forgive me? For if that is so—'

'No!' Eleanor cried. She just managed to resist the temptation to put her hands over her ears. 'I have no wish to punish you, Kit, but...' her voice sank to a whisper '...I cannot remain married to you. I am sorry.'

There was a silence.

'I, too, am sorry.' Kit spoke very formally now. 'I was under the impression that we wanted the same things. I thought that tonight we had achieved some kind of understanding and that in time, at least—' He broke off.

'It is for the best,' Eleanor said helplessly. 'You may be free to achieve the family that you wish and I shall also be free to go where I choose and do—' She stopped, unable to go on. She could feel his gaze on her, direct and angry, but also very perceptive. Too perceptive. Eleanor felt acutely vulnerable. She got to her feet.

'I must go…'

'Oh no,' Kit said smoothly. He caught her arm. 'Oh no, my dear. You cannot make so outrageous a demand as this without justifying your reasons! I want to understand you. I *need* to understand…'

Eleanor looked into his eyes and recoiled from the anger and pain she saw there. If she had ever doubted that Kit loved her she had her answer now—she had smashed all of his hopes and expectations with her words. The pain of it was tormenting her as well, yet she could not explain to him. Her fear was stronger than all else; fear that she could never give him what he wanted.

They gazed at each other for what seemed like forever, then the angry light faded from Kit's eyes.

'Nell…' His voice was impossibly gentle. 'What is this all about? I cannot believe that it is truly what you want—'

Eleanor evaded his eyes. 'It has to be—'

'It does not!' Kit's hands tightened fiercely and she winced. 'I do not understand! I could have sworn that you had feelings for me—that you were not indifferent! Yet now you suggest this…' His hands dropped away. 'Eleanor, look at me and tell me that this is what you want.'

Eleanor forced her eyes to meet his for the briefest of seconds. 'It is what I want, Kit,' she said tonelessly.

Kit stepped back meticulously, as though his presence too close to her was a contamination. Eleanor felt the cold seeping through her bones. She started to shiver convulsively.

'Very well.' Kit sounded almost calm, and looked it, but for the tight line of his lips and the hard expression in his eyes. 'I hear what you say, my lady. Now hear this. I do not believe your reasons and we will talk of them again. Further, I do not agree to the annulment of our marriage. Do you understand me? There shall be no annulment!'

With a sudden, violent movement he had sent his empty wineglass spinning from the mantelpiece to smash into fragments in the hearth. Eleanor flinched.

'You are right,' Kit said quietly. 'You had better go.'

Eleanor's legs managed to carry her as far as her own bedchamber, where she sank down on the bed and shook uncontrollably. Her mind was numb, dazed. She wondered why she had not considered that Kit would respond as he had. Had she expected him to agree to an annulment so easily when she would not even give him the honest reason why she wanted one?

Eleanor covered her face with her hands. She had been dishonest and cruel to both Kit and herself. She knew that he deserved the truth, deserved to know both about his lost child and her terror of losing another or of never being able to have more children... Yet she had locked that grief and fear so deep within herself that even now she could not tell him. He had gradually stripped away all of the barriers that remained between them until they were in a position where they could have started to rebuild their love. Instead she had told him that she wanted nothing of it…

With a sob, Eleanor curled up, wrapped her arms about herself and at last gave way to her tears.

When Eleanor woke up her head felt the size of a marrow and her eyes appeared to have been gummed together. At first she felt inclined to stay in bed, pull the covers over her head and pretend that nothing was wrong, but her feelings of misery could not be ignored. Although the bed curtains were drawn she could see that it was broad daylight and she decided instead to get up and do something—anything—to stave off her unhappiness rather than to lie there and wallow in it. A tear escaped unbidden from the corner of her eye and slid down on to the pillow, and that decided her. She jumped out of bed. She simply could not lie around feeling sorry for herself. It would give her too much time to think.

She rang the bell for Lucy, then saw her reflection in the mirror and regretted it. She looked dreadful and the maid would not scruple to tell her so. All Lucy's cunning ministrations would be wasted this morning, for Eleanor doubted if she would look anything other than wan and ugly.

Sure enough, Lucy almost dropped the can of hot water when she came into the bedroom.

'Oh! Oh, ma'am! Are you ill? You look quite dreadful!'

'Thank you, Lucy,' Eleanor said tiredly. 'I am not

ill, though my head aches a little. Pray make me as presentable as you can.'

A full hour later, washed, combed, curled and anointed with rose-petal cream, which Lucy swore would revive her complexion, Eleanor tiptoed downstairs. As soon as she set foot in the hall, the door to the drawing-room opened and Kit emerged. Eleanor felt her heart plunge as she saw him. He looked even worse than she did.

'Good morning, Eleanor.' He spoke distantly. 'I would appreciate it if you would spare a moment to speak with me.'

Eleanor shuddered. If Kit had reviewed his situation and was now prepared to agree to the annulment she did not really want to hear it and if he had not and wanted to discuss the matter further, she did not want that either. On the other hand, she could scarcely refuse his request. He held the door open and she went into the room with great reluctance, hearing the door click closed behind her.

After a moment, Kit said: 'I have been thinking all night about what you said, Nell. Is it still your wish that our marriage be annulled?'

Eleanor bit her lip hard. 'It is.'

She saw Kit's shoulders slump slightly, as though he had been hoping for a different reply. She could say nothing else.

'I see.' Kit's voice was steady. 'Your reasons?'

'I have told you—' Panic clutched at Eleanor's throat. She was not sure she could bear to rehearse all this again. 'I believe our marriage was too hasty! We should be given a second chance—'

'Is there then someone else you would prefer to marry?' Kit asked, almost as though she had not spoken. 'Is that what this is about, Eleanor?'

'No!' Eleanor burst out. 'How can you think such a thing, Kit? It was you I was thinking of—'

'How kind of you,' Kit said, with such cutting sarcasm that Eleanor had to swallow hard to quell more tears, 'but I cannot believe your altruistic motives, my love! There is something else here; something I am determined to discover. Yet you swear you do not intend it just to punish me—'

'No!'

'Though surely that is exactly what you are doing now.' Kit's quiet words silenced her. 'I am sorry, Eleanor, but I do not believe your reasons. I know there is something else—something I am determined you will tell me…'

Eleanor turned away so her face should not betray her. 'There is nothing else.' Her voice was muffled. 'This is for the best…'

Kit made a slight gesture. 'I will ask you again later. And again and again if I must.' He gave her a slight bow. 'I am going out now. Good day, Eleanor.'

When he had gone out Eleanor sank down on the sofa and wrung her hands. She was not sure how much of this she could bear. If Kit insisted on asking her, time after time, sooner or later she would give something away…

Eleanor jumped up. Waiting for the inevitable

seemed intolerable. If she could just get away for a while…

She hurried back up the stairs, calling for Lucy as she went. The startled maidservant found her pulling the portmanteau out of a cupboard and hauling it up on to the bed.

'Lucy, we are going to Trevithick for a space,' Eleanor puffed. 'London bores me! I need to get away!'

'Yes, madam…' The maid caught the other end of the case. 'Is that a good idea, madam?'

Eleanor frowned at her. 'Certainly it is! Pray fetch all my dresses and fold them up…'

Lucy looked flustered. 'Will you need your evening gowns in the country, ma'am?'

'The day dresses!' Eleanor snapped. Suddenly she was possessed with a panicky urgency to be away. 'Walking dresses, promenade dress—'

'Your riding habit, my lady?'

'Oh, I will get all the clothes!' Eleanor said in exasperation. She felt strange—hot and fearful, yet cold at the same time. 'Fetch my underwear, Lucy! This need not take us long!'

As the maid sped away to open the drawers, the bedroom door swung open and Kit appeared in the aperture.

'What is all this feverish activity for?'

Kit walked straight into the bedroom and Eleanor realised that once again Lucy had forgotten to close the door. The maid was now standing, hands full of stockings and chemises, her mouth half-open.

'Lucy, please leave us!' Eleanor snapped. This was one occasion on which the maid could not possibly misinterpret the animosity between husband and wife. Kit was looking at Eleanor and at the portmanteau and his expression was cold enough to freeze water.

Eleanor bit her lip. She knew that she should have bided her time until she was certain that Kit was out of the house, but in her anxiety to be away she had overlooked his presence.

'Just what is going on here?'

Kit came up to her. His gaze swept over the portmanteau and the pile of clothes, and fastened on Eleanor's guilty face. She closed her eyes in anguish.

'I see.' Kit said politely, drawing his own conclusions. 'Did you have any particular destination in mind, my love?'

'I thought to visit Trevithick for a space,' Eleanor said, in a rush. 'It would be better to go away and we may put it about that it is for my health...'

'I see that you have it all worked out,' Kit remarked, in a tone that brought the colour into Eleanor's pale face. 'Have you already spoken to your brother about this?'

'No,' Eleanor flushed. 'I have spoken to no one...'

'So this is entirely your own idea.' Kit was watching her implacably. 'I am so very glad that I discovered it before it was too late! I should have been quite annoyed to be put to the trouble of searching various inns for you—again!' He paused. 'I take it that you were actually planning to travel alone?'

'I was intending to take Lucy with me!' Eleanor

snapped, deliberately misunderstanding him. 'I thought that we had sorted out *that* particular disagreement, my lord—'

'I thought that we had sorted out many,' Kit returned, 'but it seems that I was wrong.'

Eleanor sat down heavily on the edge of the bed. 'Well, now that you are aware of my plans, do you not think that it is a good idea? I cannot stay here—'

'Why not?' Kit enquired, with a lift of an eyebrow.

'Well, because…' Eleanor floundered a little.

'Because we have disagreed over a point of principle?' Kit asked. 'I assure you, my dear, I *require* you to stay here and discuss the matter with me— again and again, until we have it clear! It is out of the question for you to leave London!'

Eleanor frowned slightly. 'You mean—you refuse to let me go?'

'Exactly. Indeed I would go further.' Kit smiled. 'I forbid you to go. In leaving this house you will be going against my express wishes.'

'In leaving the house!' Eleanor shot to her feet.

'Without my permission, yes. I cannot be sure that you will not run off, you see.' Kit smiled gently. 'Come come, my dear, it will not be so bad! I am happy to accompany you to balls and breakfasts, and once we have resolved our differences you may come and go as you please…'

'That is blackmail!' Eleanor said in a stifled voice. 'I have to agree with you or become a prisoner in my own home!'

Kit strolled over to the window and looked down

into the street. 'You do not have to agree with me, you have to explain your own position.' He shot her a look. 'That is not unreasonable! I know that there is something you are keeping from me and I want to know what it is and how it pertains to our marriage! Is that so surprising?'

Eleanor did not reply. She clenched her fists, then forced herself to calm down and let her breath out on a long sigh.

'Oh! This is of all things intolerable. Am I then to be allowed visitors in my…prison?'

Kit laughed. 'There is no need to be so melodramatic! Life carries on much as it has done before, the only difference being that I am waiting for you to explain yourself. The remedy is in your own hands, my dear. Do you wish to talk about it now?'

They looked at each other. Eleanor was the first to drop her gaze.

'Very well then,' Kit said expressionlessly. 'Will you dine with me tonight or do you prefer to take a tray up here, my love?'

Eleanor was silent. She understood that for the rest of the morning and afternoon she would be confined to the house, or even to just her room. She would have no company, she would not be allowed out, she would have time to sit and think…and think. She raised her chin.

'Here, I thank you, my lord,' she said. 'I do not wish for your company.'

Eleanor ate her solitary dinner whilst trying not to think of Kit downstairs eating his alone at the huge polished dining-table. She did not think he had gone out, although she was not sure. Once the meal was taken she tried to read a book for a little but found her attention straying all the time. Eventually she realised that she would have to go down and play the piano. It was the only way to soothe her feelings—or try to soothe them.

This evening a fire was burning in the music-room and the candles stood ready to be lit, as though someone had anticipated that she would need to play. She took a stand of them over to the piano and sat down, her fingers straying over the keys, playing little melancholy tunes until the familiar melodies took her and she played the Bach cantatas one after another, losing herself in the precision and the feeling. This time Kit did not come in to see her and she remained undisturbed. But later, as she was preparing for bed, there was knock at the door and Kit came in. And this time he was in only his breeches and shirt.

'My lord—' Eleanor began.

Kit looked at her. There was a glitter in his eyes that made her nervous. She wondered suddenly if he were drunk.

'It occurs to me that I have been unconscionably patient with you, my love,' Kit said. He put the candlestick down on the dresser and came to sit on the edge of the bed. His gaze wandered over her thoughtfully, considering the tumbling dark hair, her pale face and the nervous pulse Eleanor could feel beating in the hollow of her throat. She drew the bedclothes up to her chin and clutched them there. Kit smiled.

'As I was saying…' there was a caressing tone in his voice now that made her shiver '…we are married, Eleanor, and the fact that we consummated that marriage before rather than after the wedding is…' he shrugged '…almost immaterial. You do know that an annulment is not easily granted? One of the grounds is impotence and that…' he smiled '…would be ridiculous and I cannot believe that you would expect me to agree to it. I have the rights of a husband and have shown considerable forbearance, not to say restraint, in not exercising them sooner—'

'We had an agreement!' Eleanor whispered. 'You swore you would not force yourself on me…'

Kit nodded. 'So I did. I did not promise not to seduce you, however. You know as well as I that I could have done so but two nights ago—or before that if I had not been so scrupulous!'

Eleanor closed her eyes briefly. She knew it was true and it was pointless to deny it.

'That being the case,' Kit continued, 'I find myself in something of a quandary. You see, Eleanor…' he plucked one of her hands from the coverlet and held it in his, stroking the back of it gently with his thumb '…I want you very much. I have done so since the moment I first saw you and certainly from the moment I came back. So…' he paused, looking at her '…I certainly do not feel able to agree to an annulment—under the circumstances.'

Eleanor screwed her face up. 'Kit, please…'

'No.' There was a note in Kit's voice that silenced her. 'I do not pretend to understand what is going on here, Eleanor, and you do not choose to tell me. Well, I cannot force you to do so, but I can put your resolve to the test. So I shall.' He leant forward and kissed her very softly. 'We shall soon see how set on an annulment you truly are…'

Eleanor made a small, piteous noise. 'Kit, that is not fair—'

'It is perfectly fair.' Kit sounded implacable. 'Since you refuse to speak to me this is the only approach I can take. You have only to have the courage of your convictions—whatever they may be…'

Eleanor knew that it was not that simple. In fact it was not simple at all. She knew it but she could not seem to focus on it, for Kit was kissing her again, ending both thinking and discussion. His mouth took hers in short, sharp little kisses that stole her breath. There was little of love in them and everything of desire and possession, but Eleanor still felt herself weakening. Her lips parted irresistibly beneath his and he kissed her again, with a deeper kiss that was slow and hungry this time. Eleanor let the coverlet fall from her fingers and caught hold of Kit's arms as much to steady herself as to draw him closer. The linen of his sleeve was rough beneath her fingers and she clutched it for dear life, but he sat back a little.

'You can stop me, you know, Eleanor. After all, I gave you my word. All it requires is for you to tell me to stop…'

'Yes…' Eleanor whispered. She was not at all sure

what she was saying, but it certainly was not that he should stop. She could tell him that in a little while, perhaps. After he had kissed her some more…

There was a pause, then Kit pulled her to him again, teasing her lips apart with his tongue so that Eleanor caught her breath and he moved quickly to take her mouth completely. His hand tangled in her hair, tilting her head so that he could taste her to the full. She felt as though she was falling, tumbling down into a pool of the most desperate desire. This was so sweet and she had longed for it. Tell him to stop… Well, there was plenty of time.

Kit put his hand to the bow at the neckline of her nightgown and pulled the ribbon hard. It uncurled into his fingers. He eased the gown gently to her waist, dropping a kiss on the curve of Eleanor's bare shoulder. She shivered, a rose blush colouring her skin, then closed her eyes as she felt Kit cup one breast in the palm of his hand and bend to kiss its tight crest.

He sucked gently, first one breast then the other. Eleanor gave a small whimper of pleasure and almost fell backwards into the yielding softness of the mattress. Kit followed, leaning over to repeat his caresses with fingers and tongue, driving coherent thought even further from Eleanor's mind. It had been a long time and she had ached for him, and under the onslaught of her senses her conscious mind was quiescent, her fears stilled.

Kit drew the rest of the nightgown away from her so that she was lying on the coverlet, quite naked, her senses so dazed that she was utterly unselfconscious.

Kit leant over her again, kissing her softly, tenderly. She was as innocent as when he had first taken her to his bed, her eyes slumberous with passion as she looked at him from beneath heavy lids.

'Kit…'

'Yes? Do you wish me to stop now?'

'No, but…' He saw her frown and bent his lips to touch the fullness of hers again, unable to resist. They were warm, damp and already swollen from his kisses. After a moment her eyelids flickered closed again.

Kit parted her lips with his own, touching his tongue to hers. She was not passive—she accepted his caresses with pleasure and responded with a shy hesitancy that excited him more than the calculated embraces of the courtesans had ever done. Nevertheless, Kit mastered his own desire. This was all about Eleanor. He would never discover the truth if he blundered on, intent only on satisfying his own needs. He had waited this long and he could wait longer if it meant that he could claim his wife at the end and solve this perplexing mystery of the annulment.

He pressed soft kisses gently against her neck and the hollow of her shoulder, watching all the time for a sign that Eleanor was uncomfortable with his attentions, waiting for a clue to her fears. It seemed that the reverse was true. She moved beneath his caresses with evident pleasure; her skin was pink and flushed with desire. Kit trailed kisses down her throat to the upper swell of her breasts. She moaned softly. He took one nipple in his mouth again, flicking it teasingly with his tongue whilst he cupped and stroked her other breast with his fingers. The touch and taste of her satin skin and Eleanor's avid response were almost enough to drive him to the edge, but he concentrated hard on his predicament rather than his feelings. Unfortunately—or fortunately—he had not pushed her hard enough yet. There was more to learn…

He allowed his lips to drift lower, across the sensitive skin of her stomach. In the candlelight her skin was pale golden, soft but firm. Kit's fingers brushed across her thighs, softly parting her legs, subtly, so subtly stroking the soft, sensitive skin.

'Eleanor?'

An incoherent murmur was his only reply. Kit smiled and did not even bother to ask the question.

When he finally stole a caress at the burning centre of her, he was gentle and tender, watching her, revelling in her instinctive gasp of pleasure and the way she writhed on the coverlet beneath his hands. She made no move to pull away from him and after a moment Kit resumed the intimate caress. She was utterly lost in a realm of pleasurable sensation. With infinite care he parted her thighs still further and touched her again.

Eleanor shrieked, burying her face in the pillow. Her whole body went boneless, supine. Kit touched her again—and again, until she convulsed in sheer ecstasy. He no longer had any thought for anything other than the giving of pleasure—and the enjoyment it gave him to satisfy her so. At the end he rolled her

into his arms and held her close, holding her sweet
and softly scented body against his own aching one.
Now… Surely now they could be reconciled…

'I love you,' he said, very softly.

Eleanor opened her eyes and looked at him. For
what seemed like minutes her gaze was dazed and
dark, then awareness crept back and with it horror.
The colour came into her cheeks then fled as swiftly
as it had come. She pressed her hands to her face,
and burst into a storm of tears.

'No! Oh no!'

Kit was horrified. He pulled the coverlet close
about her and cradled her to him as she cried.

'Eleanor? Sweetheart? Don't cry—everything will
be all right…'

All he got in reply was a violent shake of the head
and Eleanor cried all the harder. Kit gave up any attempt to speak and just held her closer, overriding her
attempt to pull away. Eventually she started to speak.
He had to bend his head closer still and strain to hear
the words.

'This is just what I did not want to happen because
it is not fair…' Eleanor sniffed piteously. 'It is because of this that I have to go…'

Kit frowned as he tried to make sense of this. 'Why
is it not fair, sweetheart? Fair to whom? You?'

'No!' Eleanor raised her head and looked at him
angrily. 'It is not fair to you, Kit! Every man wishes
to make love to his own wife—it is only natural…'

Whilst taking issue with the first part of this sentence, Kit knew that it was certainly true in his particular case. But it still did not make sense.

'True—which we have just done—'

'No!' Eleanor said again. She sat up and the coverlet slipped. Kit tried not to look at the nakedness it revealed, for she looked like a tumbled angel and it was doing terrible things to his concentration. He wanted her so much, but this was more important. He took her hands in his.

'Sweetheart, I am sorry but I still do not understand. Surely you are not telling me that you *still* wish for an annulment?'

'Yes, I do!' Eleanor cried wildly. 'To avoid precisely this happening again…' She started to cry again.

Kit stood up abruptly and thrust one hand through his hair. He could not believe it; could not believe that she was being so stubborn, could not believe that what had seemed so sweet to him—and in the end so simple—was not the same for her. He took her by the shoulders and shook her gently.

'Eleanor, look at me and tell me that you do not love me! Look at me!'

Her head came up slowly. Her eyes were wide, her expression bruised. 'I cannot tell you that, Kit. But it makes no difference!'

Kit let his hands fall away. He felt baffled and he felt furious. 'You love me yet you still want an annulment?'

Her answer was a whispered breath. 'Yes.'

Kit looked down at her bent head. 'Then you shall

have what you want. I am too tired to fight this, Nell, when I do not understand what I am fighting.'

He went out of the room and closed the door quietly behind him. Through the bolted door to his dressing-room he could hear her crying and he almost went back to her, but in the end he did not and they both lay awake all night, on separate sides of the door, in silence.

Beth Trevithick was alone in her conservatory. It was very unusual to have time to herself, but this morning everyone had gone out and she, pleading tiredness, had snatched a few hours to herself potting cuttings for Lady Salome to take back to Devon with her. It was warm and airy in the conservatory and the scent of flowers was in the air. Beth was enjoying herself so much that she was quite annoyed to hear footsteps on the tiled floor—male footsteps, she thought, wondering if Marcus had returned early. She put down her gardening gloves and little spade in order to greet the newcomer.

It was not Marcus but Kit who came round the corner, and Beth smiled when she saw her cousin.

'Kit!' She greeted him with unalloyed pleasure. 'My dear, how delightful—and how brave of you to venture here! Is Eleanor with you?' She paused, looking at him more closely. 'Oh dear, you look quite dreadful! Whatever has happened?'

Kit did not reply. He took a seat on the cushioned bench beside the pond, and after a moment Beth came to sit beside him. She could tell something was terribly wrong—they were friends from childhood as well as cousins, and Beth knew Kit as well as she knew Charlotte. Kit was not normally profligate in his emotions, but now she knew he was building up to tell her something truly dreadful and her heart began to race with fear.

'I am only potting up some plants for Lady Salome,' she said conversationally, to give him time, 'for she wishes to have some cuttings for her own greenhouses. I do believe—'

'It is Eleanor,' Kit said abruptly, cutting across her as though she were not speaking. He swung round to look at her and Beth saw how haggard he looked in the bright morning light.

'She has asked for an annulment, Beth, and I have agreed.' Kit brought his clenched fist down on the arm of the chair with a force that made it shudder. 'I came here because I did not wish you and Charlotte to hear the news from Eleanor herself, or worse, from Trevithick. I wanted to tell you myself!'

'Kit…' Beth put a hand on his and after a moment he looked up at her, though she thought that he was not really seeing her.

'I cannot understand it.' Kit's lips set in a hard line. 'She will not tell me her true reasons yet I know that she loves me! She told me so herself! It makes no sense!' He shook his head. 'I even wondered last night if one of those so-called admirers of hers had hurt her in some manner…' he broke off, letting his breath out on an angry sigh '…yet I cannot think that true. I do not believe she has been with another man.'

He swung round, suddenly concentrating on her so fiercely that Beth almost flinched.

'Beth, you were with Eleanor during the time I was away. What happened to her?'

Beth closed her eyes briefly. From the very first she had dreaded this, knowing that one day Kit might ask her this very question, knowing that she loved her cousin and could not lie to him. Yet she knew that Eleanor loved him too and that it was Eleanor's place to tell him, not hers. But Kit had seen her hesitation now and his fingers bit into her wrist. His blue gaze narrowed on her.

'You know something, don't you! Tell me!'

'Kit, you are hurting me,' Beth said very steadily. 'Let go of me and pray keep calm, for I cannot help you if you terrify me!'

There was a moment of taut silence, and then Kit released her wrist and shook his head slowly, as though he were awaking from sleep.

'Beth, forgive me. I did not mean to hurt you, but I am half out of my mind—'

'I understand.' Beth said. She patted his hand again. 'Listen to me, Kit, and do not interrupt, no matter how tempted you are. I cannot lie to you. Yes, I do know what happened to Eleanor when you were away and no, I cannot tell you what it was. No!' She held up an imperative hand as he was about to interrupt her. 'Eleanor *must* tell you herself! Now, I will speak to her and try to persuade her, but Kit, the matter is so personal to her—and to you—that it would not be right for me to intervene. But I swear,' she took his hand in a tight grip, 'that no one has hurt her. Not in the sense that you mean. This is a matter between the two of you only. And I dare swear also…' there were tears in Beth's eyes as she looked at him '…that Eleanor loves you most truly, but she is desperately afraid, Kit. That is all I can tell you.'

There was a silence, but for the splashing of the water into the ornamental pool.

'Marcus is hosting a dinner tonight in Lady Salome's honour,' Beth said, disentangling herself a little. She sat back and smiled at her cousin.

'I understand that it is the last thing that you would wish to do, Kit, but I beg you to come and bring Eleanor with you. It is very important. I believe that many things will be revealed.'

Chapter Eleven

The party that met at Trevithick House that night was hardly in celebratory mood and it was a tribute to Lady Salome that they were all there at all. The intention was for a family dinner followed by a ball for a small and select group of friends and acquaintances, and whilst the food was good the conversation was worse than stilted.

Eleanor, who had been placed next to Justin on one side and Kit on the other, was finding it impossible to make even the slightest attempt to talk to either of them. Justin's attention was focused on Charlotte with the single-minded avidity of a starving man who can see a meal just out of his reach. Kit was polite but so distant that he might as well have been an utter stranger. Eleanor nibbled her food and felt miserable.

Further down the table, Lady Salome was chatting blithely to Marcus, who was glaring at Beth. The Dowager Lady Trevithick was surprisingly animated and had two bright spots of colour showing on her cheeks. Every so often she would surreptitiously tip some laudanum from her vial into her wineglass. Even Beth and Charlotte looked vaguely strained and were avoiding looking at their respective husbands.

The dessert had just been removed and the ladies were preparing to retire, when Lady Salome stood up.

'I should like to say a few words to you all,' she said, twinkling at them roguishly. 'It has been a great pleasure for me to have my family about me this evening and I wish to thank you all, particularly as I know you would probably not have chosen to be at the same table could you avoid it!'

There was some movement around that very table as various members of the family shifted uncomfortably. Lady Salome had a talent for making them sound like difficult children.

'And it is for that very reason that I intend to right some wrongs this evening!' Lady Salome continued grandly. 'Vengeance is mine, I shall repay, saith the Lord! But tonight, my dears, I shall do the repaying!'

'Oh Lord,' Marcus said, under his breath.

Eleanor shot him a reproving look. She was glad that he was about to get his comeuppance. 'Marcus, hush! This is a serious matter!'

'At the beginning of the year I accompanied my brother St John to Ireland on a mission he was undertaking on behalf of the Bishop of Exeter.' Lady Salome said, casting her gaze down sorrowfully. 'I think you all know now that the trip was a disaster and that St John has subsequently retired. What you do not know...' she paused for effect '...is that whilst we were in Ireland we were beset by difficulties that

I was unable and St John—sadly—incapable of rectifying. Personal and financial difficulties…' She let the sentence trail discreetly away.

There was a silence. Kit moved slightly in his seat. Lady Salome turned to him.

'I know that you had no wish for this to be disclosed, my dear Christopher, but I can be silent no longer! It pains me to see the unhappiness in this family! Where there is discord, let me bring harmony! Where there is feuding, let me spread peace!'

Eleanor bit her lip, surprised by an unexpected urge to laugh. There was no doubt that Lady Salome was playing to the gallery. Everyone had turned to look at Kit now, and he did not seem very pleased about it. She made an instinctive move to place a reassuring hand on his arm, and then drew back. No doubt the last thing that he would wish was for reassurance from her.

Marcus raised his eyebrows. 'I infer that Mostyn has rendered you some service that we are unaware of, Aunt?' He sounded as displeased as Kit looked. 'You have us all on tenterhooks! Pray enlighten us, if you please!'

'Certainly, dear boy!' Lady Salome said cheerfully. 'It was my good fortune to encounter Christopher in Ireland. He was on the point of returning to this country and…' she smiled at Eleanor '…a much desired reunion with his wife. I importuned him to help us—I do not believe we need the precise financial and personal details do we, Marcus?—and Christopher was honourable enough to put our needs before his

own, most pressing, circumstances. I need hardly
point out what a sacrifice this was for him, nor the
troubles that ensued—'

Kit held a hand up. 'Dear Lady Salome, you have
embarrassed me quite enough! I am sure your audience has all the information it needs!'

This time the silence around the table was explo-
sive. Marcus's face was a picture. Beth caught
Eleanor's eye and pulled an expressive face.

'You silence me, ma'am,' Marcus said, at length.
'Perhaps this would be an opportune moment for the
ladies to retire? The gentlemen may then…ah…
clarify a few matters…'

Eleanor sat irresolute. She did not like the thought
of leaving Kit alone with both Marcus and Justin for
it felt a little like throwing him to the lions. Her support was unlikely to be what he wanted, however.
Beth was coming to take her arm with an encouraging
word and a smile for Kit, whilst Charlotte had fixed
Justin with such a speaking look that Eleanor almost
felt sorry for her cousin. The ladies went out, Lady
Salome lending the Dowager an arm to lean upon.

'Oh, I do hope everything will be well!' Eleanor
fretted, as they took their places in the drawing-room
and waited for the tea to be served. 'I could not bear
it if they came to blows and made matters all the
worse!'

Beth squeezed her arm. 'All will be well! I am
confident that Marcus will behave as a gentleman
ought and will apologise to Kit! And if he does not I
shall never forgive him!'

'I confess I shall be glad that matters may revert to normal,' Charlotte said, casting a glance at the Dowager to make sure that she was out of earshot. 'These last few days have been very difficult! Not so much the...' she blushed, 'the *denial*, if you understand me, but the tensions it created! Why, I had to stab Justin quite hard with my embroidery needle yesterday to encourage him to desist in his attentions!'

Beth laughed. 'I understand you! I shall not be sorry either! But who would have thought that Lady Salome would spring such a surprise!' Her gaze fell on Eleanor.

'You are very quiet tonight, Nell, and you look very poorly. Very poorly indeed! Charlotte, does not poor Eleanor look positively sickly—'

'Yes, she does, Beth dear,' Charlotte said comfortably, 'but I do not think it will help Eleanor feel any better for you to keep repeating it! Come here, Nell, and sit by me.' Charlotte patted the sofa.

Eleanor sat, feeling rather uncomfortable. If Charlotte only knew what she had done to Kit she doubted she would be so friendly. Eleanor dreaded having to explain herself to Beth and Charlotte—both of them knew what had happened during Kit's absence and both of them had been the most stalwart of friends, but she suspected that she would be pushing their understanding by asking them to condone her demand for an annulment. Once or twice during the evening she had felt their gaze upon her and almost thought that they knew, but perhaps that was only her conscience making her feel guilty. Perhaps it was cowardly of her, but for now she was determined to keep quiet.

'As well as the comfort of reverting to normal in our behaviour to our husbands, it will be a relief to have the whole family united,' Beth said, making Eleanor feel much worse. 'I confess there were times when I thought it impossible to lay our quarrels to rest, but now I have real hope…'

Eleanor shifted and fidgeted on the sofa. The thought of ruining Beth's hopes of a united family made her feel quite ill. It seemed that as soon as they had achieved harmony she would spoil it all again. She had planned to approach Marcus for help tomorrow.

'Do you think Lady Salome has finished with us all yet?' she whispered, casting a glance across the room to where Lady Salome and the Dowager were chatting over the teacups. 'I have the most lowering notion that she has something else up her sleeve!'

Beth fixed her with a very direct look. 'You sound as though you are afraid of something, Nell!' she said acutely. 'And perhaps you should be, for I do not believe that Lady Salome has finished at all! Indeed I think that she has only just begun!'

By the time that the gentlemen rejoined them, the guests had started to arrive and Beth and Marcus went off to greet them whilst the others went through to the ballroom. Eleanor, who had expected to see at least a trace of constraint in Justin and Kit's behaviour, was a little taken aback to find them conversing with ease and a male camaraderie that left her feeling

ever-so-slightly excluded. It was, as Beth would have
said, quite typical.

Kit and Charlotte went off to dance, Justin stood
up with Beth and Marcus led Lady Salome out, leaving Eleanor with a lingering sense of exclusion as she
took a rout chair and sat the dance out at her mother's
side. So now the entire family were on great good
terms—except for herself and Kit, of course. He could
have danced with her if he had wanted, but he had
not chosen to do so. Eleanor concentrated fiercely on
the detail of her fan and told herself that she should
not be surprised. She was the one who had set a gulf
between herself and Kit and could not now complain
when he showed a coldness towards her. All the same,
she felt lonely.

The dance seemed long and gave Eleanor ample
chance to reflect on what would happen if she persisted in her demand for an annulment. The scandal
would be huge, her family might well cast her off,
and she would be alone… She was not sure that she
had the strength to pursue such a course. Yet what
was the alternative? Her eyes ached with unshed tears
as she watched Kit dancing with his sister. They made
a striking couple, so tall and fair, so at ease in each
other's company, so *happy*… She could have been
happy with Kit, if matters had fallen out differently.

'Would you like to dance, Nell?'

Marcus had returned Lady Salome to the chair at
Lady Trevithick's side and was now standing before
her, smiling slightly. Eleanor could see that a certain
element of tension had already left him. He looked

younger—and happier. Her heart felt like lead in comparison. Was she the only one left feeling miserable? But there was Kit, of course, whose misery was also entirely her fault.

She took Marcus's hand. 'Thank you, Marcus. I should like to dance.'

They joined a set that was forming.

'You are looking better, Marcus,' Eleanor said slyly. 'It must be a great relief to you that Beth will be…er…speaking to you again!'

Marcus's lips twitched. 'You knew about that, did you, Nell? I confess that that is one of the attractive aspects of the situation.' His smile faded. 'However, I believe I owe you an apology, before all else.'

Eleanor raised her eyebrows. 'Indeed, Marcus? Why is that?'

'Minx,' her brother said. 'You are well aware! I know that I have made matters very difficult for you and Mostyn these two weeks past, when they must have been difficult enough already, in all conscience! I am sorry.'

Eleanor's gaze flickered. 'It is Kit who is owed the real apology—'

'He has had one.' Marcus grimaced. 'I have seldom made a man so grovelling an apology in my life and I hate to say that he was entirely gracious about it! I think that I may appreciate him as a brother-in-law after all!'

Eleanor looked away.

'What about you, Nell?' Marcus said suddenly. His dark eyes were concerned. 'Are you happy?'

'I…Marcus…' Suddenly Eleanor's throat was dry. This seemed like the perfect opportunity to ask Marcus for an interview to discuss the annulment, but she was not at all sure that he would be sympathetic. Probably he would not have been sympathetic before his *rapprochement* with Kit, and now it was even more unlikely. She swallowed hard. Marcus was looking at her quizzically.

'What is it, Nell?'

'Stop thief!'

Everyone froze and swung around as Lady Salome's deep, throbbing accents rent the air. The string quartet wavered on for a few bars then died away and a hush fell over the ballroom. Marcus, Eleanor and the rest of the family converged on Lady Salome, who was standing like a vision of justice, pointing the finger at Lord Kemble.

'That man,' she said grandly, 'has just stolen my diamond brooch!'

'I have to admit that it was very clever of her,' Marcus said later, 'for all that I wish she would not do such things!'

The six of them were sitting in the drawing-room, taking a glass of wine to restore them after the trials of the evening. Both Lady Salome and the Dowager Viscountess had retired, leaving only the younger members of the party. Charlotte was sitting within the circle of Justin's arm and looking very happy, Beth looked relieved but tired. Only Eleanor and Kit were a scrupulous distance apart, in separate armchairs.

'I do not really understand why Lord Kemble did not simply blame Mama for giving him the brooch,' Eleanor said, a little hesitantly. 'Although I suppose it might have been something to do with the threatening manner in which you were standing over him, Marcus!'

'Can't stand the man!' Marcus said bluntly. 'If I had thought I could get away with calling him out—'

'And a very good thing you did not!' Beth said briskly. 'Matters have worked out quite for the best! Everyone is cold-shouldering Kemble, for all that he tried to pass it off as a mistake!'

There was a little silence. 'Do you think that Lady Salome deliberately left the brooch lying for Mama to find?' Eleanor asked.

It was Charlotte who answered. 'I am sure of it! I was sitting beside them but a moment before and Lady Salome was wearing it then! She must have slipped it on to the table, Lady Trevithick picked it up, and when Kemble came across to provide his usual supply of the laudanum...' She shrugged. 'There it was to hand as convenient payment!'

'Too convenient!' Justin said, with a grin. 'A neat strategy! Lady Salome is watching, realises that there are plenty of people who can testify to the fact that the brooch is in fact hers, and makes her accusation—'

'And Kemble cannot deny it is in his possession!' Marcus finished, a gleam in his eye. 'To pretend as he did that he picked it up off the floor in ignorance simply makes him look dishonest, if not an actual thief.' He sighed. 'I suppose it is better to let it go at that…'

'Of course it is!' Beth said sharply. 'We do not wish to draw any further attention to your mother's part in this, Marcus!'

Eleanor fidgeted. 'I do feel responsible for not telling anyone of Mama's thefts before now! I am so sorry, Beth…' she turned to her sister-in-law '…the Trevithick ruby bracelet is gone and it is my fault! It is simply that I could not believe it at first…'

Beth shook her head. 'I think that we all misjudged Lady Trevithick's desperation, Nell! Oh, we all laughed at her with her little bottle of laudanum and the way she was forever taking a draught, but we had no notion of how harmful it was becoming! It was only when Lady Salome explained to me just how damaging are the effects that I realised…' She stopped. 'It is all most distressing. What can we do now, Marcus?'

'I think that Mama will have to go away for a space,' Marcus said, grim-faced. 'Perhaps when we return to Trevithick and she has a new grandchild to occupy her and is away from town…'

There was another silence. No one seemed very hopeful. Thinking back, Eleanor realised that she could not remember a time when her mother had not been dependent on her little bottle of laudanum. To deprive her of it now might cause untold harm.

She got to her feet, yawning. 'I am sorry, but I must go home! It is late and I am monstrous tired!'

It was the signal for the group to break up. They

went out into the hall, Marcus and Justin discussing with Kit the possibility of meeting up the following day for a visit to Tatersalls. Beth raised her eyes to heaven.

'You would think that they had never been at odds!' she whispered to Eleanor. 'But it is fortuitous, for I *must* speak to you, Nell! It is most urgent! May I call tomorrow— Oh!'

Eleanor made a grab for her arm as Beth slipped, but it was too late. Her sister-in-law lost her footing and tumbled down on to the marble floor, letting out a little shriek as she fell. Eleanor, ashen-faced, fell to her knees beside her. The floor was slippery with candle grease and Beth was lying awkwardly, twisted on one side.

'Beth!' Eleanor grabbed her hand. 'Beth, are you hurt?'

There was a dreadful moment of quiet, and then Beth moved a little gingerly and started to sit up. She gave a groan. The others, who had frozen with shock for a brief moment, now hurried up. Marcus cradled his wife to him with such tenderness that Eleanor caught her breath.

'Beth—'

'I am all right, Marcus!' Beth spoke shakily. 'There is no harm done!'

Marcus tightened his grip. 'Are you sure you are not injured?'

'I feel perfectly well,' Beth said more firmly. 'Or at least I will do when you stop squashing me! I have not twisted my ankle nor do I feel remotely unwell. It was only a spot of grease and a minor tumble.'

'But the baby—' Marcus began.

'She will be quite all right.' Beth tried to get to her feet. 'Oof! I feel a little short of breath, that is all!'

Charlotte bustled up. She had nursed her first husband and his comrades on campaign in the Peninsula and was a staunch support in any emergency.

'Beth, keep still and do not try to rise. Marcus, can you carry her upstairs? I am sure she will be quite well, but it might be safer to send for the doctor. Justin, if you would send one of the servants…'

Within ten minutes, all was organised. A footman had run for the doctor, who appeared with great promptitude. Beth was carried up to her chamber, protesting volubly, and Kit and Eleanor were left to kick their heels in front of the fire in the drawing-room and wait for news.

Eleanor sank down on the sofa and knitted her fingers together to stop them shaking. She felt cold and vaguely sick. If Beth lost her child… But of course she would not, she *could* not… Beth was strong and the fall had only been a little one…

'I could not bear for it to happen to someone else!' she said. She missed the searching look that Kit directed at her down-bent head, the sudden stillness that held him for a moment before he went over and threw another log on the fire. He came to sit by her.

'Why do you suppose she thinks it will be a daughter?' he asked.

Eleanor blinked at him. 'I beg your pardon?'

'A daughter.' Kit smiled. 'Beth referred to the baby as ''she'' just now!'

'Oh!' Eleanor smiled. Suddenly she felt a little warmer. 'I think it is because she is determined to have a daughter first, and then a son! She said that she wanted her daughter to be first in order to give her a natural superiority when the son inherits the title—and of course, because girls are better behaved than boys!'

They smiled at each other. 'I am sure it will be a girl then,' Kit said. 'It would not dare be otherwise!'

'I am sure they will love it, whatever sex it may be!' Eleanor said. Her voice wavered a little. Kit took her hands. 'Nell. It will be all right.'

Kit's grasp was infinitely gentle and comforting. He slid an arm around her and drew her close to him, stroking her until her shivering stopped. Eleanor leaned her head against his shoulder and closed her eyes. She had not thought but to accept the comfort that he offered. Kit's arms were a haven against the world and her own fears, and she felt her body relax a little.

The door opened. They both jumped to their feet as Charlotte came in.

'Well?' Eleanor demanded.

Charlotte smiled. She looked relieved. 'Beth is very well. The doctor has said that there is no cause for alarm but that she should be careful for a few days. Naturally she is already making the greatest fuss about being confined to her bed! I hope that you will

both call tomorrow to try to distract her! She will be
the most tiresome patient otherwise!'

The journey back to Montague Street was a short
one and was accomplished mainly in silence, but
when they reached the house and Eleanor wished Kit
a good night and made for the stairs, he put a hand
out and touched her arm lightly.

'Eleanor, a moment.'

Eleanor looked at him, surprised. 'Kit?'

'May we speak?' There was something closed and
watchful in Kit's face and Eleanor hesitated. Her
emotions were still close to the surface, dangerously
so.

'I am very tired, Kit,' she said, knowing she
sounded reluctant. 'In fact, I feel exhausted! It has
been such a difficult evening—'

'A glass of wine would restore you and help you
to sleep,' Kit suggested. 'Take one with me.'

He held the door of the drawing-room open and
after a moment Eleanor joined him. The thought of a
drink was pleasant and she told herself that she need
not stay long, nor be drawn into a difficult conversation. This was no time to pursue the subject of an
annulment, for she was sure that she would simply
burst into tears and flee at the first mention of the
word. She hoped that Kit would not take advantage
of her evident distress to push his case.

Kit took her cloak from her, installed her in an
armchair and lit some of the candles from the one
branch that was already burning in the room. The

light was soft and pleasing, as was the warmth of the fire. Eleanor felt herself start to relax. It was only now that she realised how tense she had been during that dreadful episode after Beth's fall. She watched Kit covertly as he moved to pour them two glasses of wine. He did not call the servants and somehow this added to the sense of warm familiarity in the room.

Eleanor took her glass of wine from him, her fingers brushing his. She turned her thoughts aside from the intimacy of that touch, trying to keep at bay the loneliness that always dogged her now.

'Eleanor,' Kit had taken the chair across from her and was leaning forward, watching her intently. The ruby wine swirled in his glass, rich red in the firelight. 'There was something that I wished to ask you…'

Eleanor opened her eyes wide. 'Oh? Then ask it, my lord.'

Surprisingly, Kit still hesitated. He looked away, then directly at her. Eleanor felt the power of his glance and felt also the first pang of apprehension as his tension communicated itself to her. She narrowed her eyes, puzzled.

'When we were in the drawing-room after Beth had had her fall,' Kit said slowly, 'you said that you could not bear for it to happen to someone else.' He shifted slightly. 'What did you mean by that, Eleanor?'

Eleanor sat stock still. She felt nothing—no shock, no despair, no surprise. She wondered vaguely how she could have given herself away so easily when she had tried so hard and for so long not to do so. And she heard herself say lightly:

'Did I say that, my lord? I do not recall.'

'You did say that.' Kit was remorseless and she knew he would not let it go now. Fear nibbled at her stomach. He was watching her still. She shifted uncomfortably.

'I am not entirely sure what I meant...'

'I do not believe you.' Kit put his glass down. 'You meant that you could not bear for someone else to lose their baby, did you not, Eleanor?'

Eleanor closed her eyes for a moment. The firelight danced behind her closed lids.

'Eleanor, please answer me.' Kit's face was in shadow, his voice steady, and she sensed his resolve. 'Please.'

Eleanor opened her eyes, momentarily dazzled by the light. Once again, she found herself responding to that hypnotic tone. This would be easy if she kept it light and did not give too much away. Well, perhaps not easy, but it need not be too bad. And it need make no difference to the annulment...

'Eleanor?' There was an edge to Kit's voice now, ruthless, inescapable. She looked him straight in the eye.

'I was thinking about myself. I was thinking about me and about our child. Our child, Kit! The one I lost while you were away! I—' At the last moment, she was able to pull back from the brink before the whole terrible tale came tumbling out. She took a steadying breath.

Kit's mouth was set in a hard line, his face pale. 'How did it happen?'

Eleanor shrugged. 'It just…happened. No reason, not a fall, like Beth's. I hear it is not uncommon in the first few weeks. The doctor told me…'

Kit got up, thrusting his hands into his pockets, pacing across the room with all the restlessness of a caged animal.

'Were you ever going to tell me about this, Eleanor?'

Eleanor watched him with dull eyes. 'I thought not, no.'

'I see.' She could read nothing from his tone. He came across to her chair and stood close to her. Eleanor shuddered. The words broke from her and try as she would, she could not prevent them:

'I am sorry, Kit… I am sorry I lost the child…'

'Nell…' Now she could read his tone and the gentleness in it made her shake all the more. He went down on one knee beside her chair, his arms going about her softly, rocking her.

'No, it is I who am so very sorry that I was not with you when you needed me, Nell—'

Eleanor rushed on, heedless, the tears spilling down her face now.

'I told myself that I did not care, but I did! Oh, it hurt so much I could not bear it! For a while I thought I would run quite mad, and you were not there…I did all those other imprudent things and got myself into such foolish situations and it was all horrible—'

Kit held her closer still, stroking her hair. 'You did nothing that was foolish, sweetheart…'

'I was confused—'

'I understand. You have nothing with which to reproach yourself.'

'And then you came back and I was so very angry with you!' Eleanor shuddered, gasping on a sob. 'I hated you for leaving me, Kit, and then I hated you for coming back! But it was not easy…' She gave a little hiccup. 'You made it very difficult for me to dislike you, Kit!'

Kit did not answer. Her face was in the curve of his shoulder, so close that her lips could touch his skin. He smelled distractingly good. Eleanor snuggled closer.

It was several minutes later that Kit said, muffled: 'Eleanor, much as I would love to stay here all night, I am losing the sensation in my arms! If you will allow me—'

He scooped her up and transferred them both to the armchair by the fire. Eleanor rested her head against his shoulder.

'Kit, you do understand—'

'Yes.' Kit was stroking her hair. 'I am sure I would be the last person in whom you would wish to confide, mistrusting me as you did! Oh Nell—' There was a bitter edge to his voice, 'I will never forgive myself for leaving you so carelessly like that to face such things alone—'

'I had Beth and Marcus.' Eleanor said. She smiled a little. 'They were so good to me, but I made them promise never to tell…'

Kit's jaw set in a hard line. 'I understand your brother's attitude much better now, I confess. Had our situations been reversed I fear I would have put a bullet through him!'

Eleanor smiled again. She rubbed her fingers tentatively along the stubble of his cheek, revelling in the rough touch.

'Mmm. Well, this is a matter between you and me, not Marcus,' she murmured. 'Though I am glad that you have settled your differences now…'

Kit turned his head and kissed her palm, but his eyes were still serious.

'Eleanor, about the annulment…' He felt her stiffen and held her still. 'Please, my love… I *must* know. Why do you wish us to part?'

Eleanor fiddled with one of the buttons on his coat. In the exquisite relief of letting go of her secrets she had forgotten this one last matter. She was silent.

'If you are afraid,' Kit said huskily, 'then I swear I will not push you to do anything you do not wish. But Eleanor, I have been thinking that I cannot let you go! I will fight it with every breath in my body—'

Eleanor could not bear the anguish in his voice. She shook her head abruptly. 'No Kit, it was not that, though I confess I was a little frightened… When you made love to me the other night I wanted so much more, but yes, I was afraid…'

She saw him smile then. 'Nell, I promise I would never rush matters—'

Eleanor shook her head again. 'It was not that,' she said again. She sat away from him a little so that she could look at him properly. 'Sometimes I think that it is that I am afraid of everything,' she said candidly.

'I am afraid in case I conceive a child and lose it again, but I am more afraid that I may never have children.' Her eyes, dark and sad, sought his. 'The doctor tells me that it is by no means certain that I may have a family,' she said slowly. 'And you were so anxious to set up your nursery, Kit.'

There was a silence. Kit pulled her back close to him, his arms tightening about her. He did not speak.

'Kit—' Eleanor struggled upright. 'I am right, am I not? And with an annulment—'

'There will be no annulment.' She had never heard so much determination in his tone. 'It is out of the question.'

'But—'

'Eleanor.' Kit's voice was low and firm. 'There is no way of determining whether or not any man and woman will have children before they try, and you have not been told that it is impossible! And even if you had...' he held her so close that she could barely breathe '...there would be no annulment.'

Eleanor's throat felt thick with tears. She thought her heart would burst. 'But Kit, you need an heir—'

'Pray do not argue with me. If you are not to be the mother of my children then I want none.'

'That is not in the natural order of things,' Eleanor said uncertainly. 'A man needs an heir—'

'And I need a wife. This wife.' Kit held her away from him. 'Eleanor, I love you! Surely you cannot think that I would let you go and marry someone else just for the sake of begetting an heir! The thought is monstrous!'

'I do not know.' Eleanor's voice was small. 'I have struggled with this for so long that I am not sure what I feel any more! And Kit, I am so unhappy and afraid! If we…if I…were to conceive another child only to lose it again…' Her voice broke. 'You must see that I thought it simpler for us to part!'

'I understand why you believed it might be so,' Kit said, 'but I fear that I cannot agree, Nell. Whatever happens, we shall deal with it together. Which means that there shall be no separation and no annulment. Are you in agreement?'

A little smile curved Eleanor's lips. She was almost persuaded. 'Well…'

Kit shook her gently. 'Nell, I will lock you up if it is the only way to keep you!'

Eleanor looked at him. Her body, softening against his, gave him the answer. 'I do not believe that there is any need to be so medieval, my lord!'

Kit drew her close into an embrace that precluded any further discussion. After a moment, Eleanor was obliged to object.

'Kit, you are crushing me half to death!'

Kit loosened his grip and they looked at each other. 'I suppose I should let you go now,' he said reluctantly. 'It has, as you said, been a very long evening!'

Eleanor slid to her feet and Kit stood up too. She knew that he would let her go alone, if that was her wish. Despite his determination that there should be no annulment, he would not hurry her into a physical intimacy that she did not want and she loved him for it. She walked slowly over to the door and turned back to look at him. He was watching her, his expression unreadable.

'Kit,' she said slowly, 'I find I do not wish to be alone tonight. Please stay with me.'

Chapter Twelve

'I suppose I shall just have to seduce him!' Eleanor said glumly. 'I have tried everything else! Why, when we went to the masquerade last night I chose to wear my lowest cut dress and all Kit could say was would I like a scarf as the nights were still a little cold!'

'You could just tell him how you feel,' Beth said. She was sitting up in bed and eating a plate of toast and honey. 'It is easier in the long run than all this worrying. A simple statement of intent—that you would like Kit to make love to you—should do the trick!'

Eleanor stared, the colour slowly mounting to her cheeks. 'Oh Beth, I know that I have made great strides in overcoming my natural modesty, but that is surely a step too far. Of all the brazen things… Why I would have to be drunk! Or taken with the laudanum, perhaps!'

Beth grimaced. 'Well, there is plenty to spare. We found an entire bottle hidden at the back of one of your mama's drawers. She had evidently forgotten it was there!'

'I hope that she will be happy in the dower house at Trevithick,' Eleanor said slowly. The Dowager was even now packing her belongings for the remove. 'I realise that it is wise for her to leave town for a little until the talk dies down, but I cannot see that being in the country will help improve her situation! Unless the laudanum travels with her...'

Beth finished the toast and licked her fingers. 'Perhaps that is the kindest action. To forbid her it now would be cruel and probably dangerous.' She sighed. 'It is like an illness, is it not, and a problem not easily solved. Lady Salome is hopeful that Dr Wentworth in Exeter may be able to help her... But do not turn the subject, dearest Eleanor! We were speaking of you— and my cousin...'

Eleanor sighed. On the night that she and Kit had had their final confrontation, they had retired to their separate rooms and had prepared for bed with an odd sort of decorum. Eleanor had pulled the bolt back on the dressing-room door and opened the door shyly to allow Kit to come through. Then they had sat in her bed and had talked and talked. All the anger, all the frustrations, all the fears, had come out in the intimate dark, until she had fallen asleep in Kit's arms from total exhaustion. It had been an extraordinarily profound experience, far deeper than making love. And in the morning Kit had said gravely that he was happy that all was now resolved but that he felt they now needed a little time before anything else happened between them. Eleanor had been bitterly disappointed and a tiny bit relieved, but she had agreed to what he had suggested. Perhaps Kit himself needed time before they resumed a deeper relationship or perhaps he thought that she did. Worse, she might have made him so afraid of hurting her again that he would not approach her. Whatever the case, they had spent a week in the pleasantest of pastimes, driving together, walking, talking, attending the Season's balls, and it had been delightful but somehow…unfinished.

'You have no qualms, then, Nell?' Beth asked now. 'When the time comes, I mean…'

Eleanor shook her head. 'No. I trust Kit to stay with me and I love him with all my heart. If we have children I shall feel truly blessed, but if not… I shall still have Kit.' She shrugged lightly, 'To tell the truth I am a little nervous of how we get to that point…if you understand me…'

Beth laughed. 'I do! Which is why this delay is unsettling you, Nell. The anticipation—'

Eleanor laughed too. 'Well, it is pleasant, in a rather disturbing way! I shall think about your advice, Beth!' She stood up. 'Who knows, I may be able to summon up the will to tell Kit how I feel. Now, you will be wanting your maid sent up if you are to be ready for dinner. Though how you may eat it after that plate of toast—'

'Oh, I am forever hungry!' Beth said cheerfully, 'and most excited at being allowed to get out of bed! Of all the torments—to be confined here whilst everyone else is out enjoying themselves!'

'We are just happy that you are quite well,' Eleanor said feelingly, kissing her sister-in-law before she left the bedroom. 'I shall see you at dinner.'

Eleanor went slowly downstairs, turning over in her mind what Beth had said. She did not consider herself shy, precisely, but to state her wishes to Kit in so blunt a manner did seem somewhat bold. On the other hand if she did not take the initiative she might be fretting herself to flinders for days whilst she waited for Kit to take the hint. It was difficult.

They were taking dinner that evening at Trevithick House and following that with a visit to the theatre. The whole family, with the exception of the Dowager, were to make up the party and it promised to be a better-tempered experience than the previous dinner at Trevithick House. Eleanor had just reached the hall when the outer door opened and Kit came in, talking to Marcus. Eleanor thought that Kit, in buff pantaloons and a cinnamon-coloured coat, looked quite devastatingly handsome that afternoon. She watched him openly as he crossed the hall. After all, no doubt Beth would tell her that if one could not stare in open admiration at one's husband, one might as well be dead.

Kit saw her, exchanged a quick word with Marcus, and his brother-in-law clapped him on the shoulder before hurrying off upstairs, no doubt to visit Beth. Eleanor tried not to laugh. Such harmony between the Mostyn and Trevithick families was still something of a novelty.

'Eleanor, how are you?' Kit had taken her hand

now and was pressing a kiss on it like the most ardent
of suitors. Eleanor shivered pleasurably, her thoughts
returning to their earlier topic.

'I am well, thank you, my lord.' She gave him a
look from under her lashes. Once upon a time she had
been able to flirt rather well and perhaps she had not
lost the skill…

'I have a small present for you,' Kit continued. 'To
wear to the theatre tonight, perhaps?'

He produced a small posy of violets, velvet soft
and sweet-scented, and handed them to Eleanor. She
buried her nose in them.

'Oh, how lovely! Thank you, my lord.' Eleanor
stroked the petals with a gentle finger. They were soft
and smooth, and the faint perfume filled her senses,
making her feel curiously aware… It was like the sun
on your skin, or Kit's touch… She blinked.

Kit was speaking. Eleanor raised her gaze to his. 'I
beg your pardon, Kit, I was not attending. What did
you say?'

'I was asking whether you would care to travel to
Mostyn with me in a few weeks,' Kit repeated, brows
raised. 'The Season is almost at an end and your
brother and Beth are removing to Trevithick… Are
you quite well, Eleanor? You seem a little distracted
today.'

'Oh!' Eleanor blushed a little. His eyes were such
a deep blue, warm with laughter… 'Yes, well, Beth
and I have been talking too…about returning to
Devon, I mean, and I am sure it would be very pleasant…'

'Good.' Kit frowned slightly. 'You look a little flushed, my love. Are you sure you feel well enough to go out tonight?'

'Oh yes!' Eleanor gave him a melting smile. 'I am quite well, Kit!' She took a deep breath. 'I am very sorry if I appear a little *distrait*—it is simply that I was thinking of seducing you!'

Kit had half-turned away, for the front door had just opened to admit Justin and Charlotte. Eleanor saw the precise moment that her words impinged on him. He turned his head sharply and looked at her, his eyes narrowed in puzzlement as though he thought he had misheard. She gave him another, brilliant smile. There was a flash of heat in Kit's gaze as it rested on her, he looked as though he were about to speak, then bit off what he was going to say as Charlotte and Justin came up to greet them. Eleanor, reaching up to kiss Justin, saw out of the corner of her eye that Kit was still watching her. She took Charlotte's arm and moved away to the drawing-room, well satisfied.

There was no chance of private conversation after that. They were joined by Marcus and Beth and finally by Lady Salome, and went into dinner informally, chattering amongst themselves.

Eleanor was delighted to see that Kit was quite preoccupied during dinner. Twice he stopped eating altogether and a third time he almost knocked over his wine. Lady Salome, who was sitting on his left, had the greatest trouble in sustaining a conversation with him. Every so often his gaze would rest on

Eleanor and she would give him the demurest of smiles before applying herself to her food once again. She knew what was distracting him; he knew that she knew. It was definitely working… Eleanor gave a little shiver of nervous anticipation.

When they were all in the hall gathering their cloaks prior to going to the theatre, Kit caught her arm in an urgent grip and drew her to one side.

'Eleanor, did you have to initiate that topic of conversation at the precise moment when you knew we would not be able to discuss it?'

'Which topic was that, my lord?' Eleanor queried, her tone light. She could not quite meet his eyes.

Kit gave her arm a little shake. 'You know full well! Devil take it, I have thought of little else since we last spoke!'

'Oh,' Eleanor gave him a little smile, 'I do believe that is the problem, Kit! Sometimes you think far too much when you should simply…act!'

She whisked her arm out of his grip, smilingly accepted her cloak from the footman's hands and hurried out to the carriage, wondering how she had the audacity to tease her husband like this. But she had started and so she was determined to finish.

The play was *She Stoops to Conquer* by Goldsmith and had always been one of Eleanor's favourites, but tonight it seemed to drag. She was very aware of Kit sitting behind her in the box and although she could not turn around to look at him, she was sure that his attention was on her and not the play. When they reached the interval, Kit offered her his arm.

'Would you care for a stroll, my love?'

The press of people was great, for plenty were taking the opportunity to stretch their legs. Neither Kit nor Eleanor spoke at first, but she was very aware of him beside her and of the brush of his body against hers. After they had walked the length of the corridor, Kit said:

'When you said earlier that I thought too much, what did you mean?'

Eleanor gave a little sigh. This was proving more difficult that she had imagined. It seemed ironic that Kit, who had not troubled to conceal his desire for her in the past, should now prove so difficult to persuade. Without pausing for thought, Eleanor tugged his arm and pulled him behind the shelter of a huge pillar. It was hardly private but it afforded more seclusion that the theatre entrance hall.

'It is simply that if we wait until we both think that it is an…appropriate time…' Eleanor took a deep breath and pressed on, 'well, the time may never come!' She put both hands against Kit's chest. She could feel the beat of his heart beneath her palm. 'Stand closer!' she said urgently.

Kit obligingly bent closer to her. His breath stirred her hair. Eleanor resisted the urge to run her fingers along the line of his jaw.

'If you are taking care because you have no wish to frighten me…' the colour came up into her face and she stood on tiptoe so that she could whisper in his ear '…then I pray you, do not! I want you to make love to me! And please do not ask me to make it any more plain to you because I cannot!'

And before he could say another word, she had whisked out from behind the pillar and was making her way back to the box with determined step, not looking behind her.

Kit followed slowly. It was going to prove impossible to concentrate on the play now—not that he had been giving it his full attention before. From the moment that Eleanor had made her outrageous statement about seducing him, back in the hall at Trevithick House, he had been utterly incapable of focusing on anything other than that thought. He could not remember a single thing about dinner, for his entire attention had been rapt in his wife. She had looked so demure, so innocent and so wholly seductive. Deliciously so, outrageously so. And every so often, she had cast Kit a look that had said that she knew exactly what he was thinking and she wanted him to want her. She wanted him to make love to her... Kit reached the box and almost cannoned into Lady Salome in the doorway, so intent was he in his own thoughts. After making his apologies he resumed his seat, and looked at Eleanor. She had cast him one swift glance as he had come in and was now making conversation with Beth, but there was a colour in her cheeks and a sparkle in her eye that he could not miss. She was wearing a pink dress with a modest décolletage and one dark ringlet was resting in the hollow of her shoulder. Kit's fingers itched to touch it.

In fact he had been aching to touch her for what

seemed like weeks now. This latest abstinence he had laid upon himself, sternly abjuring himself to do the gentlemanly thing and not to hurry Eleanor, not to press his attentions on his wife when they were so recently reconciled. But now… Kit shook his head a little to try to displace the images that seemed to be running riot in his brain. It was no good. The figures on the stage were pale and unreal in comparison to the vision of Eleanor as he had seen her stretched out on her bed. He had to take her home and they had to go now. Except that there were still two acts of the play to go… Kit almost groaned aloud.

By the time the play ended he felt as though several days had passed. Then there were the farewells to the rest of the family, the arrangements to meet the following day, the business of sending for the carriages… It seemed that every delay was designed to add to his torment. He could smell Eleanor's faint perfume as she stood beside him; he could feel the brush of her hair against his shoulder. He wanted to kiss her senseless and instead he was obliged make polite conversation whilst Eleanor and Beth and Charlotte discussed at endless length the plan to go shopping the following day. By the time it finished he would have happily traded half his fortune to see his sister and his cousin in Hades.

Eleanor was well aware of Kit's impatience as she discussed arrangements with Beth and Charlotte. He positively vibrated with irritation and she suspected that she knew the cause—her plan to engage his interest was working exceptionally well. And now she had to deliver what she had promised. It felt quite curious, as though she had deliberately let a predatory animal out of its cage and now could not restrain it. Not that she wanted to, of course, but she knew that eventually there would be a price to pay. What she could not decide was whether eventually would arrive too soon—or not soon enough.

She did not look at Kit and an edge of nervousness made her spin out the farewells as long as she could. Soon it was impossible to delay any longer, however. Kit's hand was imperative on her arm as he helped her up into the carriage. He installed her in the corner then sat next to her rather than opposite, as was customary. Eleanor tried to appear casual and yawned delicately. Kit raised an eyebrow.

'Did you enjoy the play, my love?' he asked politely. 'I seem to remember it as one of your favourites.'

'Oh it is.' Eleanor cast him a sideways look. Her heart was beating rather fast. Surely he did not intend to commence his seduction in a carriage? Or did he?

'I fear I found myself oddly distracted tonight, my lord!' she said slowly. 'I was not as drawn in as usual.'

She could not see Kit's face in the darkness but she heard him laugh. 'Is there anything that I might do to help your powers of concentration, sweetheart? You need only say the word!'

Eleanor's heart not only speeded up, it skipped a

beat. 'Well, I do not know… Yes, perhaps you might…'

In reply, Kit caught her up in his arms and pulled her to him. He stopped with his mouth an inch away from hers.

'You have been teasing me all evening, my love—'

Eleanor wriggled. 'That is true, but—'

'No buts. Now you have to make good your words.'

Kit bent closer until his lips touched hers lightly. Eleanor leaned into him, grasping the lapels of his coat to hold him to her when the movement of the carriage threatened to pull them apart. After a moment she felt him slide a hand round behind the curls at her neck, holding her to him as his mouth explored hers, slowly and deeply. Eleanor felt the world start to spin around her; her senses reeled. She had spent the whole day imagining what it would be like and now the reality transcended both her memories and her dreams. Now there were no barriers between them, no misunderstanding and no bitterness. Now there was only sweetness—and longing.

The carriage jolted over a rut and broke them apart. Eleanor fell back against the cushions, and Kit followed, trapping her body beneath his, claiming her mouth again in a fiercely demanding kiss.

'Kit…' When she could speak at last, Eleanor was moved to protest. 'We are in the carriage!'

'And?' Kit sounded amused.

'And…' Eleanor struggled to sit upright and after a moment he shifted sufficiently to allow it, 'and I do not wish to be seduced in a carriage—at least not on this occasion!'

'You have considered it for a future occasion then?' Kit questioned.

'Well,' Eleanor smiled to herself, 'I confess I had thought about the possibility!' She smoothed her gloves down demurely. 'Along with the drawing-room and the conservatory—'

In reply, Kit tumbled her back into his arms and kissed her with a thorough slowness and a heat that threatened to melt on the spot. When the coach drew up in Montague Street she allowed Kit to help her down and did not demur when he put an arm about her, for her legs were still trembling a little. In the entrance hall, Carrick came forward to take their coats, then hesitated, clearly embarrassed.

'Excuse me, my lord, but there is a small matter of business which I must draw to your attention—'

Kit's face was a picture. Eleanor very nearly laughed.

'Good God, Carrick, can it not wait? It is near midnight and I am anxious to retire—'

Eleanor could tell that Kit was trying to erase the impatience from his voice but he was not quite succeeding. The butler hovered.

'I am sorry, my lord. It will not take long.'

Kit cast Eleanor a speaking look. 'My apologies, my dear. If you wish to retire—'

'I think I shall go to the music-room and play for a little,' Eleanor said, suddenly reckless. 'I am in the mood for a passionate piece—'

She saw the flash of desire in Kit's eyes before he turned away and gestured to Carrick to follow him to the study. Eleanor hurried across the hall and into the music-room. The piano was waiting and nothing but Beethoven would do. She closed her eyes and plunged into the music.

She did not even hear Kit come in, nor the click of the door closing. The first intimation she had that she was not alone came when she felt Kit brush aside the curls at the base of her neck and plant a kiss against the sensitive skin uncovered there. Eleanor shivered abruptly, opened her eyes and broke off in the middle of the music.

'Enchanting,' Kit murmured. He drew her to her feet. 'And very, very passionate, my love.'

'What did Carrick want?'

'Oh…' Kit did not sound remotely interested. 'He had a urgent letter for me from St John Trevithick, settling his debts. Which will please your brother, my love, since I refused to take payment from him no matter how he urged it upon me. But I do not really wish to speak of that. Tell me…' He was touching her hair again, entwining a curl about his finger before he released it again, 'did the music-room feature on your list of places suitable for seduction?'

Eleanor's throat dried. 'No…' She whispered.

'Hmm, a pity.' Kit sounded thoughtful. 'Would you like to reconsider?'

Before Eleanor could reply, Kit had bent his head to kiss her, the touch of his lips once again driving out any other thought from her mind. This kiss was tender but no less disturbing for that. The slow, sure passion of it made Eleanor quiver with anticipation, the hardness of Kit's body against her own yielding softness was desperately distracting. She was shaking; she leaned back for support, feeling the edge of the piano hard against the small of her back. A second later Kit had caught her about the waist and placed her so that she was sitting on the piano top. She could feel the smoothness of the polished wood beneath her skirts and caught the edge to steady herself.

'Kit, what on earth—'

'I'll show you…'

'Oh!' The word was driven from Eleanor with a mixture of shock and wicked pleasure, as Kit, suiting actions to words, slid the gown and chemise from her shoulders. The height of the piano had changed their relative positions and he did not even need to bend down to disrobe her. Eleanor felt his hands on her bare waist, above the material of her bodice, and then his lips traced a leisurely path across the bare skin that he had exposed, to brush the upper slope of her breast with the lightest of touches. He moved in closer and Eleanor felt the weight of his body force her thighs apart under her silken skirts. Then his mouth was at her breast.

Eleanor trembled, closing her eyes. This was exquisite torture, and pinned here on the piano's smooth surface, she felt strangely vulnerable and at his mercy. Kit's hand traced the curve of her breast before his lips followed the path of his fingers, teasing, tormenting, making her skin shiver. The searing touch reduced her to desperation and she caught him to her, running her fingers into his hair.

'Kit, please—'

In answer he slipped one hand beneath her skirt to stroke the soft skin of her inner thigh. Eleanor wriggled desperately and slithered straight off the piano top into Kit's arms.

'So now you may add the music-room to your list for the future.' Kit's voice was husky. His hands closed about her waist again and slid her down the whole, hard length of him. 'I just wanted to demonstrate the potential. But now—' He swiftly rearranged her bodice, 'Now, I fear, my dearest Eleanor, that I can wait no longer. I want to take you to bed, for neither the carriage nor any other location can do justice to what I have in mind tonight.'

He swept her up in his arms, and threw the music-room door open. The entire servants' hall appeared to be lined up outside, making no pretext whatsoever of doing any sort of work. Kit merely grinned.

'We do not wish to be disturbed,' he said, and took the stairs two at a time.

'You might as well have made a public announcement,' Eleanor said drowsily, much later, as she lay naked in her husband's arms. 'Indeed, you did make a public declaration—'

Her words were cut off as Kit kissed her triumphantly, his hands sliding to cup her breasts in a gesture of possession that set her trembling again with an echo of the passion that had so recently subsumed them. Kit propped himself up on one elbow and looked down at her, brushing the hair tenderly away from her face.

'There is no shame in that. I want everyone to know how much I love you, Nell…'

Another blissful interlude followed this affirmation. Eleanor twisted beneath him, running her hands over his chest, fascinated by the feeling of hard muscle beneath her fingers, revelling in his warmth and the scent of his skin. She turned her lips against his shoulder, bit him gently and heard him groan.

'Nell… No, don't distract me! Keep still, you minx!'

Kit caught both her hands in one of his, restraining her innocently erotic caresses, and rolled her into his arms.

'Listen to me, Nell. I want to be quite sure that this is the right thing—'

Finding her hands captured, Eleanor pressed tiny butterfly kisses against his chest. 'Sure? Can you be more sure than this, Kit?'

Kit moved to trap her beneath him. 'Then if you are still happy—'

'Oh yes…' Eleanor freed her hands and slipped her arms about him, stroking the smooth skin of his back. 'I do not believe I could be happier…'

She tilted her head to kiss him, parting her lips beneath his, touching her tongue tentatively to his. She could feel the coiled tension of desire in his body again, see the concentrated, passionate heat in his eyes. It thrilled her that he wanted her so much. She wriggled down, her hair spilling over the pillow to entwine them both in its silken bonds. Kit drew her hard against him, her breasts pressed against his chest, his mouth plundering hers ruthlessly as his hands moved over her. Each movement was intense, gentle and demanding by turn as he set out to learn her body all over again. Again and again. Eleanor felt weak at the thought.

'Nell, look at me…'

Eleanor opened her eyes and looked at him, half-fearful of drowning in the intense light in Kit's blue eyes. The blissful sweetness was building inside her now, demanding release. She arched against him.

'Kit…'

He took her then, with a mixture of exultant demand and exquisite tenderness that made her ache with pleasure. And when it was over she slept in his arms, utterly confident that he would always be there when she awoke. No fear of the future could ever touch her now.

Epilogue

It was a week later and Eleanor was sitting in the garden when Carrick announced that Lady Salome Trevithick had called to see her. That redoubtable lady swirled across the lawn in a dress of green taffeta adorned with diamonds, and came to rest under the canopy where Eleanor was reading *Guy Mannering*. She had paid another visit to the circulating library the day before and was forced to admit that reading was a far more enjoyable pastime than she had previously imagined. Really, it was very absorbing indeed.

'My dear Eleanor!' Lady Salome bent to kiss her. 'Here I am come like a *deus ex machina* to put everything right for you and I find you have no need of my help! You look radiant, my love! Am I to infer that All Is Well?'

Eleanor blushed. 'Yes, I thank you, ma'am! Kit and I are reconciled, and in no small part due to your plotting!'

Lady Salome dismissed this with a wave of her hand. 'I do my poor best! But I am glad to see that no more of my interference is needed here!'

She sat back. 'Now that your mama is to retire to the country and this foolish family feud is finished, I find there is little for me here. I shall be returning to Fairhaven Island in a couple of days. My work is done!'

Eleanor sighed. 'We shall miss you, Aunt, although I do not believe that we shall be far behind you! Kit and I plan to retire to Mostyn Hall at the end of the Season, but up until then we shall scandalise the *Ton* by being quite hopelessly in love!'

There was a hint of a tear in Lady Salome's eye. 'Bless you, my dear,' she said gruffly. 'Well, I have kept you from your husband quite long enough! And as I see he is coming to join you now, I will take my leave. But first, I had something for you. I was helping your mama to pack this morning and I found these at the back of one of her drawers…'

She was groping around in her reticule and emerged, brandishing a handful of paper triumphantly.

'Here you are! Letters for you, my love! Well, I must be away.'

She dropped the letters into Eleanor's lap, bent to kiss her again, and swept away across the lawn, meeting with Kit on the edge of the terrace and stopping to engage him in conversation.

Eleanor picked up the letters in some confusion.

She could see that they were addressed to her, and at
Trevithick House, and that they had been opened. She
unfolded the first one.

> My dear love
> Forgive me for leaving you so suddenly and
> without a word. I had no intention of this… Pray
> seek my sister's help until I may return and I
> swear it will not be for long… Forgive me, my
> love…

Eleanor let the letter sink slowly back into her lap.
Lady Salome and Kit were still talking on the terrace,
although Kit was looking across the garden towards
her. Eleanor picked up a second letter.

> My dearest Eleanor
> I can scarce bear to imagine what you are think-
> ing of me by now, alone and friendless as I have
> left you. I think of you every day, no, every mo-
> ment of every day, and long for that time when
> we will be together. I imagine you reading my
> letter and hope from the bottom of my heart that
> you will forgive me… I love you…

Eleanor remembered the Dowager railing against
her marriage, intent on an annulment, desperate for
her to marry Kemble. She thought of her mother reading Kit's letters secretly and hiding them away from
the one person for whom they had been intended. She
thought of Kit, honour bound not to tell her why he

had to delay, and of the Dowager telling her that her husband had abandoned her and had never loved her and that he was a rogue and a scoundrel. She picked up the last letter.

My dearest love
I know of nothing to say other than that I love you so dearly and count the days until I may be back with you. I love you… I love you…

The letter blurred a little and a fat tear dropped onto the paper. Eleanor wiped her eyes. She was smiling and crying at the same time. She saw Kit take his leave of Lady Salome and start down the steps towards her. She got to her feet. The letters fell to the ground. Eleanor could not tear her gaze away from Kit. As he drew closer she saw that the urgency in her own stance had somehow communicated itself to him. He started to hurry towards her just as Eleanor started to run—positively run—across the grass to him. They met in the middle and Kit swept her up in his arms and spun her round, before setting her back on her feet and looking into her face.

'Eleanor?' He touched a gentle finger to her tear-stained cheek. 'What has happened? What is the matter?'

'Nothing!' Eleanor said. She smiled radiantly at him and flung her arms around his neck so that she could reach up to kiss him. 'I love you, Kit! There is nothing the matter at all!'

* * * * *

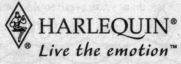

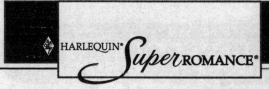

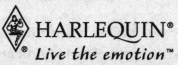

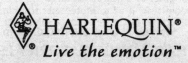

ITCHIN' FOR SOME ROLLICKING ROMANCES SET ON THE AMERICAN FRONTIER? THEN TAKE A GANDER AT THESE TANTALIZING TALES FROM HARLEQUIN HISTORICALS

On sale September 2003

WINTER WOMAN by Jenna Kernan
(Colorado, 1835)

After braving the winter alone in the Rockies, a defiant woman is entrusted to the care of a gruff trapper!

THE MATCHMAKER by Lisa Plumley
(Arizona territory, 1882)

Will a confirmed bachelor be bitten by the love bug when he woos a young woman in order to flush out the mysterious Morrow Creek matchmaker?

On sale October 2003

WYOMING WILDCAT by Elizabeth Lane
(Wyoming, 1866)

A blizzard ignites hot-blooded passions between a white medicine woman and an amnesiac man, but an ominous secret looms on the horizon....

THE OTHER GROOM by Lisa Bingham
(Boston and New York, 1870)

When a penniless woman masquerades as the daughter of a powerful marquis, her intended groom risks it all to protect her from harm!

Visit us at www.eHarlequin.com

HARLEQUIN HISTORICALS®

HHWEST27

LOOKIN' FOR RIVETING TALES ABOUT RUGGED MEN AND THE FEISTY LADIES WHO TRY TO TAME THEM?

From Harlequin Historicals

July 2003

TEXAS GOLD by Carolyn Davidson

A fiercely independent farmer's past catches up with her when the husband she left behind turns up on her doorstep!

OF MEN AND ANGELS by Victoria Bylin

Can a hard-edged outlaw find redemption—and true love—in the arms of an angelic young woman?

On sale August 2003

BLACKSTONE'S BRIDE by Bronwyn Williams

Will a beleaguered gold miner's widow and a wounded half-breed ignite a searing passion when they form a united front?

HIGH PLAINS WIFE by Jillian Hart

A taciturn rancher proposes a marriage of convenience to a secretly smitten spinster who has designs on his heart!

Visit us at www.eHarlequin.com

HARLEQUIN HISTORICALS®